This House Is Haunted

Also by John Boyne

NOVELS
The House of Special Purpose
The Absolutist
Mutiny: A Novel of the Bounty
Next of Kin
Crippen
The Congress of Rough Riders
The Thief of Time

NOVELS FOR YOUNGER READERS
The Terrible Thing that Happened to Barnaby Brocket
Noah Barleywater Runs Away
The Boy in the Striped Pajamas

NOVELLAS
The Dare
The Second Child

For more information on John Boyne and his books,
visit his Web site at www.johnboyne.com

THIS HOUSE IS HAUNTED

JOHN BOYNE

Other Press
New York

Copyright © John Boyne 2013

First published in Great Britain in 2013 by Doubleday,
an imprint of Transworld Publishers

Production Editor: Yvonne E. Cárdenas
This book was set in 11.25 pt Giovanni Book by Falcon Oast Graphic Art Ltd.

10 9 8 7 6 5 4 3 2

Library of Congress Cataloging-in-Publication Data

Boyne, John, 1971-
This house is haunted / by John Boyne.
pages cm
ISBN 978-1-59051-679-9 (paperback) — ISBN 978-1-59051-680-5 (eBook)
1. Governesses—Fiction.   2. Family secrets—Fiction.   3. Haunted houses—
East Anglia (England)—Fiction.   4. Ghost stories, English—19th century—
Fiction.   5. East Anglia (England)—Fiction.   I.   Title.
PR6102.O96T49 2013   823'.92—dc23
2013012034

For Sinéad

Chapter One

London, 1867

I BLAME CHARLES DICKENS for the death of my father.

In tracing the moment where my life transformed from serenity to horror, twisting the natural into the unspeakable, I find myself seated in the parlour of our small terraced home near Hyde Park, observing the frayed edges of the hearth rug and wondering whether it might be time to invest in a new one or try to repair it myself. Simple, domestic thoughts. It was raining that morning, an indecisive but unremitting shower, and as I turned away from the window to catch my reflection in the looking glass above the fireplace, I grew disheartened by my appearance. It was true that I had never been attractive but my skin appeared paler than usual, my dark hair wiry and unkempt. There was a certain hunched aspect to my shoulders as I sat, my elbows propped upon the table, a teacup positioned between my hands, and I tried to relax in an attempt to correct my posture. I did something foolish then—I smiled at myself—hoping that a manifestation of contentment would improve the rendering, and was startled when I noticed a second face, much smaller than my own, staring back at me from the lower corner of the mirror.

I gasped, a hand to my breast, then laughed at my folly, for the image I observed was nothing more than the reflection of a portrait of my late mother that was pinned to the wall behind my chair. The mirror was capturing both our likenesses side by side and I did not benefit from the comparison, for Mother was a very beautiful woman, with wide, bright eyes where mine were narrow and pallid, a feminine jawline where mine tended towards harsh masculinity, and a slender build where my own had always felt outsized and absurd.

The portrait was a familiar one, of course. It had been hanging on that wall for so long that perhaps I never really noticed it any more, in the way that one often ignores familiar things, like seat cushions or loved ones. However, that morning her expression somehow captured my attention and I found myself lamenting her loss anew, despite the fact that she had passed from this world to the next more than a decade before, when I was little more than a child. And I wondered then about the afterlife, about where her spirit might have settled after death and whether or not she had been watching over me all these years, taking pleasure in my small triumphs and grieving for my numerous mistakes.

The morning fog was beginning to descend on the street outside and a persistent wind was forcing its way down the chimney, tracking a path along the loose stonework within and diminishing only slightly as it entered the room, forcing me to wrap my shawl more closely around my shoulders. I shivered and longed to return to the warmth of my bed.

I was pulled out of my reverie, however, by a cry of delight from Father, who was sitting across from me, his herrings and eggs half-eaten, scanning the pages of the *Illustrated London News*. The issue had been lying unread since the previous

Saturday on a small table in that same room in which we sat, and I had intended on discarding it that morning, but some impulse had made Father decide to glance through its pages over breakfast. I looked up in surprise—it sounded as if something had passed his throat the wrong way—but his face was flushed with excitement and he folded the paper in two, tapping it several times with his fingers as he passed it across to me.

"Look, my dear," he said. "The most wonderful thing!"

I took the newspaper and glanced at the page he had indicated. The article seemed to have something to do with a great conference that was scheduled to take place in London before Christmas in order to discuss affairs related to the North American continent. I read through a few paragraphs but quickly became lost in the political language, which seemed designed both to provoke and intrigue the reader simultaneously, before looking back at Father in confusion. He had never before shown any interest in American matters. Indeed, he had professed his belief on more than one occasion that those who lived on the opposite side of the Atlantic Ocean were nothing more than barbarous, antagonistic scoundrels who should never have been permitted independence, an act of disloyalty to the Crown for which the name of Portland should for ever after be damned.

"Well, what of it?" I asked. "You don't plan on attending as a protester, surely? The museum would take a very dim view of your engaging in political matters, I think."

"What?" he asked, confused by my response, before shaking his head quickly. "No, no," he said. "Not the article about those villains. Leave them well alone, they have made their beds and they may lie in them and be damned for all I care. No, look to the left. The advertisement at the side of the page."

I picked up the paper again and realized immediately what he was referring to. It was announced that Charles Dickens, the world-famous novelist, would read from his work the following evening, Friday, in a Knightsbridge speakers' hall, a venue no more than a half hour's walk from where we lived. Those who wished to attend were advised to come early, as it was well known that Mr. Dickens always attracted a substantial and enthusiastic audience.

"We must go, Eliza!" cried Father, beaming in delight and taking a mouthful of herring to celebrate.

Outside, a slate fell from the roof, unsettled by the wind, and crashed in the yard. I could hear movement in the eaves.

I bit my lip and read the advertisement again. Father had been suffering from a persistent cough that had weighed heavily on his chest for more than a week, and it was showing no sign of improvement. He had attended a doctor two days before and been prescribed a bottle of some green, glutinous liquid which I had to force him to take but which did not, in my view, appear to be doing much good. If anything, he seemed to be growing worse.

"Do you think it's wise?" I asked. "Your illness has not quite passed yet and the weather is so inclement. You would be sensible to remain indoors in front of the fireplace for another few days, don't you agree?"

"Nonsense, my dear," he said, shaking his head, looking dismayed that I might deny him this great treat. "I'm almost entirely recovered, I assure you. By tomorrow night I shall be myself again."

As if to belie that statement he immediately let forth a deep and sustained cough that forced him to turn away from me, his face growing red, his eyes streaming with tears. I ran to the kitchen and poured a glass of water, set it before him and he took a deep draught, finally smiling at me with an expression that suggested mischief. "It's just working its way out of my system," he said. "I assure you that I'm improving by the hour."

I glanced out the window. Had it been springtime, had the sun been shining through the branches of the blossoming trees, I might have felt more persuaded by his argument. But it was not springtime, it was autumn. And it seemed imprudent to me that he would risk further ill health for the sake of hearing Mr. Dickens speak in public when the novelist's words could be more honestly located between the covers of his novels.

"Let's see how you feel tomorrow," I said, an attempt at conciliation, for surely no decision needed to be reached just yet.

"No, let us decide now and be done with it," he insisted, setting the water aside and reaching for his pipe. He tapped the remains of last night's fug into his saucer before refilling it with the particular brand of tobacco that he had favoured since he was a young man. A familiar scent of cinnamon and chestnuts drifted through the air towards me; Father's tobacco held a strong infusion of the spice and whenever I detected it elsewhere it always recalled the warmth and the comfort of home. "The museum has permitted me to remain away from my post until the end of the week. I shall stay indoors all day today and tomorrow and then in the evening we shall don our greatcoats and go together to hear Mr. Dickens speak. I would not miss it for the world."

I sighed and nodded, knowing that for all he relied upon my advice, this was one decision upon which he was determined to have his way.

"Capital!" he cried, striking a match and allowing it to burn for a few seconds to disperse the sulphur before holding it to the chamber and sucking on the bit so contentedly that I could not help but smile at how much pleasure it afforded him. The darkness of the room, coupled with the mixed light from candles, fire and pipe, made his skin seem ghostly thin and my smile diminished slightly to recognize how much he was ageing. When had our roles altered so much, I wondered, that I, the daughter, should have to grant permission for an outing to him, the parent?

Chapter Two

FATHER HAD ALWAYS been an impassioned reader. He maintained a carefully selected library in his ground-floor study, a room to which he would retire when he wanted to be alone with his thoughts and memories. One wall housed a series of volumes dedicated to his particular study, entomology, a subject that had fascinated him since childhood. As a boy, he told me, he rather horrified his parents by keeping dozens of samples of living insects in a glass box in the corner of his bedroom. In the opposite corner he kept a second display case, exhibiting their corpses *post mortem*. The natural progression of the insects from one side of the room to the other was a source of great satisfaction to him. He did not want to see them die, of course, preferring to study their habits and interactions while they were still alive, but he was industrious in keeping a series of journals relating to their behaviour during development, maturity and decomposition. Naturally the maids protested at having to clean the room—one even resigned in protest at being asked—and his mama refused to enter it. (His family had money back then, hence the presence of domestics. An older brother, dead many years by now, had squandered the inheritance and so we had enjoyed few such extravagances.)

Gathered next to the volumes describing the life cycles of queen termites, the intestinal tracts of longhorn beetles and the mating habits of strepsiptera, was a series of dossiers that gathered his correspondence over the years with Mr. William Kirby, his particular mentor, who had offered him his first paid employment in 1832, when Father had just acquired his majority, as an assistant at a new museum in Norwich. Subsequent to this, Mr. Kirby had taken Father with him to London to help with the establishment of the Entomological Society, a role which would in time lead to his becoming curator of insects at the British Museum, a position he loved. I shared no such passion. Insects rather repelled me.

Mr. Kirby had died some sixteen years earlier but Father still enjoyed re-reading their letters and notes, taking pleasure in following the progress of acquisition which had led the society, and ultimately the museum, to be in possession of such a fine collection.

All of these, "the insect books" as I facetiously referred to them, were shelved carefully, with a curious order that only Father truly understood, on the wall next to his desk. Gathered together on the opposite wall, however, next to a window and a reading chair where the light was much better, was a much smaller collection of books, all novels, and the most dominant author on those shelves was of course Mr. Dickens, who had no peer in Father's mind.

"If only he would write a novel about a cicada or a grasshopper instead of an orphan," I remarked once. "Why, you would be in heaven then, I think."

"My dear, you are forgetting *The Cricket on the Hearth*," replied Father, whose knowledge of the novelist's work was second to none. "Not to mention that little family of spiders who set up home in Miss Havisham's uneaten wedding cake. Or Bitzer's lashes in *Hard Times*. How does he describe them? *Like the antennae of busy insects*, if memory serves. No, insects appear regularly throughout Dickens" work. It is only a matter of time before he devotes a more substantial volume to them. He is a true entomologist, I believe."

Having read most of these novels myself, I am not so certain that this is true, but it was not for the insects that Father read Dickens, it was for the stories. Indeed, the first time I remember Father smiling again after Mother's passing, in the wake of my return from my aunts' home in Cornwall, was when he was re-reading *The Posthumous Papers of the Pickwick Club*, whose protagonist could always reduce him to tears of laughter.

"Eliza, you must read this," he said to me in my fourteenth year, thrusting a copy of *Bleak House* into my hands. "It is a work of extraordinary merit and much more attuned to the times than those penny fancies you favour." I opened the volume with a heavy heart which would grow heavier still as I tried to discern the meaning and intent of the lawsuit of Jarndyce *vs.* Jarndyce, but of course he was quite right, for once I had battled through those opening chapters the story opened itself up to me and I became deeply sympathetic to the experiences of Esther Summerson, not to mention utterly captivated by the romance pursued between her and Dr. Woodcourt, an honest man who loves her despite her unfortunate physical appearance. (In this, I could relate quite well to Esther, although she had of course lost her looks to the smallpox while I had never found mine in the first place.)

Prior to his bout of ill health, Father had always been a vigorous man. Regardless of the weather, he walked to and from the museum every morning and evening, discounting the omnibus that would have taken him almost directly from our front door to the museum entrance. When, for a brief few years, we had the care of a mongrel dog named Bull's Eye, a far kinder and more temperate creature than Bill Sikes' mistreated companion, he would take further exercise twice daily, taking the dog into Hyde Park for a constitutional, throwing a stick for him in Kensington Gardens or allowing him to run free along the banks of the Serpentine where, on one occasion, he claimed to have spotted the Princess Helena seated by the waterside weeping. (Why? I do not know. He approached her, enquiring after her health, but she waved him away.) He was never late to bed and slept soundly through the night. He ate carefully, did not drink to excess, and was neither too thin nor too fat. There was no reason to believe that he would not live to a good age. And yet he did not.

Perhaps I should have been more forceful in attempting to dissuade him from attending Mr. Dickens' talk but in my heart I knew that, although he liked to give the impression that he deferred to me on domestic matters, there was nothing I could say that would prevent him from making the journey across the park to Knightsbridge. Despite his ardour as a reader, he had never yet had the pleasure of hearing the great author speak in public and it was well known that the performances the novelist gave on stage were the equal, if not the superior, of anything which might have been found in the playing houses of Drury Lane or Shaftesbury Avenue. And so I said nothing, I submitted to his authority, and agreed that we might go.

"Don't fuss, Eliza," he said as we left the house that Friday evening when I suggested that, at the very least, he should wear a second muffler for it was shockingly cold out and, although the rain had held off all day, the skies were turning to grey. But Father did not like being mollycoddled and chose to ignore my advice.

We made our way, arm in arm, towards Lancaster Gate, passing the Italian Gardens on our left as we bisected Hyde Park through the central path. Emerging some twenty minutes later from the Queen's Gate, I thought I saw a familiar face appearing through the fog and, when I narrowed my eyes to make out the visage, I gasped, for was this not the same countenance that I had seen in the mirror the previous morning, the reflection of my own late mother? I pulled Father closer to me, stopping on the street in disbelief, and he turned to look at me in surprise just as the lady in question appeared from the miasma and nodded a greeting in my direction. It was not Mother of course—how could it have been?—but a lady who might have been her sister, or a cousin, for the resemblance around the eyes and brow was uncanny.

The rain began almost immediately then, falling heavily, great drops tumbling on our heads and coats as people ran for shelter. I shivered; a ghost walked over my grave. A large oak tree a little further along the pavement offered shelter and I pointed towards it but Father shook his head, tapping his index finger against his pocket-watch.

"We'll be there in five minutes if we hurry," he said, marching along the street faster now. "We might miss it entirely if we seek refuge."

I cursed myself for having forgotten my umbrella, which I had left by the front door during the business about the muffler, and so we ran through the forming puddles towards our destination unprotected and when we arrived, we were soaked through. I shivered in the vestibule, peeling my sodden gloves from my hands, and longed to be back in front of the fireplace in our comfortable home. Beside me, Father began a fit of coughing that seemed to build from the very depths of his soul and I despised those other entrants who glanced at him contemptuously as they passed. It took a few minutes for him to recover and I was for hailing a hansom cab to take us home again but he would hear none of this and marched ahead of me into the hall, and what, in the circumstances, could I do but follow?

Inside, perhaps a thousand people were gathered together, equally damp and uncomfortable, a stench of wet wool and perspiration pervading the atmosphere. I looked around, hoping to find a quieter part of the room for us to sit, but almost every chair was taken by now and we had no choice but to choose two empty seats in the centre of a row, surrounded by shivering, sneezing audience members. Fortunately we did not need to wait long, for within a few minutes Mr. Dickens himself appeared to tumultuous applause and we stood to receive him, cheering loudly to his evident delight, for he stretched his arms wide as if to take us all into his embrace, acknowledging the wild reception as if it was entirely his due.

He showed no sign of wanting the ovation to subside and it was perhaps five minutes more before he finally moved to the front of the stage, waving his hands to indicate that we might suspend our admiration for a few moments, and permitted us to take our seats once again. He wore a sallow expression and his hair and beard were rather dishevelled but his suit and waistcoat were of such a rich fabric that I felt a curious urge to feel the texture beneath my fingers. I wondered about his life. Was it true that he moved as easily in the back alleys of London's East End as he did in the privileged corridors of Balmoral Castle, where the Queen in her mourning had reputedly invited him to perform? Was he as comfortable in the company of thieves, pickpockets and prostitutes as he was in the society of bishops, cabinet ministers and leaders of industry? In my innocence, I could not imagine what it would be to be such a worldly man, famous on two sides of the ocean, beloved by all.

He stared out at us now with a hint of a smile on his face.

"There are ladies present tonight," he began, his voice echoing across the chamber. "Naturally I am delighted by this but also distressed for I hope that none of you are of the sensitive disposition that is peculiar to your sex. For, my dear readers, my friends, my *literati*, I do not propose to entertain you this evening with some of the more preposterous utterances of that delightful creature Sam Weller. Nor do I plan on uplifting your spirits through the bravery of my beloved boy Master Copperfield. Neither shall I seek to stir your emotions through a retelling of the last days of that unfortunate angel Little Nell Trent, may God have mercy on her soul." He hesitated, allowing our anticipation to build, and we watched him, already captivated by his presence. "Instead," he continued after a long pause, his voice growing deep and mellifluous now, the words emerging slowly, "I intend to read a ghost story that I have only recently completed, one which is scheduled to appear in the Christmas number of *All the Year Round*. It is a most terrifying tale, ladies and gentlemen, designed to stir the blood and unsettle the senses. It speaks of the paranormal, of the undead, of those pitiful creatures who wander the afterlife in search of eternal reconciliation. It contains a character who is neither alive nor deceased, neither sentient nor spirit. I wrote it to chill the blood of my readers and despatch ghouls into the beating heart of their dreams."

As he said this a cry went up from halfway down the hall and I turned my head, as did most of those in attendance, to see a young woman of about my own age, twenty-one, throwing her hands in the air and running down the aisle in fright. I sighed and secretly despised her for disgracing her sex.

"Should any other ladies wish to leave," said Mr. Dickens, who appeared to be delighted by this interruption, "might I urge you to do so now? I would not like to interrupt the flow of the story and the time has come for me to begin."

At these words, a small boy appeared from the side of the stage, approached the novelist and offered a low bow, before thrusting a sheaf of pages into Mr. Dickens' hand. The boy ran off, the writer glanced at what he held, looked about him with a wild expression on his face and began to read.

"Halloa! Below there!" he shouted in such an extraordinary and unexpected roar that I could not help but jump in my seat. A lady behind me uttered an oath and a gentleman on the aisle dropped his spectacles. Apparently enjoying the reaction that his cry had caused, Mr. Dickens paused for a few moments before continuing, whereupon I quickly found myself entranced by his tale. A single spotlight illuminated his pale face and his tone fluctuated between characters, describing fear, confusion and distress with only a slight change of modulation to his tone. His sense of timing was impeccable as he said one thing that made us laugh, then another that made us feel unsettled and then a third that made us leap in fright. He portrayed the two characters at the centre of the story—a signalman who worked by a railway tunnel and a visitor to that place—with such gusto that one almost believed that there were two actors on stage performing either role. The tale itself was, as he had suggested in his introduction, a disconcerting one, centring on the signalman's belief that a spectre was informing him of calamities to come. The ghost had appeared once and a terrible crash had ensued; he had appeared a second time and a lady had died in the railway carriage as it passed. It had appeared a third time more recently, gesticulating wildly, urging the signalman to get out of the way, but as yet no misfortune had occurred and the nervous fellow was distressed at the thought of what horror might lie ahead. I considered Mr. Dickens rather devilish in the manner in which he took pleasure in stirring the emotions of his audience. When he knew that we were scared, he would incite us further, building on the threat and menace he had laid out for us and then, when we were certain that a terrible thing was about to happen, he would let us down, peace would be restored and we who had been holding our collective breaths in anticipation of some fresh terror were free to exhale and sigh and feel that all was well in the world once again, which was when he took us by surprise with a single sentence, making us scream when we thought we could relax, terrifying us into the depths of our very souls and allowing himself a brief smile at how easily he could manipulate our emotions.

As he read, I began to fear that I might not sleep that night, so certain was I that I was surrounded by the spirits of those who had left their corporeal form behind but had not yet been admitted through the gates of heaven and so were left to trawl through the world, crying aloud, desperate to be heard, causing disarray and torment wherever they went, uncertain when they would be released to the peace of the afterlife and the quiet promise of eternal rest.

When Mr. Dickens finished speaking, he bowed his head and there was silence from the audience for perhaps ten seconds before we burst as one into applause, leaping to our feet, crying out for more. I turned to look at Father who, rather than appearing as thrilled as I had anticipated, wore a pale expression, a sheen of perspiration gleaming on his face, as he inhaled and exhaled in laboured gasps, staring at the floor beneath him, his fists clenched in a mixture of determination to recover his breath and a fear that he might never do so.

In his hands, he clutched a handkerchief stained with blood.

Departing the theatre into the wet and cold night, I was still trembling from the dramatics of the reading and felt certain that I was surrounded by apparitions and spirits, but Father seemed to have recovered himself and declared that it was quite the most enjoyable evening he had spent in many years.

"He's every bit as good an actor as he is a writer," he pronounced as we made our way back across the park, reversing our earlier walk, the rain starting yet again as we marched along, the fog making it almost impossible for us to see more than a few steps ahead of ourselves.

"I believe he often takes part in dramatics," I said. "At his own home and the homes of his friends."

"Yes, I've read that," agreed Father. "Wouldn't it be wonderful to be invited to—"

Another coughing fit overtook him and he struggled for air as he bent over, assuming an undignified position on the street.

"Father," I said, putting my arm around his shoulders as I attempted to right him. "We must get you home. The sooner you are out of those wet clothes and lying in a hot bath the better it will be."

He nodded and struggled on, coughing and sneezing as we leaned on each other for support. To my relief the rain came to an abrupt halt as we rounded Bayswater Road for Brook Street, but with every step I took I could feel my feet growing more and more soaked through my shoes and dreaded to think of how wet Father's must be. Finally we were home and he forced himself into the metal bathtub for a half hour before changing into his nightshirt and gown and joining me in the parlour.

"I shall never forget tonight, Eliza," he remarked when we were seated side by side by the fire, sipping on hot tea and eating buttered toast, the room filled again by the scent of cinnamon and chestnuts from his pipe. "He was a capital fellow."

"I found him truly terrifying," I replied. "I enjoy his books almost as much as you, of course, but I wish he had read from one of his dramatic novels. I don't care for ghost stories."

"You're frightened by them?"

"Unsettled," I said, shaking my head. "I think any story which concerns itself with the afterlife and with forces that the human mind cannot truly understand risks disquiet for the reader. Although I don't think I've ever experienced fear in the way that others do. I don't understand what it is to be truly frightened, just how it feels to be disconcerted or uncomfortable. The signalman in the story, for example. He was terrified at the horror he knew was sure to come his way. And that woman in the audience who ran screaming from the hall. I can't imagine what it must feel like to be that scared."

"Don't you believe in ghosts, Eliza?" he asked and I turned to look at him, surprised by the question. It was dark in the room and he was illuminated only by the glow of the reddened coals that made his eyes appear darker than usual and his skin glow with the colour of the sporadic flames.

"I don't know," I said, uncertain how I truly felt about the question. "Why, do you?"

"I believe that woman was an imbecile," declared Father. "That's what I believe. Mr. Dickens had barely even begun to speak when she took fright. She should have been excluded from the start if she was of such a sensitive disposition."

"The truth is I've always preferred his more realistic tales," I continued, looking away. "The novels that explore the lives of orphans, his tales of triumph over adversity. Masters Copperfield, Twist and Nickleby will always hold a greater place in my affections than Mr. Scrooge or Mr. Marley."

"*Marley was dead, to begin with,*" stated Father in a deep voice, imitating the writer so well that I shuddered. "*There is no doubt whatever about that.*"

"Don't," I said, laughing despite myself. "Please."

I fell asleep quite soon after going to bed but it was a fitful and unhappy sleep. My dreams were supplanted by nightmares. I encountered spirits where I should have undertaken adventures. My landscape was dark graveyards and irregular vistas rather than Alpine peaks or Venetian canals. But nevertheless I slept through the night and when I woke, feeling groggy and out of sorts, the morning light was already coming through my curtains. I looked at my wall clock; it was almost ten past seven and I cursed myself, knowing that I would certainly be late for work and still had Father's breakfast to prepare. However, when I entered his room a few minutes later to see whether his condition had improved in the night, I could see immediately that he was far more ill than I had previously realized. The rain of the evening before had taken hold of him and the chill seemed to have entered into his very bones. He was deathly pale, his skin damp and clammy, and I took great fright, dressing immediately and running to the end of our mews where Dr. Connolly, a friend and physician of long standing, lived. He came back with me and did everything in his power, I have no doubt of that, but he told me there was nothing we could do but wait for the fever to break, or hope that it would, and I spent the rest of the day by Father's bedside, praying to a god who did not often trouble my thoughts, and by early evening, when the sun had descended again to be replaced by our perpetual and torment-ing London fog, I felt Father's grasp of my hand grow weaker until he slipped away from me entirely, gathered quietly to his reward, leaving me an orphan like those characters I had spo-ken of the night before, if one can truly be called an orphan at twenty-one years of age.

Chapter Three

Father's funeral took place the following Monday morning in St. James's Church in Paddington and I took some comfort in the fact that half a dozen of his co-workers from the British Museum, along with three of my own colleagues from St. Elizabeth's School where I had employment as a teacher of small girls, attended to offer their sympathies. We had no living relatives and so there were very few mourners, among them the widow who lived next door to us but who had always seemed loath to acknowledge me in the street; a polite but shy young student whom Father had been mentoring in his insect studies; our part-time domestic girl, Jessie; and Mr. Billington, the tobacconist on Connaught Street who had been providing Father with his cinnamon-infused tobacco for as long as I could recall and whose presence made me feel rather emotional and grateful.

Mr. Heston, Father's immediate superior in the Department of Entomology, held my right hand in both of his, crushing it slightly, and told me how much he had respected Father's intellect, while one Miss Sharpton, an educated woman whose employment had initially caused Father some disquiet, informed me that she would miss his lively wit and excellent humour, a remark that rather astonished me but which I nevertheless found consoling. (Was there a side to Father that I did not know? A man who told jokes, charmed young ladies, was filled with *bonhomie*? It was possible, I supposed, but still something of a surprise.) I rather admired Miss Sharpton and wished that I could have had an opportunity to know her better; I was aware that she had attended the Sorbonne, where she was awarded a degree, although naturally the English universities did not recognize it, and apparently her own family had cut her off on account of it. Father told me once that he had asked her whether she was looking forward to the day when she would get married and thus not have to work any more; her reply—that she would rather drink ink—had scandalized him but intrigued me.

Outside the church, my own employer, Mrs. Farnsworth, who had taught me as a girl and then hired me as a teacher, informed me that I must take the rest of the week to grieve but that hard work could be an extraordinary restorative and she looked forward to welcoming me back to school the following Monday. She was not being heartless; she had lost a husband the year before, and a son the year preceding that. Grief was a condition that she understood.

Mercifully, the rain stayed off while we laid Father to rest but the fog fell so deeply around us that I could barely make out the coffin as it descended into the ground and, perhaps a blessing, I missed that moment when one is aware of laying eyes on the casket for the final time. It seemed to be simply swallowed up by the mist, and only when the vicar came over to shake my hand and wish me well did I realize that the burial had come to an end and that there was nothing left for me to do but go home.

I chose not to do so immediately, however, and instead walked around the graveyard for a time, peering through the haze at the names and dates etched into the tombstones. Some seemed quite natural—men and women who had lived into their sixtieth or, in some cases, their seventieth years. Others felt aberrant, children taken while they were still in their infancy, young mothers buried with their stillborn babies in their arms. I came across the grave of an Arthur Covan, an erstwhile colleague of mine, and shuddered to remember our one-time friendship and his subsequent disgrace. We had developed a connection for a brief period, Arthur and I, one that I had hoped would blossom into something more, and the memory of those feelings, combined with the knowledge of the damage that troubled young man had caused, only served to upset me further.

Realizing that this was not perhaps a sensible place for me to linger, I looked around for the gate but found myself quite lost. The fog grew thicker around me until I could no longer read the words on the headstones, and to my right—extraordinary thing!—I was certain I heard a couple laughing. I turned, wondering who would behave in such a fashion here, but could see no one. Uneasy, I reached a hand out before me and could make nothing out beyond my gloved fingertip. "Hello," I said, raising my voice only a little, uncertain whether I truly wanted a response, but answer came there none. I reached a wall where I hoped for a gate, then turned and almost fell over a group of ancient headstones piled together in a corner, and now my heart began to beat faster in anxiety. I told myself to be calm, to breathe, then find the way out, but as I turned round I let out a cry when I was confronted by a young girl, no more than seven years of age, standing in the centre on the path, wearing no coat despite the weather.

"My brother drowned," she told me and I opened my mouth to reply but could find no words. "He was told not to go towards the river, but he did. He was disobedient. And he drowned. Mama is sitting by his grave."

"Where?" I asked, and she stretched a hand out, pointing behind me. I spun round but could see no lady through the vapour. I looked back only to discover the girl turning on her heels and breaking into a run, disappearing into the mist. Panic rose inside me; it might have developed into an hysteria had I not forced myself to walk quickly along the paths until finally, to my great relief, I was returned to the street, where I almost collided with an overweight man I was quite certain was our local Member of Parliament.

Walking home, I passed the Goat and Garter, a public house I had of course never entered, and was astonished to observe Miss Sharpton seated by the window, drinking a small porter and engrossed in a textbook while she made notes in a jotter. Behind her I could see the expressions on the men's faces— naturally, they were appalled and assumed that she was some sort of deviant—but I suspected that their opinions would have caused her not a moment's concern. How I longed to enter that establishment and take my place beside her! Tell me, Miss Sharpton, I might have said, what shall I do with my life now? How can I improve my position and prospects? Help me, please, for I am alone in the world and have neither friend nor benefactor. Tell me what I should do next.

Other people had friends. Of course they did; it was the natural way of things. There are those who are comfortable in the company of others, with the sharing of intimacies and common secrets. I have never been such a person. I was a studious girl who loved to be at home with Father. And I was not pretty. In school, the other girls formed alliances which always excluded me. They called me names; I will not repeat them here. They made fun of my unshapely body, my pale skin, my untamed hair. I do not know why I was born this way. Father was a handsome man, after all, and Mother a great beauty. But somehow their progeny was not blessed with similar good looks.

I would have given anything for a friend at that moment, a friend like Miss Sharpton, who might have persuaded me not to make the rash decision which would nearly destroy me. Which still might.

I looked through the window of the Goat and Garter and willed her to glance up and spot me, to wave her arms and insist that I join her, and when she failed to do so I turned with a heavy heart and continued for home, where I sat in my chair by the fireplace for the rest of the afternoon and, for the first time since Father's death, wept.

In the late afternoon, I fed some more coals on to the fire and, determined to achieve some sort of normality, made my way to the butcher's shop on Norfolk Place, where I purchased two pork chops. I wasn't particularly hungry but felt that if I lingered at home all day without food I might sink into an inexorable melancholy and, despite the early nature of my grief, I was determined that I would not allow this to happen. Passing the corner shop I even decided to treat myself to a quarter pound of boiled sweets and picked up a copy of *The Morning Post* for later perusal. (If Miss Sharpton could attend the Sorbonne, after all, then surely I could at least familiarize myself with the events of our own nation.)

Back home again, my spirits sank to a new low when I realized my error. Two pork chops? Who was the other chop for? My habits had superseded my needs. I fried them both, however, ate the first mournfully with a boiled potato, and fed the second to the widow-next-door's spaniel, for I could not bear either to save it for later or to eat it now. (And Father, who loved dogs, would I'm sure have been delighted by my charity.)

As evening fell, I returned to my armchair, placed two candles on a side table, the bag of boiled sweets on my lap, and opened the newspaper, flicking through it quickly, unable to concentrate on any stories and almost ready to throw the entire thing on the fire when I came upon the "Situations Available" page, where a particular notice caught my attention.

An "H. Bennet," of Gaudlin Hall in the county of Norfolk, was advertising for a governess to attend to the care and education of the children of the house; the position needed to be filled without delay by a qualified candidate and the remuneration was promised to be satisfactory. Applications should be despatched immediately. Little more was said. "H. Bennet," whoever he was, did not specify how many children required supervision, nor did he offer any details regarding their ages. The whole thing lacked a certain elegance, as if it had been written in haste and submitted to the newspaper without proper consideration, but for some reason I found myself drawn to the urgency of the appeal, reading it from start to finish over and over, wondering what this Gaudlin Hall might look like and what kind of fellow H. Bennet might be.

I had only been outside London once in my life and that was a dozen years before, when I was nine years old, in the immediate aftermath of my mother's death. Our small family had lived together in a state of considerable harmony during my early childhood. My parents had a marked characteristic that distinguished them from those of most of my school friends: they were affectionate towards each other. The things which seemed natural in our home—the fact that they parted every morning with a kiss, that they sat side by side in the evening reading their books rather than in separate parlours, that they shared a bedroom and laughed together and were unsparing in how often they touched or shared a joke or simply remarked upon how happy they were—were alien in the homes of others. I knew this quite well. On the rare occasions when I visited the houses of neighbouring girls, I found a distance between their parents, as if they were not two people who had met and fallen in love, exchanged intimacies and joined each other at an altar with the purpose of spending their lives together, but a pair of strangers, cell mates perhaps, thrust into a mutual confinement with little in common except the decades that they were forced to endure each other's company.

My parents could not have been more different in their behaviour, but if their affection towards each other was obvious, it was as nothing compared to the fondness they displayed towards me. They did not spoil me; staunch Anglicans both, they believed too much in discipline and self-restraint for that. But they delighted in my presence and treated me with great kindness and we were a happy group until, when I was eight, they sat me down and informed me that I was to have a younger brother or sister in the spring. Naturally they were delighted, for they had hoped for a long time to be blessed with a second child and, with the passing of the years, they had grown to believe that it was not to be. But to their great delight, they announced that our small family of three would soon expand to four.

I confess that when I look back on those months, I did not comport myself with as much dignity as I wish I had. I did not feel the same degree of joy that my parents felt at the notion of welcoming a baby into our home. I had been an only child for so long that selfishness may have hidden in my heart and displayed itself in unruly passions on a number of occasions. Indeed, so ill behaved was I, so uncharacteristically naughty, that Father took me aside during the last month of Mother's confinement and told me that I was not to worry, that nothing would change, for there was enough love in our house to be shared with a new baby, and that I would look back one day and find it hard to imagine how I had ever done without this younger brother or sister, whom I should very soon grow to love.

Sadly, this expectation, which I had begun to come around to, was not to be fulfilled. Mother struggled during her delivery, giving birth to a second daughter who, within a few days, would be lying in a coffin, safe in the arms of the lady who had carried her for nine months, under a headstone that read: *Angeline Caine, 1813–1855, beloved wife and mother, and baby Mary.* Father and I were now alone.

Naturally, given his great love for my mother, Father struggled in the immediate aftermath of her death, secluding himself in his study, unable to read, barely eating, succumbing too often to the vice of alcohol, neglecting his work and his friends and, most importantly of all, me, a situation which, had it been allowed to continue, might have led us both in time to the workhouse or the debtors' gaol, but fortunately matters were taken in hand by the arrival of Father's two elder sisters, Hermione and Rachel, who appeared unannounced on a visit from Cornwall and were shocked to discover the conditions in which their brother and niece were now living. They took it upon themselves to clean the house from top to bottom, despite Father's protests. He tried to chase them out with a sweeping brush, as one might expel some unwanted vermin, but they were having none of it and refused to leave until the obvious decline of our living standards could be reversed. They took charge of Mother's clothes and personal effects, saving some of the more precious items—her few pieces of jewellery, for example, a pretty dress that I might grow into in a decade or so—and distributing the rest among the poor of the parish, an act which drove Father into a fury but, wise and temperate ladies, they took little notice of their brother's anger and simply got on with things.

"We refuse to pander to self-indulgence," they informed me as they took charge of our pantry, disposing of the food that had gone stale and replacing it with fresh produce. "We have never been ones to wallow in misfortune. And you must not wallow either, Eliza," they insisted, sitting on either side of me and attempting to balance kindness and understanding with disapproval of our new, slovenly ways. "Your mother has passed, she is with the Lord now, it is a sad and terrible thing but there it is. Life for you and our brother must go on."

"Life, as I know it, is at an end," replied Father bitterly, standing in the doorway and making us jump in surprise for we had not realized that he was eavesdropping on the conversation. "My only wish now is to join my dear Angeline in that dark place from which no man may return."

"Stuff and nonsense, Wilfred," said Aunt Rachel, standing up and marching across to him, hands on her hips, her expression one of fury mixed with compassion, both emotions struggling to attain the upper hand. "I've never heard such rot in all my days. And don't you think it cruel to say such a thing in front of the child when she has already suffered such a terrible loss?"

Father's face descended into the very picture of misery—he did not wish to cause me further pain but was suffering so badly that he could not resist his self-indulgent language—and when I looked at him and he turned away, unable to meet my eyes, I burst into tears, feeling for all the world that I wanted nothing more than to run out on to the street and leave this place as far behind me as I could, to disappear into the nameless crowds of London and become an indigent, a traveller, a nobody. Before I knew it my aunts were fussing around the both of us, chastising us and comforting us in equal parts, trying to control their natural frustration. It soon became clear that Father was too deeply lost in grief to take care of me and so it was decided that I should return to Cornwall with Aunt Hermione for the summer, while Aunt Rachel stayed in London to minister to her younger brother, a decision which turned out to be a very sensible one, for I spent a happy summer in the country, coming to terms with my loss and learning to cope with it, while somehow Aunt Rachel brought Father back from the depths of his despair to a place where he could take charge of his life, his responsibilities and his daughter once again. By the time I returned to London in the autumn and we were reconciled to each other, it was clear that the worst was over. We would miss Mother, of course, and we would speak of her often, but we had both grown to understand that death was a natural phenomenon, albeit a sorrowful one for those left behind, but one that every man and woman must accept as the price we pay for life.

"I let you down, I fear," Father told me when the two of us were alone in the house again. "It will not happen another time, I promise you that. I will always look after you, Eliza. I will keep you safe."

We made a happy, if somewhat resigned, pair in our home from that day on. Naturally, I attended to the domestic duties. I took charge of the cooking while Father's salary allowed us to

employ a maid-of-all-work, a Scottish girl called Jessie, on two
afternoons a week, when she would clean the house from top
to bottom and complain about the pains in her back and the
arthritis in her hands, although she was only a year or two older
than I. Despite her cantankerous nature, I was grateful that we
could afford her, for I hated cleaning with a passion and she
took that duty away from me.

At St. Elizabeth's School, which I had attended since girl-
hood, I had always been an excellent student, and soon after
completing my education, I was offered the position of teacher
to the small girls, a position that suited me so well that it became permanent within six months. I took great pleasure in
my young charges, who were between five and six years of
age, teaching them the rudiments of sums and spelling, the
history of the Kings and Queens of England, while preparing
them for the more difficult subjects which would be theirs to
endure at the hands of Miss Lewisham, into whose calloused
hands I would deliver them, trembling and crying, within
twelve months. It was difficult not to form an attachment to
my small girls. They had such pleasant dispositions and were
so entirely trusting when it came to their dealings with me,
but I learned early on that if I was to thrive as a teacher—and
I took it for granted that I would always be a teacher, for marriage seemed unlikely given the fact that I had no fortune,
no particular place in society and, worst of all, a face that my
aunt Hermione once said could curdle milk ("I don't mean it
unkindly, child," she added, noticing my disquiet, leaving me
to wonder how else she could possibly have meant it)—then
I must balance affection with resilience. This notion, however,
sat fine with me. I would live as a spinster, I would have my
small girls to teach and the summer holidays perhaps to take

a little trip—I dreamed of visiting the French Alps or the Italian city of Venice and would occasionally wonder whether I might even find paid employment as a lady's companion during the summer months—I would take care of Father and our house. I would sympathize with Jessie about her numerous inflammations and ask her whether or not she had seen to the skirting boards yet. I would not worry about suitors, who in turn would certainly not worry about me, and I would face life with a seriousness of intent and a positive outlook. And for all this, I was content and happy.

The only slight change in these circumstances came about with the arrival of Arthur Covan as instructor to our oldest girls and with whom, as I mentioned, I formed a particular friendship. Mr. Covan arrived to us from Harrow and was taking a year's experience in teaching before heading up to the Varsity to read classics. Arthur made me laugh—he was a fine mimic—and flattered me with his attentions. He was a handsome boy, a year younger than me, with a mop of dark hair and a ready smile. To my shame I allowed myself the most indulgent fantasies of what it might be like if we were to "step out" together, although he never did anything to encourage this delusion. And even when it all came out a few months later, when his name was in the papers and the public was baying for his blood, I still could not find it in myself to condemn him fully, although naturally I never spoke to him again. And then, of course, he took his own life. But no more of that now. I was speaking of my position at St. Elizabeth's, not indulging in sentimental daydreams.

It was only now, with Father gone, that it occurred to me how alone I truly was and whether this simple plan for my future would be enough to satisfy all my needs. My aunts had passed away in the intervening years. I had no siblings to take care of, and none who might take care of me, no cousins in whose lives I might take an interest, and none who might take an interest in mine. I was entirely alone. Should I disappear in the middle of the night, should I be murdered as I walked home from school one day, there was no one who would miss me or question my withdrawal from society. I had been left a solitary figure.

Which, perhaps, is why the advertisement for the governess position in Norfolk seemed like such an inviting opportunity.

Should I have waited longer before making my rash decision to leave? Perhaps, but I was not in my right senses, so struck was I by the grief which had fallen upon my mind. And a knock on the front door a little later in the evening sealed the matter when I was confronted by a thug of a man who called himself Mr. Lowe—a fitting name—who informed me that the house I had grown up in did not in fact belong to Father, but that we were mere tenants, an assertion he backed up with incontrovertible paperwork.

"But I thought it would be mine now," I said in astonishment and he smiled at me, revealing a row of yellow teeth and one black one.

"It can be if you want it," he declared. "But here's the rental figure and I expect my money every Tuesday without fail. Your father never let me down on that score, may God have mercy on his soul."

"I can't afford that," I said. "I'm just a schoolteacher."

"And I'm a businessman," he snarled. "So if you can't, then you best pack your things. Or take in a lodger. A quiet girl, that is. No men. I won't run a bawdy house."

I flushed, humiliated, and felt an urge to kick him. I knew not why Father had never told me that the house did not belong to him, nor why he never asked me to contribute to the rent when I found employment. At any other time I would have been deeply upset by this but it seemed at that moment like just one more trauma and, recalling the notice in the newspaper, I sat down later that night and wrote my letter of application, dropping it into the post-box first thing the following morning before I could change my mind. Tuesday and Wednesday were busy days—I sorted through some of Father's effects and, with Jessie's help, organized his bedroom in such a way that it betrayed few signs of its previous occupant. I wrote to Mr. Heston at the museum and he replied immediately to accept my offer of Father's insect books and correspondence. I placed all of Mr. Dickens' novels in a box and hid them away at the back of a wardrobe for I could not bear to look at them now. And then, on Thursday morning, a letter made its way back to me from Norfolk, expressing satisfaction with my qualifications and offering me the position without interview. I was surprised, of course. The advertisement had stressed urgency but for all that H. Bennet knew, I could have been completely wrong for the job, and yet he seemed content to place the well-being of his children in my hands.

Of course, I was uncertain whether or not such a radical transformation of my life was sensible, but now that the offer was there, I believed that a change of circumstances could be just the thing, and met with Mrs. Farnsworth in her office later that morning, tendering my notice, which she accepted with a great deal of irritability on her part, pointing out that I was leaving them high and dry in the middle of the school year and who could she possibly find to tutor the small girls at such short notice? I accepted the blame and rather played on my grief, nefarious creature, in order to avoid further scolding, and finally she could see that my mind would not be changed and reluctantly shook my hand and wished me well for the future. I left St. Elizabeth's that afternoon torn between feelings of excitement and utter terror.

By Friday, less than a week since Father and I had made our way towards Knightsbridge in pouring rain, not even a full seven days since Mr. Dickens had entered the speakers' hall to discover more than a thousand of his loyal readers huddled together, steaming with perspiration, I had closed up our house, dismissed Jessie with a week's pay in lieu, and was seated on a train to a county I had never visited, to work for a family I had never met in a position I had never held before. To say that this was an eventful and emotional week would be to understate matters considerably. But to suggest that it was any more shocking than what was to come over the weeks that followed would be simply a lie.

Chapter Four

IT WAS A SURPRISINGLY sunny day when I left London. The city had contrived to kill my beloved father, but now that it had succeeded in its cruel adventure it was satisfied to be benevolent once again. I felt an antipathy towards the place as I left, an emotion that surprised me, for I had always loved the capital, but as the train pulled out of Liverpool Street Station, the sun pouring through the window and blinding my eyes, I thought it harsh and unfair, an old friend who had turned on me for no good reason and whom I was now happy to see the back of. At that moment I believed that I could lead a contented life and never lay eyes on London again.

Seated opposite me in the railway carriage was a young man of about my own age and although we had not spoken since boarding the train I allowed myself several surreptitious glances in his direction, for he was rather attractive, and I found that, however hard I tried to look away and focus my attention on the passing fields and farmlands, I kept being drawn back to his face. He reminded me of Arthur Covan, that's the truth of it. As we pulled into Colchester, I noticed that he grew rather pale and his eyes filled with tears. He closed them for a few moments, perhaps hoping to stem their tide, but when he opened them again a few fell down his cheeks and he used his handkerchief to wipe them away. Catching me looking at him, he ran a hand across his face and I felt a desperate urge to ask him whether he was quite all right, whether he might like to talk for a little while, but whatever hurt was lingering in his heart, whatever trauma was causing him to lose control of his emotions, was not to be shared, and once the train pulled out of the station, he stood up, embarrassed by his display, and moved to a different carriage.

Of course, with the benefit of hindsight, I can see that the decisions I made that week were impulsive and foolish ones. I was lost in shock, my entire world had fallen apart over the course of seven days, and where I should have taken solace in my work, in my school, in my small girls, and yes, even in the company of the likes of Mrs. Farnsworth and Jessie, I made the hasty decision to uproot myself from everything I had ever known, the streets around Hyde Park where I had played as a child, the Serpentine that still filled me with memories of Bull's Eye, the twists and turns of the laneways that would lead me from home to the familiarity of my classroom. I was desperate for change, but the curtains of that dark room up-stairs that had claimed both my parents' lives, and the life of my infant sister, might have been opened, the windows might have been flung wide, it might have been aired thoroughly with good, honest London air, it might have been redecorated and made inviting once again, a place to live and not to die. I was leaving all of these things behind and going to a part of the country I had never visited, and to do what? To be a gov-erness to who knew how many children for a family who had not even sent an agent to meet with me before offering me the position. Foolish girl! You might have stayed. You might have lived a life that was happy.

The sun of London gave way to a cold wind in Stowmarket which blew against the train and made me feel rather unsettled, and by the time we reached Norwich in the early evening that in turn had been exchanged for a thick fog, the kind of pea-souper which reminded me of home, despite the fact that I was doing all I could to put that place out of my mind. As we came closer to Thorpe Station, I pulled the letter I had received the previous morning from my bag and read it thoroughly for perhaps the tenth time.

> Gaudlin Hall,
> 24 October 1867
>
> Dear Miss Caine,
> Your application received with gratitude. Your experience acceptable. You are offered paid employment as Governess, by rates and conditions specified in the *Morning Post* (21st October number). You are expected on the evening of the 25th, by the five o'clock train. The Gaudlin man, Heckling, will collect you in the carriage. Please do not be tardy.
> Sincerely,
> H. Bennet

On reading it again, it struck me, as it had on every previous occasion, how curious a letter it was. The phrasing was so hurried, and once again there was no mention of how many children would be under my authority. And who was this "H. Bennet" who omitted the requisite "*esq.*" after his name? Was he a gentleman at all, or perhaps the head of a diminished household? What was his business? There was nothing to tell me. I sighed and felt a degree of anxiety as the train pulled into the station but determined to be strong, no matter what lay ahead. That, at least, would stand me in good stead in the weeks that followed.

I descended the train steps and looked around. It was almost impossible to see anything through the murky greyness of the fog but the direction that the other passengers were walking in assured me that the exit might be found if I followed them, and I began to walk even as I heard the doors of the train carriages slamming shut again for the return journey and the signal-man's whistle. Several people were running past me, making haste to board the train before it departed and, perhaps unable to see me through the mist, one collided with me, knocking my case from my hand and letting her own fall at the same time.

"Excuse me," she said, not sounding particularly apologetic, but I did not mind too much for it was obvious that she did not want to miss her train. I reached for her suitcase, which had fallen to my left, and handed it across to her, and as I did so I noticed the monogrammed initials, etched red in the dark-brown leather. *HB*. I stared at them, wondering briefly why those initials meant something to me. At that moment I caught the lady's eye and it seemed almost as if she knew me, for she stared with an expression of recognition, one that mingled pity with regret, before pulling the case from my hand, shaking her head quickly and disappearing into the fog and the carriage ahead.

I stood there, surprised by her rudeness, and then remembered why "HB" had seemed so familiar. But it was ridiculous, of course. A coincidence, nothing more. England must be littered with people with those initials.

Turning round now, I grew rather disoriented. I walked in the direction of what I believed to be the platform exit but as there were no passengers either departing or boarding trains from here, it grew difficult to be sure whether or not I was correct. To my left, the engines of the train returning to London were growing noisier as it prepared to depart; to my right, there was another track and I could hear the sound of a second train approaching. Or was it just behind me? It was hard to know. I turned round and gasped; which way should I walk? There was noise everywhere. I reached a hand out, try-ing to feel my way along, but nothing was where I expected it to be. The sound of voices began to grow louder around me and now there were people again, pushing past with their suitcases and valises, and how could they see where they were going, I wondered, when I could not even see my own hand stretched out before my face? I had not felt so unsettled since the afternoon in the graveyard, and a panic rose inside me, a sense of great terror and foreboding, and I thought that if I did not march forward with intent, then I would be left on this platform for ever, unable to see or breathe, and that I should live out my days here. And so, taking my heart in my hands, I lifted my right foot and started to press forward once again just as a great whistling noise—the sound of the sec-ond train—increased to a violent scream and to my horror I felt a pair of hands on my back, pushing me forward with a sharp thrust, and I stumbled, ready to fall headlong just as a third hand gripped my elbow, pulled me back quickly, and I stumbled over my feet towards a wall where, almost immedi-ately, the fog began to disperse a little and I could make out the man who had dragged me so violently from where I had been standing.

"Good God, miss," he said, and I could see his face now; it was kindly and fine-featured; he wore a rather elegant pair of spectacles. "Didn't you see where you were going?" he asked. "You nearly stepped out in front of a train. You would have been killed."

I stared at him in confusion and then looked back towards the place from which he had pulled me and sure enough the second train was screeching to a halt. Had I made another step forward I would have fallen beneath it and been crushed to death. I felt faint at the idea.

"I didn't mean to—" I began.

"Another moment and you would have been under it."

"Someone pushed me," I said, staring directly into his face. "A pair of hands. I felt them."

He shook his head. "I don't think so," he said. "I was watching you. I could see which way you were going. There wasn't anyone behind you."

"But I felt them," I insisted. I stared at the platform, swallowed hard and turned back to him. "I felt them!" I repeated.

"You've had a shock, that's all," said the man, apparently dismissing this idea, and me as an hysteric. "Can I get you anything for your nerves? I'm a doctor, you see. Some sweet tea perhaps? There's a little shop over there, it's nothing much of course but—"

"I'm fine," I said, shaking my head and trying to compose myself. He must be right, I decided. If he was watching and there was no one there, then I must have imagined it. It was the fog, that was all. It was playing games with my mind. "I must apologize," I said finally, trying to laugh the incident away. "I don't know what came over me. I felt quite dizzy. I couldn't see anything."

"Good job I caught you," he replied, grinning at me, displaying a very even set of white teeth. "Oh dear," he added. "That does sound terribly pompous, doesn't it? Like I'm hoping that you'll pin a medal for bravery on my lapel."

I smiled; I liked him. A ridiculous thought occurred to me. That he would say that I should abandon the idea of Gaudlin altogether and come with him instead. Where? I did not know. I almost laughed at the absurdity of it. What was wrong with me that day? First the young man on the train and now this. It was as if I had taken leave of all my morals.

"Oh, here's my wife now," he said after a moment and I turned to see a young, pretty woman approaching us, an expression of concern on her face as her husband explained what had just happened. I tried to smile.

"You should come home with us," said Mrs. Toxley, for that was the couple's name, as she stared at me with honest concern on her face. "You're really quite pale, you know. You could probably do with a pick-me-up."

"You're very kind," I said, wondering whether I could do such an unlikely thing, whether it was appropriate or not. Perhaps they would allow me to be governess to their children, if they had any, and I would not have to go to Gaudlin Hall at all. "I'd very much like to, only—"

"Eliza Caine?"

A voice from our left made us all turn in surprise. A man was standing there. He was in his early sixties, I should say, roughly dressed with florid features. He did not appear to have shaved in several days and his hat was an inadequate match for his overcoat, making him appear slightly ridiculous. I could smell tobacco on his clothes and whisky his breath. He scratched his face and his fingernails displayed themselves dark and dirty, stained as yellow as his teeth, and he didn't say another word, waiting for me to reply.

"That's right," I said. "Do I know you?"

"Heckling," he replied, prodding his chest with his thumb several times. "Carriage is over here."

And with that he turned away in the direction of the afore-said carriage and I was left with my bags, my saviour and his wife, who both turned to stare at me, a little embarrassed by the scene and the extraordinary rudeness of the man.

"I'm the new governess," I explained. "At Gaudlin Hall. He's been sent to fetch me."

"Oh," said Mrs. Toxley, looking at her husband, who, I no-ticed, caught her eye for a moment before looking away. "I see," she added after a long pause.

An uncomfortable silence settled over us—at first I thought that I had offended the Toxleys in some way but then I realized that this was impossible, for I had said nothing untoward, I had merely explained who I was—but their warmth and generos-ity of a moment before had been suddenly replaced by anxiety and discomfort. What odd people, I thought as I retrieved my case, thanked them both and made my way towards the car-riage. And they had seemed so affable before!

As I walked away, however, something made me glance back in their direction and I saw that they were staring at me as if there was something they wanted to say but could not find the words. Mrs. Toxley turned to her husband and muttered some-thing in his ear but he shook his head and looked distinctly uncertain about what was required of him.

Again, hindsight is a wonderful thing, but I look back now and I think of that moment, I think of Alex and Madge Toxley standing there on the platform at Thorpe Station and I want to scream at them, I want to run and shake them, I want to look them squarely in their faces and say, you knew, you knew even then. Why didn't you say something? Why didn't you speak?

Why didn't you warn me?

Chapter Five

I CLIMBED INTO THE back of Heckling's carriage, my suitcase placed securely in the rear, and with a great roar that seemed to build from somewhere deep inside his being, the Gaudlin man urged the horse, Winnie, forward. I felt a strong desire to glance behind once again at the Toxleys—their curious behaviour, coupled with my near accident on the platform, had unsettled me greatly—but resolved to remain calm and resilient. Whatever nerves were attacking me could, I felt, be put down to the fact that I was in an unfamiliar county away from the only city I had ever known, and that it would take time for me to feel comfortable in these new surroundings. I could not allow my mind to play tricks with me. This was the start of a new life; I determined to be optimistic.

"Is the mist always this thick?" I asked, leaning forward in the carriage in an attempt to make conversation with Heckling, who showed no sign of wanting to make conversation with me. The fog, which had dissipated slightly on the platform during my conversation with the Toxleys, had grown dense again as we began our journey and I wondered how he could see well enough to navigate accurately the roads that would eventually lead us to our destination, a few miles to the west of the Norfolk Broads. "Mr. Heckling?" I said, when he showed no sign of offering a response, and this time I was sure I could make out a certain stiffening in his shoulders. "I asked whether the mist is always this heavy."

He turned his head slightly and rotated his jaw in a rather unpleasant fashion, as if he was chewing on something, before shrugging and turning back to the road.

"Always been this thick, I s'pose," he offered. "Long as I can remember anyway. Summertime, it's not so bad. But now, aye." He considered this and nodded his head. "We make do."

"You're Norfolk born and bred, I expect?" I asked.

"Aye."

"You must like it here then."

"Must I?" he muttered, his voice deep and filled with a mixture of boredom and irritation. "Aye, I expect I must. If you say so, that is."

I sighed and sat back in the seat, unwilling to engage with him if he was going to be so cantankerous. Father, in addition to his dislike of Americans, the French and the Italians, had not cared greatly for the people of Norfolk and I knew that Heckling, who was certainly no Barkis and was proving himself entirely unwilling, would have irritated him greatly. During his time at the Norwich museum he had found them suspicious and discourteous, although it was possible that they simply did not care for the idea of a young Londoner arriving in their town to do something that a local boy could perhaps have done just as well. It was a coincidence that we should both spend time working in this county and I wondered whether I might have a chance to visit the museum that he and Mr. Kirby had established together, little more than fifty miles away.

Sitting back now, I watched as the scenery, what little I could see of it anyway, passed by. The carriage was rather comfortable and I was glad of that. A thick blanket had been left on the seat and I laid it across my lap, settling my hands atop and feeling quite contented. As the roads over which we passed were rather bumpy it would have been a much more difficult journey had not the seating been so exquisite, which gave me every reason to believe that my employer was a man of substantial means. I fell to thinking about H. Bennet and the life that I was going towards. I prayed that the home would be a happy one, that the Bennets would be a loving couple and that their children, however many there might be, would be kind and welcoming. I had no home of my own now, after all, and assuming that the employment worked out and they took to me as I hoped to take to them, then Gaudlin Hall might be where I resided for many years to come.

In my mind, I pictured a large house with many rooms, something rather palatial, with a spiralling driveway and lawns that went on as far as the eye could see. I think I based this entirely on the fact that my host's name was Bennet and I associated this with the young lady at the heart of *Pride and Prejudice*. Her story had resolved itself in an extraordinary mansion, Mr. Darcy's home at Pemberley. Perhaps these Bennets would have earned similar good fortune? Although of course Elizabeth and her sisters were part of a fiction and this, the house that I was travelling towards, was not. Still, as I reached out and ran my hand against the thick fabric of the carriage seat, it did pass through my mind that they must be moneyed at least, and that should mean that Gaudlin was something special.

"Mr. Bennet," I said, leaning forward again and wiping my face, for a thin drizzle of rain had begun to fall. "He is in business, I suppose?"

"Who?" asked Heckling, holding fast to his reins, keeping a close eye on the dark road ahead.

"Mr. Bennet," I repeated. "My new employer. I wondered what he does for a living. Is he in business perhaps? Or . . ." I struggled to think of an alternative. (I barely even knew what "in business" meant, other than the fact that a great many men seemed to describe themselves thus and seemed unwilling or unable to define the term in more intelligible ways.) "Is he the local Member perhaps? I understand that a great many wealthy families offer the head of the household to Parliament."

Heckling deigned to turn now and he fixed me with an irritated expression. Truthfully, he looked at me as if I was a dog, scampering about his feet, desperate for attention, yapping and pawing at him when all he wanted was to be left alone with his thoughts. Another in my position might have looked away but I held his glance; he would not intimidate me. I was to be governess, after all, and he was merely the Gaudlin man.

"Who be he?" he asked finally in a contemptuous fashion.

"Who be who?" I replied, then shook my head, annoyed by how quickly I was adopting his Norfolk style. "What do you mean by *who be he*?" I asked.

"You said Mr. Bennet. I don't know any Mr. Bennet."

I laughed. Was this a trick of some sort? A game that he and the other servants had invented to make the new governess feel ill at ease? If it was, it was cruel and malicious and I wanted no part of it. I knew from teaching my small girls that if one showed the slightest sign of vulnerability at the start then one was lost for ever. I was made of stronger stuff than that and was determined to show it.

"Really, Mr. Heckling," I said, laughing a little, trying to keep my tone light. "Of course you do. He sent you to collect me, after all."

"I were sent to collect you," agreed Heckling. "But not by no Mr. Bennet."

A sudden rush of wind forced me back in my seat as the rain started to fall in heavier drops and I wished that Heckling had brought the covered carriage rather than the open one. (Foolish girl! I was still adrift in my notions of Pemberley. In my mind there was an entire fleet of carriages waiting at Gaudlin Hall for me, one for every day of the week.)

"Did the housekeeper send you then?" I asked.

"Mr. Raisin sent me," he replied. "Well, Mr. Raisin and Miss Bennet anyway. Between them, I s'pose."

"And who, pray tell," I asked, "is Mr. Raisin?"

Heckling stroked his chin and, with the approach of evening, I could see the manner in which his dark whiskers were turning to grey in the moonlight. "Lawyer fellow, i'nt he," he said.

"A lawyer?" I asked.

"Aye."

I considered this. "But whose lawyer?"

"Gaudlin lawyer."

I said nothing, simply placed these facts together in my mind and considered them for a moment. "Mr. Raisin is the family solicitor," I said, more for my own benefit than his. "And he instructed you to collect me from the station. Well, who is this Miss Bennet then? She is the master's sister perhaps?"

"What master?" asked Heckling and, really, I had had quite enough by now.

"The master of Gaudlin," I said with a sigh.

Heckling laughed, then seemed to think better of it. "Ain't no master of Gaudlin," he said finally. "Not no more. Missus took care of that, di'nt she?"

"No master?" I asked, wondering what ridiculous game he was playing with me. "But of course there's a master. There must be. Who is this Miss Bennet if not some relative of the master? Why, she is the one who employed me, after all. I assumed she was head of the household but according to you she holds no such position."

"Miss Bennet were now't more than a governess," he said. "Just like you. Now't more, now't less."

"But that's ridiculous. Why would the governess advertise for a new governess? It's quite beyond her responsibilities."

"She were leaving, weren't she?" explained Heckling. "But she wouldn't go till she found someone new. I took her in carriage to t'station, she got out, told me to wait, said you'd be along shortly and here you are. To take her place. Winnie here din't have more than ten minutes to rest."

I sat back, open-mouthed, uncertain what to make of this. It sounded ridiculous. According to this man, this driver, Gaudlin Hall had no master, my position had been advertised by the previous incumbent, who, upon knowing that I had arrived in the county, saw fit to leave it immediately. What sense could such a thing make? I decided the man must be mad or drunk or both and resolved not to discuss this with him any further and simply sit back, keep my own counsel, and wait until I arrived at our destination, at which point matters would surely be explained.

And then I remembered. *HB*. The woman who had collided with me after I disembarked the London train. It must have been her. H. Bennet. She had looked at me and seemed to know me. She must have been watching for a young woman who fitted my description, satisfied herself that I was she, and then made her escape. But why would she do such a thing? It was extraordinary behaviour. Quite incomprehensible.

Chapter Six

I MUST HAVE DOZED off shortly after this for I was soon in a fit-ful, uncomfortable sleep. I dreamed that I was back in my school, or rather something resembling St. Elizabeth's but not entirely the same, and Mrs. Farnsworth was there, speaking to my small girls, while Father was seated in the back row engaged in conversation with someone I identified as Miss Bennet, although she did not bear the same physical charac-teristics as the woman on the platform. Where she had been stocky and red-haired, the woman in my dream was dark and beautiful with Mediterranean features. No one would speak to me—it was as if they did not see me at all—and from there things grew rather more hazy and descended into a blend of strangeness and mystery, in the way that dreams will, but I fancy that I was asleep for some time for when I woke it was even darker than before, night-time now, and we were turning on to a narrow laneway that opened out finally to present a view of two extraordinary iron gates.

"Gaudlin Hall up yonder," said Heckling, pausing the horse for a moment and indicating some place in the distance, al-though it was impossible to see it clearly through the darkness of the night. I sat up in my seat, adjusting my skirt beneath the blanket, aware of a stale, dry taste in my mouth and the heaviness of my eyes. My clothes were rather wet now and I regretted the fact that I would be meeting my new employers—whoever they were—for the first time in such a bedraggled state. I had never been an attractive woman but worked on my appearance to present the best possible aspect; such refinements were lost to me now. I hoped that they would excuse me quickly to my room after my arrival so that I could make some basic repairs.

My idea of a long driveway was not inaccurate and it took a few minutes for the house to come fully into sight. It was no Pemberley, that was for sure, but it was a grand country house nevertheless. Tall and imposing, the exterior bore a certain Baroque splendour with two wings jutting out from an impressive front portico, and I suspected that it was seventeenth century in origin, one of those houses whose design was influenced by the European fashions after the Restoration. I wondered how many bedrooms there might be inside—at least a dozen, I imagined—and whether or not the ballroom, for there was sure to be one in a house of this size, was still in use. Of course, I was in no way accustomed to this style of living and it rather excited me to imagine myself residing in such a place. And yet there was something frightening about it too, some darkness that I assumed would be washed away by the coming morning. But as I stared at my new home, I felt a curious urge to ask Heckling to turn the carriage around and drive me back to Norwich, where I might sit on a bench at Thorpe Station until the sun came up and then return to London, a job badly done.

"Now, Winnie," said Heckling as we pulled up at the front door and he descended, his boots crunching in the gravel as he moved to the back of the carriage to remove my suitcase.

Realizing that the man did not have the manners to open the door for me, I reached down to the handle to twist it. To my surprise, it would not budge. I frowned, recalling how lightly it had given way when I boarded the carriage in the first place, but now it appeared to be sealed fast.

"Staying in there, are you?" asked Heckling, ignorant fellow, standing on the opposite side of the carriage and making no move whatsoever to come to my aid.

"I can't get out, Mr. Heckling," I replied. "The door appears to be jammed."

"Now't wrong wi' it," he said, coughing some horrendous mess up from the base of his throat and spitting it on the driveway. "Turn it, that's all."

I sighed and reached down once again for the handle—where were the man's manners, after all?—and as I tried to twist it, I had a sudden reminiscence about one of my small girls, Jane Hebley, who had taken against school one day for some silly reason and refused to emerge from the girls' bathroom. When I attempted to open it from the outside she held it tightly and, resilient in her determination, managed to stay in there for several minutes before I was able to wrench it open. That was how this felt now. It was a ridiculous notion, of course, but it felt as if the harder I tried to twist the handle, the tighter some unseen force held it shut from the outside. Had I not been outdoors, and had Heckling not been the only other soul in sight, I would have sworn that someone was playing tricks with me.

"Please," I said, turning round to glare at him. "Can't you help me?"

He swore a blasphemy under his breath, dropped my suitcase on the ground without ceremony and walked around, and I stared at him irritably, wondering why he was being so difficult. I looked forward to him trying the door for himself so he would see that I was not some foolish woman who did not know how to turn a handle, but to my surprise, the moment he reached out for it, it opened easily, quite as easily as it had when I had first boarded the carriage a couple of hours earlier.

"Ain't too difficult," he grumbled, walking away, refusing even to offer me his hand as I descended, and I simply shook my head, wondering what on earth was wrong with me. Had I been turning it the wrong way? It was ridiculous, after all. The door had been sealed shut. I could not open it. And yet he could.

"Gaudlin Hall," he said as we made our way towards the front door. He pulled a heavy rope and I heard the bell ringing within, at which time he placed my suitcase on the step beside me and tipped his hat. "Evening then, Governess," he said.

"Aren't you coming in?" I asked, surprised that I should just be deposited here like this, as if I was little more than a piece of luggage.

"Never do," he said, walking away. "I live out yonder."

And to my astonishment, he simply boarded the carriage and started to drive away, while I stood there, open-mouthed, wondering whether this was the manner in which all new employees were treated here.

A moment later, the door opened and I turned, expecting at last to come face to face with my new employer, whoever he or she might be.

It was not a man or woman standing there, however, but a little girl. She was about twelve years old, I thought, older than my small girls, and very pale and pretty. Her hair was curled into ringlets that hung down to her shoulders and perhaps a little further. She was dressed in a white nightdress, fastened at the neck and hanging to her ankles, and as she stood there, the candles in the hallway illuminating her from behind, she took on a spectral appearance that rather frightened me.

"Hello," she said quietly.

"Good evening," I replied, smiling, trying to put myself at ease by pretending that nothing was amiss. "I didn't expect the door to be answered by the daughter of the house."

"Oh no? Who did you expect to answer it then? The Prime Minister?"

"Well, the butler," I said. "Or the maid."

The little girl smiled. "We have fallen on diminished times," she said after a long pause.

I nodded. I had no answer to this. "Well then," I said. "Perhaps I should introduce myself. I'm Eliza Caine. The new governess."

There was an almost imperceptible roll of the girl's eyes and she opened the door wider to let me in. "It's only been a few hours," she said.

"Since what?"

"Since the last one left. Miss Bennet. Still, at least she's gone. She wanted to go, terribly. But she couldn't, of course. Not until she found someone to take her place. That was kind of her, I suppose. It does her great credit. And here you are."

I stepped inside, uncertain what to make of this extraordinary speech. Looking around, expecting her mother or father to descend the staircase despite what Heckling had said, I found myself immediately impressed by the grandeur of the house. It was very traditional and no expense had been spared on its ornamentation. And yet, for all that, it seemed to me to be a home which had been decorated perhaps several years before, and little had been done to keep it looking fresh in recent times. Still, it was clean and well ordered. Whoever took care of the place did a good job. As the little girl closed the door behind me, it sealed with a heavy sound, making me jump and turn round in fright, at which point I startled again, for standing next to her, wearing a similarly white, crisp nightshirt, was a little boy, perhaps four years her junior. I hadn't seen him before. Had he been hiding behind the door?

"Eliza Caine," said the little girl, tapping her index finger against her lower lip. "What a funny name. It sounds common."

"The working classes all have names like that, I think," said the little boy, scrunching his face up as if he was almost certain that this was true but not entirely so. I stared at him, wondering whether he meant to be rude, but he offered me such a friendly smile that I felt he was just stating the obvious. If we had to speak in terms of classes, then I supposed I was working class. I was here, after all, to work.

"Did you have a governess when you were a girl?" he asked me then. "Or did you go to school?"

"I went to school," I told him. "St. Elizabeth's in London."

"I've always wondered what that would be like," said the girl. "Eustace here would suffer dreadfully at a normal school, I think," she added, nodding in the direction of her brother. "He's quite a delicate child, as you can see, and boys can be terribly rough. Or so I've heard. I don't know any boys myself. Other than Eustace, of course. Do you know many boys, Miss Caine?"

"Only the brothers of the small girls I teach," I said. "Or taught. I was a teacher, you see."

"At the same school you attended as a girl?"

"Yes."

"My goodness," she said, smirking a little. "It's almost as if you never grew up. Or never wanted to. But it's true what I say, isn't it? About little boys. They can be terribly rough."

"Some," I said, looking around, wondering whether we were going to stand here chatting all night or whether I might be shown to my room and introduced to the adults. "So," I said, smiling at them and attempting to speak in an authoritative manner. "Here I am anyway. I wonder, could you let your mama know that I have arrived? Or your papa? They might not have heard the carriage."

I noticed the boy, Eustace, stiffen slightly as I made refer- ence to his parents but chose not to remark on it. The little girl, however, allowed her demeanour to slip a little and she bit her lip and looked away with an expression approaching, but not quite reaching, embarrassment.

"Poor Eliza Caine," she said. "I'm afraid you've been brought here under false pretences. That is a phrase, isn't it?" she added. "I read it in a book recently and rather liked the sound of it."

"It is a phrase, yes," I said. "Although I don't think it can mean what you think it means. I've been hired to be your gov- erness. Your father placed the advertisement in the *Morning Post*." I didn't care what Heckling had said; the notion that the previous governess had placed the notice was quite absurd.

"He didn't, as it happens," said the girl lightly, and now Eustace turned and pressed his small body against hers, and she put an arm around him. It was true, he was a delicate child. I thought he could break quite easily. "Perhaps we should sit down, Miss Caine," she said, leading the way towards the drawing room. "You must be tired after your journey."

I followed in astonishment, both amused and disturbed by her grown-up manner. She waited until I had sat down on a long sofa before taking her place in an armchair opposite me, as if she was mistress of Gaudlin and not the daughter of the house. Eustace hovered between us but then chose to sit at the very end of the sofa, staring at his toes.

"Your parents are home, aren't they?" I asked, sitting opposite her, beginning to wonder whether this entire position was some elaborate ruse, designed to fool a grieving young woman for no apparent reason. Perhaps the family was comprised of lunatics.

"They're not, I'm afraid," she said. "There's just Eustace and me. Mrs. Livermore comes in every day to take care of various things. She does a little cooking and leaves meals for us. I hope you like overcooked meat and undercooked vegetables. But she lives in the village. And you've met Heckling, of course. He has a cottage out near the stables. Dreadful man, don't you agree? He reminds me of an ape. And doesn't he smell funny?"

"He smells of the horses," said Eustace, grinning at me, displaying a missing front tooth, and I could not prevent myself, despite my disquiet, from smiling back.

"He does rather," I said before turning back to his sister. "I'm sorry," I said, my tone expressing my confusion. "You didn't tell me your name."

"Didn't I?"

"No."

She frowned and nodded, waiting the longest time before replying. "How rude of me," she said. "My name is Isabella Westerley. I am named for one of the great Queens of Spain."

"Isabella of Castille," I said, remembering my history.

"That's the one," she replied, apparently pleased that I knew to whom she was referring. "My mother was born in Cantabria, you see. My father, on the other hand, was born here. In this very house."

"So you're half English, half Spanish?" I said.

"Yes, if you want to talk of me in terms of fractions," she replied.

I stared at her, then looked around. There were some interesting paintings in the room—forebears of the current inhabitants, I assumed—and a rather lovely tapestry on the wall that faced out towards the courtyard, and it crossed my mind that I would enjoy studying these in more detail the following day, in sunlight.

"But you don't," I began, wondering how to phrase this. "You don't live here alone, surely? Just the two of you?"

"Oh no, of course not," said Isabella. "We're far too young to be left alone."

I exhaled a sigh of relief. "Thank heavens for that," I said. "Well, if your parents aren't here, then who is? Could you call for the adult of the house?"

To my astonishment, without moving even slightly on her seat, Isabella opened her mouth and let out an extraordinary and chilling scream. At least, I thought it was a scream until I realized that she had, in fact, simply called my name. Eliza Caine.

"What on earth?" I said, placing a hand to my breast in fright. I could feel my heart thumping in my chest. I glanced across at Eustace but he seemed unperturbed, merely staring at me, the whites of his eyes appearing very clear in the candlelight.

"I do apologize," said Isabella, smiling a little. "But you asked me to call for the adult of the house."

"And you called my name. You screamed it, in fact."

"You are the adult of the house," she insisted. "Now that Miss Bennet is gone. You've taken her place. You're the only responsible adult here."

"Ha!" said Eustace, laughing a little and shaking his head, as if his sister's statement was not one that he entirely believed. He was not the only person who seemed astonished. I could make no sense of this.

"But the advertisement—" I began, exhausted by now from explaining this.

"Was placed by Miss Bennet," said Isabella. "I told you that. You're her replacement."

"But who takes charge of things? Who, for example, settles my accounts due?"

"Mr. Raisin."

There was that name again. Mr. Raisin, the lawyer. So Heckling had not been entirely deceiving me.

"And where is this Mr. Raisin, might I ask?"

"He lives in the village. I can show you tomorrow if you like."

I glanced at the grandfather clock, beautiful piece, that was standing in the corner of the room. It was already past ten o'clock at night.

"Mr. Raisin settles everything," continued Isabella. "He pays the governess, he pays Mrs. Livermore and Heckling. He sees that we have our pocket money."

"And he reports to your parents?" I asked and this time Isabella shrugged her shoulders and looked away.

"You must be tired," she said.

"I am rather," I agreed. "It's been a very long day."

"And hungry? I'm sure there's something in the kitchen if—"

"No," I said, shaking my head and standing up abruptly. I had had enough of this for one night. "No, the motion of the carriage has unsettled my stomach a little. Perhaps it would be for the best if you just showed me to my room. A good night's sleep will settle things and then tomorrow I can find Mr. Raisin and get to the bottom of this business."

"As you like," said Isabella, standing up. The moment she did, Eustace stood too and clung close to her. She smiled at me, that mistress-of-the-house expression on her face once again. "Won't you follow me?"

We made our way upstairs. It was such a grand and elaborate staircase that I could not resist running my hand against the marble balustrade. The carpet beneath our feet was of a very fine quality too, although like everything else in the house it did not look as if it had been changed in a number of years.

"Eustace and I sleep here on the first floor," said Isabella, indicating a couple of rooms towards the end of a corridor; difficult to see in the darkness now for only Isabella was carrying a candle. "You're on the next floor up. I hope you'll be comfortable. Truly I do."

I looked at her, wondering whether she was trying to be funny, but her face bore a stoic expression and we ascended together, Isabella with her candle three steps in front of Eustace; Eustace three steps before me. I glanced at his bare feet. They were tiny and he had two cuts on his heels, as if he had been wearing shoes that were a size too small. Who looked after this little boy, I wondered, if there were no adults around? "This way, Eliza Caine," said Isabella, making her way along a corridor before opening a large oak door and stepping inside. Entering a few moments later, I appreciated the fact that she had used her own candle to light three more in the bedroom and I looked around, able to see a little better now. It was a rather nice room, large and quite airy, neither cold nor hot, and the bed looked comfortable. My sense of unease dissipated and I felt goodwill towards the children and this place. Everything would be all right in the morning, I decided. Things would become clearer then.

"Well, goodnight then," said Isabella, heading for the door. "I hope you sleep well."

"Goodnight, Miss Caine," said Eustace, following his sister, and I smiled and nodded at them both, wished them a good night's sleep and told them that I would look forward to our getting better acquainted in the morning.

When I was alone, the first time I had been alone since leaving my home that morning, I sat on the bed for a moment and breathed a sigh of relief. I looked around, uncertain whether I should burst into tears at how bizarre this day had been or laugh out loud at the absurdity of it all. When I finally unlatched my suitcase I decided against unpacking and setting my clothes away in the wardrobe and bureau just yet. That, I decided, could wait until the morning. Instead, I simply took out my nightdress and changed into it, glad to relieve myself of my wet clothes, and performed a few ablutions in the bowl that was laid out with a water jug on a side table. I pulled the curtain aside to examine my view and was pleased to see that my room was situated at the front of the house, overlooking the lawns. I tried to open the tall windows to breathe in the night air but they were sealed fast and no pressure that I put on the handles would make them open. I could see the driveway that Heckling and I had rode along streaking off into the distance, and a half-moon illuminated some of the estate that was entirely empty now. Relieved, I climbed into bed, satisfied by the spring of the mattress and the softness of the pillows. Everything will be all right, I told myself. Everything always feels better after a good night's sleep.

I blew out the last remaining candle on my bedside table and pulled the sheets up about my shoulders, closing my eyes and allowing a great yawn to escape my mouth. In the distance I could hear a rather unpleasant cry and wondered whether it was Winnie settling down for the night, but then I heard it again and it was not the sound of a horse, I could tell that much, and decided that no, it must be the wind in the trees, for it had grown even more blustery than before and the rain was starting to pound against my window. It would not keep me awake though, I decided, despite how horrible the sound that wind made, more like a woman being choked to death than anything else, for I was tired and weary after my day's journey and the confusion of the three residents of Gaudlin that I had met so far.

I closed my eyes and sighed, stretching out my body, my legs digging down deeper under the covers, and I expected that at any moment my toes would touch the wooden bedstead, but they did not and I smiled to realize that the bed was longer than I was, that I could stretch out as much as I wanted, and I did so, pleased to feel my aching limbs loosen up as they reached as far as they could, the toes dancing beneath the sheets, a sensation of the most delightful pleasure, until a pair of hands grabbed both my ankles tightly, the fingers pressing sharply against the bone, as they pulled me down into the bed and I gasped, dragging myself back up quickly, wondering what kind of terrible nightmare I had fallen into. Throwing myself from the bed, I pulled the curtains across and ripped the bedspread away but there was nothing there. I stood, my heart pounding. I had not imagined it. Two hands had gripped my ankles and pulled me. I could feel them still. I stared in disbelief, but before I could gather my thoughts the door flew open and a sharp light filled the corridor, a white, ghost-like figure standing before me.

Isabella.

"Are you all right, Eliza Caine?" she asked.

I gasped and ran towards her and the comfort of the candle. "There's something . . ." I began, uncertain how to explain it. "In the bed, there was . . . I could feel . . ."

She stepped forward and held the candle over it, examining it up and down from pillow to base. "It's entirely empty," she said. "Did you have a bad dream?"

I thought about it. It was the only sensible explanation. "I must have," I said. "I thought I was still awake but I must have drifted off. I'm sorry for waking you. I don't . . . I don't know what came over me."

"You woke Eustace, you know. He's a light sleeper."

"I'm sorry about that," I said.

She raised an eyebrow, as if she was considering whether or not she could find it in her heart to forgive me, but settled for a polite nod instead and left me, closing the door behind her.

I stood by the side of the bed for a long time, until I could convince myself that it must have been my imagination playing tricks on me, and then finally, leaving the curtains open to allow the moonlight to pour in, I climbed back into the bed, pulling the sheets around me, and slowly, very slowly, allowed my legs to stretch out once more, where they encountered nothing other than the soft sheets of the bed.

I closed my eyes, convinced that I would never sleep now, but exhaustion must have overtaken me, for when I woke again, the sun was streaming through the windows, the rain and wind had dissipated, and a new day, my first at Gaudlin Hall, was upon me.

Chapter Seven

ITT CAME AS A relief that my first morning at Gaudlin should be a
bright and sunny one, but also a surprise that a night of heavy
rain could give way to such a fine aftermath. I knew nothing of
Norfolk weather, of course, and this might have been a typical
response to an overnight storm but I could not recall when I
had last awoken to such clear skies and pleasant conditions.
In London, there was always the murk of a prodigious fog in
the air, the smell of burnt coal, the sensation that one's body
was being surreptitiously coated with some infamous parasitic
residue that would seep through the pores and sink beneath the
skin, an assassin lurking, but here, looking through the large
windows across the grounds that surrounded the house, I felt
that if I were to run outside and fill my lungs with good, honest
country air, then all my traumas of the past week would begin
to dissolve and threaten my spirits no more.

It was this optimistic sensation that lifted my mood when
otherwise it might have been deflated by apprehension and
loneliness. To my surprise I had enjoyed a good night's sleep
and the various unpleasant businesses of the previous day—my
brush with death at the train station, my difficulty in conversing

with Heckling, the uncertainty regarding my employers, that ridiculous nightmare when I went to bed (for nightmare, I was now certain, was all it could have been, a fantasy born of exhaustion and hunger)—all of these things seemed remote to me now. I was determined that today, the first day of my new life away from London, would be a good one.

The smell of cooking led me directly through a series of connected rooms on the ground floor, the odour growing stronger in each one. The drawing room where I had sat with the children the night before, a rather ornate dining room with a table that might have seated twenty, a small reading room that was filled with marvellous light, a corridor whose walls were decorated with watercolours of butterflies and, finally, the kitchen. I did not know where the Westerleys ate in the mornings for I had not yet received a thorough tour of the house but felt certain that if I followed my nose then I would find the entire family enjoying their breakfast and preparing to welcome me. Surely all this nonsense about Isabella and Eustace's parents would be sorted out then.

To my surprise, however, the kitchen was deserted, although the aromas in the air made it clear that someone had been there not long before, preparing breakfast.

"Hello," I cried, stepping towards the pantry in search of the cook. "Is there anyone here?"

But no, there wasn't. I looked around; the shelves were well stocked. There were fresh vegetables and fruit lying in baskets, and a cold store that, when opened, revealed cuts of beef and poultry encased in glass containers. A bowl of brown eggs sat beneath the window next to a loaf of nut-infused bread that had been delivered of several slices already. Pausing for a moment, wondering what I should do next, my attention was taken by the rather fine arched Romanesque window and, looking through, I observed a portly, middle-aged lady wearing what appeared to be a maid's uniform marching along the gravel in the direction of Heckling's stables, a deeply filled bag in her left hand, a coat and hat adorning her ample frame, and I wondered whether this was the Mrs. Livermore to whom Isabella had referred the night before. I had failed to ask who she was at the time, assuming that she was some type of housekeeper, but the ensemble that this lady was dressed in suggested otherwise.

I stepped across to the pantry door but struggled with the key in the lock, which was stiff and unwilling to turn, much like the windows in my bedroom which, when tried again in the morning, had proved impossible to open. I forced the door, however, and finally emerged into the grounds just as the lady turned the corner of the house and disappeared from sight. I called out, expecting her to hear me and retrace her steps, and when she did not, I followed at rather a good pace, determined to catch up with her, but when I turned the corner myself a few moments later she had vanished entirely. I looked around in astonishment— there did not seem to be anywhere that she could have gone, nor could she have made her way to the far end of the perimeter in such a short time, but the fact remained that she had been there one moment and had disappeared the next. I glanced to my left, through the clump of trees; the horse, Winnie, was standing patiently outside the stables, staring at me, fixing me with a look that unsettled me. Confused, I could think of nothing else to do but turn round and make my way back to the pantry door.

To my frustration it had closed and locked itself from the inside—how it could possibly have done this I did not know, as I had left the door wide open and there was absolutely no breeze to push it shut again—and this left me with no choice but to walk round to the front door of Gaudlin Hall, which was mercifully unlocked, and make my way back through the house to where I had begun.

I sat down at the kitchen table and frowned, wondering what I should do next. Was I to prepare my own breakfast? Had the children eaten? Were they even awake or was I expected to rouse them too? I had almost decided to go back upstairs and knock on Isabella's door when, to my horror, a pair of hands grabbed my ankles from beneath the table, much like the wicked creature in my fantasy had the night before, but before I could scream or leap from my seat, a small boy appeared from beneath and he scampered out with a mischievous grin on his face.

"Eustace," I said, shaking my head and holding a hand to my chest. "You gave me a fright."

"You didn't see me under there, did you?"

"I didn't," I replied, smiling. It was impossible to be angry with him. "I thought I was alone."

"You're never alone at Gaudlin Hall," he said. "Miss Harkness used to say that she would give a month's salary for a day's peace and quiet."

"I prefer company," I told him. "If I'd wanted solitude I would have stayed in London. But look at you," I added after a moment, standing up and taking him in from head to toe. "Don't you look smart!"

It was true; he looked very fine indeed. He was dressed in a neat pair of white trousers, a white shirt and tie and a blue serge jacket that made me want to reach out and stroke the fabric in much the same way that Mr. Dickens' waistcoat, a week earlier, had also made me long to experience the sensation of such expensive material against my fingertips. He had washed too; I could smell the rich scent of carbolic soap that emanated from his body. And his hair was neatly combed, parted at the side and held in place with a little pomade. He might have been going out on a family visit or attending church services, such was his respectable appearance.

"Mama likes me to dress well every day," he said in a confidential tone, leaning forward a little despite the fact that there was no one else in the kitchen. "She says it is the mark of a gentleman to dress at home as if one is going out. One never knows who might call, after all."

"That's true," I said. "But when I was a girl, not much older than you are now, I preferred to wear my runabout clothes when I knew we weren't planning on receiving company. I felt more at ease in them. Don't you feel uncomfortable in such finery? Particularly on a day like today, when it's so warm?"

"It's what Mama prefers," he insisted and sat down on the seat next to mine. "Would you like some breakfast? You must be hungry."

"I am, rather," I admitted. "But I haven't been able to find your cook anywhere."

"We don't have a cook," said Eustace. "Not any more. There used to be one, of course. Mrs. Hayes was her name. She smelled like soup and was forever trying to tousle my hair. I had to tell her off about it. It's taking liberties, don't you think? But she was quite a good cook," he added, nodding wisely. "Anyway, she's gone. She left. Afterwards, I mean."

"Afterwards?" I asked, but he simply shrugged and looked away. "Well, who prepares the meals if you don't have any help?"

"The governess usually. Or Isabella. My sister is quite a good cook actually. I tease her that she will end up in service one day but whenever I do she hits me so I think I ought to stop."

I stared around in astonishment, suppressing an urge to laugh at this intolerable situation. Was I to undertake every job in this house? There had been no mention of cooking in the advertisement, although I was beginning to realize just how deceptive that notice had been.

"But this is insupportable," I declared, throwing my hands in the air. "I don't know where anything is; I don't know what you children like to eat. And there has definitely been someone cooking here this morning. I can smell it in the air."

"Oh," said Eustace, marching over to the cooker and opening the door to look inside. "You're right. Look, there's two breakfasts waiting for us here. Hurrah! Isabella must have made them already. She can be quite thoughtful when she's not being violent. We should eat them before they become disgusting."

I laughed, despite myself. What an odd thing to say, I thought. But sure enough, there were two plates of food warming inside the cooker and I lifted them out using a dishcloth to save my hands and placed them on the table. There was nothing too elaborate there, a couple of sausages and slices of bacon, some scrambled egg. Any capable person could have cooked this but somehow, from Isabella's hands, it looked almost indigestible. Perhaps it had been resting in the cooker for too long.

"And what about Heckling?" I asked as we began to eat, trying hard to make my first question sound innocent so my second would be answered. "Where does he eat?"

Eustace shrugged his shoulders. "In the stables, I expect," he said. "With the horses."

"And the other lady? The maid?"

"What maid?"

"I saw her this morning, making her way across the grounds. Where does she eat?"

"We don't have a maid."

"Now don't be false, Eustace," I told him, trying to keep my tone light. "I saw her, not ten minutes ago. I followed her outside but lost sight of her."

"We don't have a maid," he insisted.

"Then who was the lady with the handbag and the uniform who passed by the pantry window? Did I simply imagine her into being?"

He didn't say anything for a moment and I resolved not to rush him. Let him answer in his own time, I decided. But do not speak again until he does.

"I don't know much about her," he said finally. "She comes and goes, that's all. I'm not supposed to speak to her."

"Who says so?"

"My sister."

I thought about this. "And why is that?" I asked. "Do Isabella and Mrs. Livermore not get along? Her name is Mrs. Livermore, isn't it? Isabella mentioned someone of that name last night."

He nodded.

"And are they not friends?" I continued. "Is there an argument between them?"

"I don't know why you think we're bad children," said Eustace suddenly, frowning as he put his knife and fork down on the table. He stood up and stared at me with a dark expression. "You've only just met us, after all. I think it very unfair that you call me false and say that my sister causes fights when this time yesterday you didn't even know either of us."

"But I don't think that at all, Eustace," I said, reddening a little. "You're a very polite boy, that's for certain. I didn't mean to hurt your feelings. I was just . . . well, I don't know, but I'm sorry for it anyway. And I'm certain that if Isabella and Mrs. Livermore are not friends then there must be a reason for it. She seems as well mannered as you are."

"Mama believes that we should speak well and act in a decorous fashion," he replied. "She insists upon it. She won't allow either of us to be naughty. She gets very angry when we are."

"And where is she, your mama?" I asked, wondering whether I might get more information out of him now in the cold light of day. "I'm so looking forward to making her acquaintance."

He turned away and breathed heavily through his nose. "Aren't you going to eat your breakfast?" he asked. "It will get cold and then everything will have been for nothing."

I looked down at it but the sight of the eggs spilling out across the meat turned my stomach a little. "I don't think I will just now," I said, pushing the plate away. "My stomach is still a little upset after my journey yesterday. I'll eat something later on."

"Isabella will be insulted," he said in a deep voice and I stared at him, uncertain how to respond.

"Well," I said eventually. "I'll simply have to apologize to her, won't I?" I smiled and leaned in, trying to make a friend of him. "Why do you look so worried anyway, does she have a wicked tongue on her? Will she scold me?"

"Certainly not," he replied, pulling away. "She won't say anything."

"Nothing at all?"

"Isabella says we must never say what we're thinking."

"But why ever not?" I asked. He breathed heavily through his nose and looked down at the table, scratching at a groove in the wood with the tip of his thumb. "Eustace," I insisted. "Why shouldn't you say what you're thinking?"

"Isabella says it's best if we don't talk about it to anyone," he muttered.

"Talk about what?" I stared at him, feeling an overwhelming urge to shake him. "Eustace, what do you mean? What is it you're not telling me?"

He looked up at me, those brown eyes set in a sea of whiteness that could melt the hardest of hearts, and opened his mouth, only to seal it shut again as his glance told me that something, or someone, was standing behind me.

I leaped out of my chair in fright and spun round, uttering an oath under my breath for the girl had been standing so close that I wondered how I had not felt her presence behind me.

"Good morning, Eliza Caine."

"Isabella," I said, gasping in surprise. She was as well dressed as her brother—the lace dress she wore might have been something she would put on for a wedding or an appointment at court—and her hair was hanging loose around her shoulders, carefully brushed. "I didn't hear you come in."

"I hope Eustace hasn't been boring you with silly stories," she said, standing perfectly still, her expression one of pure tranquillity. "Little boys can be terribly dramatic, don't you think? They make things up all the time. And they lie. That's a scientific fact. I read about it in a book."

"I don't lie," insisted Eustace. "And I'm not a little boy. I'm eight."

"That is quite young," I said, turning to him, and he frowned, displeased. I immediately regretted having said that. It would have been kinder to have simply agreed with him.

"If you're not going to eat that," said Isabella, nodding at my food, "should I give it to the dogs? They live out there with Heckling by the stables and would be grateful for it even if you're not. It's a sin to waste good food, after all."

"Yes, I suppose so," I said. "I do appreciate your making it for me but I'm afraid I don't have much of an appetite this morning."

"None of you governesses ever do," she replied, lifting the plate from the table and marching out the back door. "It's the most extraordinary thing. I don't know how any of you manages to stay alive."

"Isabella!" cried Eustace, and I stared at him, startled that he should seem so appalled by her choice of words, and when I looked back at his sister even she looked a little unsettled.

"I only meant . . ." she said, her composure fading for once. "Obviously, I didn't . . ." She shook her head quickly, as if dismissing all memory of the dialogue, and smiled at me. "I'll give it to the dogs," she repeated. "They'll be delighted and consider me their greatest friend."

And with that she vanished out into the courtyard, leaving Eustace and me alone together again. He still looked scandalized by what she had said, which I thought something of an overreaction. After all, it was just a turn of phrase. She hadn't meant anything by it. I went over to the sink and turned the taps on, washing my hands thoroughly in the freezing water.

"Can you tell me," I asked, "where Mr. Raisin's office is? The solicitor your sister spoke of last night."

"Somewhere in the village, I believe," Eustace said. "I haven't been myself but I'm sure he has an office there."

"And is it far? The village?"

"Oh no. And it's a straight road, it's impossible to get lost. Did you want to see him?"

I nodded. "I think it's important that I do," I said. "Particularly since your parents are not here to greet me. I might go down there now. How long will it take me to walk?"

"There's a dandy-horse in the front courtyard," he said. "You can take that if you like. You'll be there in about fifteen minutes if you do."

A dandy-horse! I liked the idea of that. Mrs. Farnsworth had brought herself to school every morning on one, oblivious to the stares of Londoners who felt that a lady should not be seen on such a contraption, and so enamoured with it was I that she had allowed me to use it on several occasions and I had managed to pick up the rudimentary skills quite quickly. To board one now seemed like an adventure and the fresh morning breeze would do me the world of good. It might knock some of the silliness out of my head.

"And what will you do this morning, Eustace?" I asked. "While I'm gone, I mean?"

"I have tasks," he said, employing his mysterious tone once again, and then stood up and abruptly left the kitchen. I laughed. He was a peculiar little boy but I liked him very much already.

Chapter Eight

I MADE MY WAY out to the front of the house, where, just as Eustace had said, a dandy-horse was propped up against one of the columns, its heavy wooden frame and seat pivoted over two strong wheels. I wheeled it away, throwing my leg over the saddle as I began to progress down the driveway, hearing the pebbles crunch beneath me. To my surprise, considering I had only been at Gaudlin Hall for little more than twelve hours, I felt a curious sense of relief at putting distance between the house and myself.

Eustace wasn't wrong in his directions or timings. The journey towards the village was a pleasant one, my mood improving considerably as I made my way along twisting lanes, the recently harvested fields turning to green on either side of me, the fresh air blowing in my face and offering me a sense of well-being. Why would anyone live in London, I wondered, dirty, fog-fouled, smog-smothered London, with its murderers and its streetwalkers and its criminality on every corner? The stinking, twisting river polluting our bodies, the empty palace mourning its absentee Queen, the calamitous weather, the striking workers, the filth in the streets. Here, in Norfolk, I might have been in another world entirely. It was idyllic. And the countryside provided not the dispiriting experience of the previous night at the hall. No, there was something far more enriching to be discovered on this land, and as I made my final turn and the path opened up into a picturesque country village I felt, for the first time since Father's death, that the world was a good place and my part in it was to be valued.

Arriving at the village, I left the dandy-horse propped up against the church railing and looked around, determined to discover what kind of place my new home was. I was here to find Mr. Raisin's office, of course, but was under no pressure of time so a little investigation of this new locale seemed appropriate. The church itself was quite striking, not large but with an intelligent design that made the most of its footprint, and I took a few moments inside to examine the carvings, the elaborate ceiling work and an enormous stained-glass window, which presented an image of Moses standing atop Mount Horeb, removing his sandals and turning away as the face of God appears in the burning bush before him. It was very beautiful and I wondered whether the glazier was a local man or whether the window had been imported from elsewhere. I could recall Father taking me once, when I was a child, to Whitefriars to see the production factory of Powell & Sons, the intricacy of whose designs rather fascinated me, as did the signature monk design they placed in the corner. I leaned forward now to see whether any similar autograph had been included here and noticed an image of a swallow-tailed butterfly, similar to those I had seen in the corridor at Gaudlin Hall, and I wondered whether this was an insect peculiar to the region. Father would have known, of course.

The church was quiet, the only other person present being an elderly lady seated at the furthest edge of a pew halfway down the aisle, who turned her head to look at me, nodded and smiled, but then seemed to think better of it for her expression darkened as she turned away. I thought nothing of it—she must have been in her late eighties and was quite possibly touched in the head—and continued to wander along the nave, where I found a small chapel with room for perhaps a dozen church-goers before a plain altar, and sat down. Looking around, I was struck by the gruesome nature of some of the carvings, violent creatures with crazed eyes staring back at me, griffins and trolls, figures that seemed more appropriate to medieval folklore than a place of worship.

Behind me, I heard steps approaching, but when I turned round, a chill passing through my body, they became quieter and finally vanished. The elderly lady had gone now but the footsteps could not have been hers, for she had a pair of canes propped beside her seat and these steps were vigorous and youthful.

I stood up and made my way along the aisle to a lectern, where a book was open before me, a collection of biblical verses presented one for every day of the year, and I read the lines for that day: *Then I heard the Lord say to the other men, "Follow him through the city and kill everyone whose forehead is not marked. Show no mercy! Have no pity! Kill them all—old and young, girls and women and little children. But do not touch anyone with the mark."*

The lines disturbed me and I turned as an organ in the upper gallery began to play and then, quite suddenly, stopped, and I felt that I had spent enough time and made my way quickly outside and into the graveyard, where I examined the headstones, most of them for elderly people, a few unfortunate children, a fresher grave for a young woman named Harkness who had died only a few months previously. She was only a couple of years older than I, poor soul, and I felt a rush of unease at this intimation of mortality. I paused—why did that name mean something to me?—but my memory failed me and I walked on.

Returning to the street, I noticed a small tea shop on the corner and, realizing how hungry I was, since I had barely eaten any of the breakfast that Isabella had prepared for me, I stepped inside and ordered a pot of tea and a scone with some of their locally made gooseberry jam.

"New to the area, are you, miss?" asked the young girl behind the counter as she served me. She had a rough look to her, a childhood spent in manual service I thought, but wore a welcoming expression, as if she was pleased to have some company. The dimples in her cheeks offered her a certain charm but her eyes were a little askew, the left looking directly at me, the right pupil positioned towards the edge of the socket, and it took from her; it was difficult not to stare. "Or are you just passing through?"

"I'm here to stay, I hope," I told her. "I only arrived last night so thought I should take a look at the village this morning. You have a lovely tea shop here. Do you run it alone?"

"It's me mam's," she explained. "Only she's taken to her bed with one of her sick headaches so Muggins is left alone to run things."

"That must be terribly hard," I said, hoping to ingratiate myself with the local tradespeople. "It gets rather busy at lunchtime, I imagine."

"Easier when she's not here, if I'm honest," said the girl, scratching her head furiously. "She don't half make mountains out of molehills. No, when I'm on my own I can just get things done. Do you know what I mean, miss? I have my ways and she has hers and sometimes the two just don't fit together."

"I do, most certainly," I said, smiling and offering her my hand. "Eliza Caine," I said. "It's a pleasure."

"And you, miss," she replied. "Molly's the name. Molly Sutcliffe."

She stepped back behind the counter and I took a seat by the window, relishing my tea and scone, watching the world go by. A copy of the *Illustrated London News* had somehow found its way here and was lying on the table next to mine and I reached for it but then changed my mind; it was that newspaper, after all, which had advertised Mr. Dickens' reading, and had Father not seen it, he would most likely still be with me. I had turned against the paper on account of it. Instead, I simply watched the villagers as they passed along the street. I noticed a vicar, a surprisingly young man, tall and thin, making his way towards the church, a small puppy in tow. The pup could not have been more than a couple of months old and was still accustoming himself to his lead for he stopped regularly, twisting his head to try to bite through the cord to set himself free, but the vicar was diligent, never pulling the dog along too fiercely, and stopping every so often to pat him and whisper affectionately in his ear, at which point the dog would offer licks and kisses so that trust could be established. On one of these occasions, as he stood up again, the vicar glanced in my direction and our eyes met and he shrugged his shoulders, smiling, and I found myself laughing and continuing to watch the pair as they made their way through the gates of the churchyard.

Finishing my tea, I stood up, paid my bill and thanked Molly. She picked up my empty cup and saucer from the table and said that she hoped she would see me in there again, only not to mind if her mother was around and shouting because she could be a tartar when she wanted to be.

"I'm sure I'll be back often," I told her. "I'm the new governess at Gaudlin Hall so I expect I will be in and out of the village on a regular basis."

The moment I said this, the tea cup slipped out of her hands and fell to the floor, smashing into a dozen or more pieces.

"Oh dear," I said, looking down at it. "I hope it wasn't valuable."

Molly, however, was not looking at the broken cup but staring at me instead with a ghastly expression on her face. All the friendliness and warmth of a moment before had left her now and she continued to stare silently as I stood there, uncertain what on earth was the matter with her, until she finally composed herself, shook her head and stepped quickly away, reaching for a dustpan and brush, with which she proceeded to clear up the wreckage. She did not turn back to look at me and I guessed that she was embarrassed by her clumsiness.

"Well, goodbye then," I said, turning and walking away, wondering why her mood had altered so quickly, but I had little time to think of it for as I stepped out on to the street a milk-float came by and, had I exited a moment or two later, I am sure that the horses would have run me over. I gasped, took a moment to recover my wits, and resolved that I should watch where I was going in future. It didn't matter if this was a small village, one never knew where danger might lie.

I continued to walk along the street, not entering any of the stores but looking through the windows at the products on show. This was a habit I had developed a year or so before in

London, when I would stroll down Regent Street, looking at the fine goods in the stores aimed at the quality, things I could never have afforded but which filled me with desire. Here in Gaudlin I passed a rather nice greengrocer's with a display of fruit and vegetables that was quite unlike anything I had ever seen before. Local produce, no doubt. How fortunate to live near farmland, I thought, where the food must always be wholesome. This in turn led me to thinking of Isabella and the congealed breakfast. I hoped that dinner would be an improvement on this; it might be sensible if I prepared it myself. The window of a dressmaker's store presented a view of another mother and daughter duo, one helping a lady decide about a particular dress, the other seated behind her sewing machine, her mouth containing so many pins that I hoped no one would startle her, lest she swallow one or more of them. A cake shop presented a bounty of delights and I wondered whether I might bring some back home with me—home! What a strange word to employ about Gaudlin Hall; as if that place could ever be a home to me—to endear myself to the children and then, finally, on this side of the road, just after a village pump from which some small children were drinking, I discovered a small mahogany plaque outside a door engraved with the words *Alfred Raisin, Solicitor-at-Law; Discerning Clients*, and smoothed down my coat, settled my hat firmly on my head, and stepped inside.

A young man was seated at a desk and he looked up from his ledger as the bell rang over the door. He was a rather odd-looking individual, prematurely balding, with fat, rosy cheeks and whiskers that were in need of grooming. A dark smudge of ink sat, unobserved by him, beneath his left eye. He took his spectacles off, replaced them on his nose once again and laid his pen down. I noticed that his hands were covered in black marks and the cuffs of his shirt would surely present his wife with a challenging task come washday.

"Can I help you, miss?" he asked.

"I hope so," I replied. "Are you Mr. Raisin?"

"Cratchett," he said, shaking his head. "Mr. Raisin's personal clerk."

I struggled with an urge to laugh. "Cratchett?" I said.

"That's right, miss," he replied defensively. "There is something amusing about my name?"

I shook my head. "I do apologize," I said. "I was thinking of another clerk called Cratchett. In the ghost story, *A Christmas Carol*. Have you read it?"

He stared at me as if I had suddenly started to speak an ancient Russian dialect and shook his head. "I don't have much time for reading," he said. "My clerking keeps me busy enough for reading. Them as has time to read should do so, I expect. But not me."

"Well, you have heard of it at least."

"I have not," he said, shaking his head.

"You've never heard of *A Christmas Carol*?" I asked, astounded, for the short novel had been a popular success. "By Charles Dickens."

"No, miss. I'm not familiar with the gentleman."

I burst out laughing, certain that he was playing some elaborate joke, and his face turned red with anger. He had never heard of Charles Dickens? Was such a thing possible? Had he heard of Queen Victoria? The Pope in Rome?

"Well, it doesn't matter," I said, feeling a little embarrassed, for the manner in which he looked at me suggested that he took any perceived slights against his character terribly seriously. "I wonder whether I might speak with Mr. Raisin. Is he available?"

"Do you have an appointment?"

"I'm afraid not. Is it necessary to make one?"

Cratchett glanced at his watch and frowned. "He has a meeting with an important client on the hour," he said. "I can ask him if he can fit you in now but you'll have to be quick with your business. Name please?"

"Eliza Caine," I said and he nodded and took himself off to a different room while I stood staring around me. There was no place to sit and nothing of interest to look at. I picked up a copy of that morning's *Times* that lay on Cratchett's desk and glanced at the headlines. Another murder in Clerkenwell. A young girl this time. And another, in Wimbledon. A middle-aged man who was known to police. Also, a small child had gone missing in Paddington Station and the Prince of Wales was due to make a visit to Newcastle.

"Miss Caine?" said Cratchett, returning now, and I dropped the newspaper, feeling as if I had been discovered doing something I shouldn't. His eyes followed to the desk and he seemed displeased by my rooting among his things. "Come with me, won't you? Mr. Raisin can spare you five minutes if you promise to be quick."

I nodded. "Five minutes will be perfectly adequate," I said, not believing that for a moment. I suspected that I had enough questions to fill ten times that amount but five minutes would have to do for a start. I followed him into the next room, which was far more luxurious than the antechamber, and he closed the door behind me. By the window stood a large oak desk, covered in documents, neatly arranged, and as I entered a man stood up from behind it and came towards me, offering his hand. He was in his late thirties, neatly presented with a tired if kindly expression on his face. Rather handsome too, if one's tastes ran to the older gentleman.

"Alfred Raisin," he said, offering a polite bow. "I believe you wanted to see me. I'm afraid I don't have much time today though. I don't know if Cratchett said but—"

"Yes, I understand perfectly," I replied, taking the seat that he offered me opposite his desk as he returned to sitting behind it. "I have come on a chance, that's all. I hoped you'd make time for me."

"Of course, Miss . . . ?"

"Caine," I said. "Eliza Caine."

"And you're new to Gaudlin? I don't believe I've seen you before."

"That's right," I said. "I arrived only last night. By the London train to Norwich and then Mr. Heckling brought me here in the carriage."

"Heckling," he replied, looking a little surprised. "You don't mean the—"

"Yes, the stable man out at Gaudlin Hall," I explained. "I'm the new governess."

He put both hands to his face and pressed the fingertips against his closed eyes for a moment, as if he was thoroughly exhausted, then sat back and stared at me as much in curiosity as surprise. He stood up, then glanced at his watch and shook his head.

"It won't do," he said. "I forgot that I have an appointment with . . . with . . . with Mr. Hastings from Bramble Lodge. I can't talk now."

"Please," I said. "It won't take long."

"I'm sorry, Miss Caine, but—"

"Please," I insisted, raising my voice. A long silence ensued between us. He continued to stare and I turned away, noticing a rather lovely clock set inside a wooden boat on the mantelpiece. It was elaborately carved, really a thing of some beauty, and I felt an urge to walk over, release it from its mooring and run my finger along the woodwork.

"The new governess," he said, sitting back down at last with a sigh. "Indeed. Arrived already."

"You knew I was coming then?" I asked, turning back to him.

"Miss Bennet said something about it," he replied, dissembling, I thought. "Well, rather more than something. She was here not three days since, seated in that same seat that you find yourself in now. She told me she was leaving. I had rather hoped I might persuade her otherwise."

I felt suddenly uncomfortable and knew not why. I did not like the notion that I was sitting in that woman's chair. It made no sense—it was not as if she had died there—but I shifted awkwardly and wished that we could repair to the couches that were situated along the walls of the office.

"Which is more than she told me," I replied. "Mr. Raisin, I come to you in a state of some confusion. I understood that I was being hired by a family to be governess to their children. However, I arrived last night to discover that neither Mr. nor Mrs. Westerley is available, that neither of them is even *in situ* at Gaudlin Hall, and that the previous governess boarded the train that I disembarked in order to avail herself of its return journey. I'm quite at a loss as to what is going on."

Mr. Raisin nodded and sighed. He smiled at me and offered something like a shrug. "I can imagine that would be quite bewildering, Miss Caine," he said.

"You imagine correctly, sir."

"So," he said, making a temple of his fingers before his nose, "how can I help you?"

I hesitated, wondering why he needed to ask such a ludicrous question. "Well," I said, feeling a sense of irritation grow in me now, "I was informed that you take care of financial matters relating to the estate."

"I do," he agreed. "I do indeed." He sat up suddenly. "Ah, I think I understand now," he said. "You're concerned for your salary? You need have no worries on that point, Miss Caine. You may collect your weekly stipend here, at this office, every Tuesday morning. Cratchett will have everything ready for you. The accounts are in perfect order."

"It's not my salary I'm thinking of," I said, although I must admit that had been at the back of my mind too; I did not have many savings of my own, after all, only what I had managed to put aside from my work at St. Elizabeth's, and a few hundred pounds that Father had left me in his will and I had determined never to touch this capital but to avail myself of the interest instead. I needed paying if I was to survive.

"As for the other household expenses," he continued, "you need not give them a second thought. The local grocer here organizes the food and has it sent up. All the invoices from the stores come directly to me and are settled promptly. Heckling's wages, Mrs. . . . ." He coughed and corrected himself. "Any wages that need paying. We take care of them all here. There's really nothing for you to worry about other than the obvious."

"The obvious?" I asked. "And what obvious is that?"

"Why," he said, smiling at me as if I was a perfect fool, "taking care of the children, of course. Who else would do that, if not the governess?"

"Their parents?" I suggested. "I assume that I am not to be left alone with Isabella and Eustace indefinitely. Their parents will be on hand soon?"

Mr. Raisin looked away, his expression becoming troubled. "Did Miss Bennet say that in her advertisement?" he asked.

"Well, no," I admitted. "But I naturally assumed—"

"The truth is that Miss Bennet had no business placing that advertisement without consulting me first. I couldn't believe my eyes when I picked up the *Morning Post* and saw it there. We had words on the subject, Miss Caine, I don't mind telling you that. Strong words. But she was determined to leave. I suppose I can't blame her in a way but—"

"Why?" I asked, leaning forward. "Why can't you blame her?"

"Well," he said, struggling now for an answer. "She didn't settle here, that's all. She wasn't happy. She wasn't *local*," he added, stressing the word.

"Mr. Raisin, *I* am not local," I said.

"No, but perhaps you will fit in better than that lady did." He glanced at his watch. "Heavens, is that the time already? I'm sorry to rush you out, Miss Caine," he said, standing up and ushering me to my feet. "But as I said, I do have another appointment."

"Of course," I replied, frustrated by his evasions but rising now and allowing him to lead me to the door. "But you still haven't answered my question. About Isabella and Eustace's parents. When can I expect to see them?"

He stared directly into my eyes now and his forehead crinkled in dismay. There was a long pause and I swore that I would not break it; he would speak first or I would be damned.

"Did you come to Gaudlin alone?" he asked me and I raised an eyebrow, startled by the abrupt change of subject.

"I beg your pardon," I said.

"I wondered whether you have a companion with you, that's all. Or a parent perhaps? An older brother?"

"I have no siblings, Mr. Raisin, no friends, my mother died when I was a girl and my father passed away to his reward a little over a week ago. Why do you ask?"

"I'm so sorry," he said, reaching out and touching my arm, a gesture of such honest intimacy that it rather took my breath away. "About your father, I mean," he added. "The loss of a loved one is a terrible thing."

I opened my mouth to reply but found that I had no words. His hand remained on my elbow and to my astonishment I felt great consolation from his tenderness. I glanced at it, he followed my eyes, and took his hand away abruptly, coughing and turning away. Finally, trying to recover my wits, I repeated my question as to the whereabouts of the Westerley parents.

"I can't say," was the rather disappointing answer he finally gave me. "Miss Caine, you do like children, don't you?"

"What?" I asked, astonished by such a question. "Yes of course I like children. I was a teacher of small girls in London."

"And you like the Westerley children? I know you've only just met them, but you like them?"

I thought about it. "They're a little unusual," I said. "But very bright. The girl is a study. The boy is a charm. I'm sure we'll get along famously in time."

"Then all I ask is that you take care of them, Miss Caine. That is what you are hired to do. To take care of them, educate them a little if necessary. The boy, anyway. As for the rest . . ." And here he opened his arms wide as if to suggest that there was nothing more that he could do. I wondered for a moment whether he expected me to throw myself into them. (And, as ridiculous as it might sound, I had half a mind to do that very thing.)

I sighed. The interview had been entirely unsatisfactory and I felt no closer to understanding my situation than before. But there seemed little choice but for me to leave. Out on the street I felt a great sense of frustration but, on the journey back to Gaudlin Hall, this began to dissipate and I told myself that it didn't matter, I had established myself with Mr. Raisin and I could pay another visit in the future, and another if necessary, to learn more about my responsibilities. I would make an appointment. If I had an appointment for half an hour, say, then he could hardly eject me on to the street within five minutes.

Alfred Raisin. I thought it a beautiful name.

The journey back to the Hall was more difficult than the one to the village, which surprised me rather for it was neither uphill nor downhill either way; the road was for the most part perfectly flat, like so much of the Norfolk countryside. I made my way through the large gates that marked the beginning of the property, the same spot where Heckling had paused for a moment the night before to afford me a view of the estate through the trees. I felt a great wind begin to rise suddenly, despite the fact that it was still a sunny morning. As I steered towards the house, this wind grew stronger and stronger, pushing me backwards, until finally I had no choice but to give in, disembark and wheel the dandy-horse by hand the remaining distance.

In the courtyard, struggling to open my eyes fully with the force of the gale blowing against me, I noticed that the front door was ajar. I made my way towards it, besieged by the wind, which seemed determined to keep me from the house, and as I ascended the three steps that led to the entrance, it slammed hard in my face. I gasped. Was there someone behind there, one of the children perhaps, playing a game with me? Eustace had hidden himself behind the door the previous night; was he at this nonsense again?

I reached for the bell but my arm could not fight through the growing storm. How is this possible, I wondered, when I am so close to the wall? I should be sheltered from the wind, not being bullied by it. I forced my hand forward but it was too strong and seemed angry with me now, for it lifted me off my feet entirely, pushing me away from the house, and I fell backwards, tripping over the steps, stumbling to prevent myself from falling over as it pushed and pushed and pushed, and it was all I could do to stay erect until finally it lifted me once again and I tumbled over, my right leg dragging along the stones until I could feel the skin being lifted from my knee, at which point I let out a great cry, a scream, which in turn coincided with the sound of the front door being opened and the wind suddenly, as quickly as it had started, dissipating, dying down, fading away.

"Eliza Caine!" cried Isabella, walking towards me, her younger brother following her a few feet behind. "Why are you lying there like that?"

"Look at all the blood," said Eustace in a hushed, reverent tone, and I stared down at my leg, which was very bloody indeed around the kneecap, although I knew immediately that nothing was broken, that it would only need to be cleaned up, the wound washed and bandaged, and all would be well. But still I was shocked by what had happened, particularly by the fact that the air had entirely changed now and there was not so much as a breeze to be felt, let alone the near tornado that had pushed me away from Gaudlin Hall and tried to force me as far from the building as possible.

"The wind," I said, staring at the children, who did not have so much as a hair out of place. "The wind! Couldn't you feel it, children? Didn't you hear it?"

Chapter Nine

O VER THE DAYS that followed, matters at Gaudlin Hall appeared to settle down and, to my relief, no further disturbing incidents took place. I remained unsettled by how little I knew about the Westerley family and why I was being left alone with Isabella and Eustace for so long, but put my disquiet to one side as I began to forge a relationship with the children. True to his word, my wages were made ready for me at Mr. Raisin's office the following Tuesday, counted out and checked by the clerk, Cratchett, who seemed to have taken against me entirely, but when I asked for another appointment with his employer I was informed that Mr. Raisin was away from Norfolk on business and that it was beyond Cratchett's abilities to place an appointment in the book without that man's prior agreement. Throughout this exchange, because of the manner in which Cratchett's eyes kept darting back and forth to the door behind him, I grew convinced that Mr. Raisin had not in fact left the county but was instead seated behind his desk in the next room, unwilling to see me, a source of great disappointment to me. However, as I could not possibly have challenged what he said without sounding like an hysteric, I simply informed him that I would be back, that I could not leave matters as they stood, and left, frustrated.

I made several attempts to track down the elusive Mrs. Livermore too but to no avail. If I rose at eight, I would see her with her coat on and her bag in her hand marching down the driveway away from the house; if I rose half an hour earlier she would leave half an hour earlier. She appeared to have made it her business not to engage with me in any way, although I had no doubt that she knew full well there was a new governess on the premises. On the one occasion when I happened to look out the kitchen window and see her nearby I ran outside, but, just as with our earlier encounter, she turned a corner and apparently vanished into nothingness, leaving me wondering whether or not I had imagined her presence. At moments like this, I began to ask myself whether the Norfolk air was playing tricks with my mind.

Despite all these concerns, however, I found that I was beginning to enjoy life at Gaudlin Hall. Naturally, I still thought of Father frequently and, on occasion, particularly at night, alone in my room, his memory would move me to tears, but I was growing accustomed to the loss and learning to cope with my grief. Long walks in the gardens that surrounded the house helped with this. I consoled myself with the knowledge that he had, for the most part, led a happy and intellectually stimulating life, and had known true love twice, once from his wife and once from his daughter. When I returned, my lungs filled with clean air, my legs a little tired from the exercise, my spirits always seemed improved and I experienced a sense of optimism for this new life in which I found myself.

As much as I enjoyed the comfort of my new surroundings, however, I was frustrated by the musty air in my bedroom and my continued inability to open the window. It was tall with a pointed arch at the top, much like a lancet window only wider, separated from both floor and ceiling by no more than about three feet and divided down the centre into two halves which, in theory, should have opened to allow the room to be aired. Seeing Heckling making his way through the courtyard one afternoon, his dog, Pepper, scampering around at his heels, I decided to tackle him about it.

"That window don't open," he told me, shrugging his shoulders and looking at me indifferently, as if he could not quite believe that I would have the stupidity to think it might.

"But of course it opens, Mr. Heckling," I said. "There are two handles, waiting to be turned. But nothing I do can make them budge. Perhaps they need a little oil?"

"Mr. Westerley sealed that window shut," he told me, chewing something abhorrent, the disgusting sounds of mastication making me want to put as much distance between him and me as I could. "Poured hot tar into the lock, didn't he? So as no one could ever open them again."

I stared at him, uncertain whether or not he was playing me for a fool. "Why on earth would he do such a bizarre thing?" I asked.

"He said it were too draughty. He did it to half the windows in the Hall. Check if you don't believe me. It don't cost nothing to heat a place that size, you know. And money don't last for ever. Them as has it likes to spend it, don't they?"

I sighed. It seemed a ridiculous thing to do, particularly frustrating now that the air in my room was beginning to grow so stale. I didn't like the idea of leaving my door open—I preferred my privacy and did not want the children to believe that they had free run of the place; I was only too aware that children liked to rummage in other people's possessions—and simply wanted to ventilate it daily. My sleep had been unsettled and I believed that the staleness of the atmosphere was contributing to this.

"Your wages are being paid correctly every week, Mr. Heckling?" I asked, seizing the opportunity to ask him a few more general questions, for whenever he saw me approaching, he would turn his back and walk in the opposite direction. On one occasion he had even mounted the horse, Winnie, and charged away; extraordinary behaviour. He narrowed his eyes, chewing his lip and thinking about this before nodding.

"Aye," he said. "Worried about that, were you?"

"Not at all," I replied, blushing a little but looking him in the eye; I was determined not to be intimidated by this man. "Of course, Mr. Westerley leaves all these matters in the hands of Mr. Raisin, doesn't he?"

"Aye. So far as I know."

"Do you think we'll be seeing him any time soon?"

"Mr. Raisin?" he asked, shrugging. "No special reason why we should. If you want to see him, you should—"

"Mr. Westerley," I said, correcting him, even though I was certain he knew exactly whom I had meant. I thought for a moment that he was going to smile, a rare thing, but he clearly thought better of it. He looked down at Pepper, who was sitting on his haunches now, his head turning from one of us to the other as we conversed. The thought occurred to me that I might get more sense out of the dog than the man.

"I should think it unlikely," he replied eventually. "I best get on, miss. Pepper needs his run or he gets belligerent."

"He must be very preoccupied if he cannot even return to see his children," I remarked. "And as for Mrs. Westerley, well,

I cannot imagine how she could stay away from them. They're such treasures."

He barked some type of laugh now and spittle hit me in the face, forcing me to rear backwards in disgust as I wiped it away. Naturally the brute didn't even think of apologizing.

"Treasures," he said, shaking his head. "That's one way to put it, I suppose." He laughed again; he was clearly tickled by the notion.

I watched him as he made his way down the driveway, picking up the occasional stick and throwing it for the dog to run after and retrieve. I made a pact with myself that I would not turn away until he vanished from sight, and finally, perhaps aware that I was watching him, he paused at some distance from me and turned round, his eyes fixed on mine, and we watched each other, two employees of this house, waiting to see who would give in first. He was too far away for me to read his expression but when he picked up another stick, a larger one, and held it aggressively in his hand, the dog jumping up and down in anticipation, I felt a chill run through me and, turning away, cursed myself for my inability to stare the brute down.

Chapter Ten

THE CHILDREN AND I ran our daily studies from the school-room, which was situated at the end of the second-floor corridor and up a small flight of steps. It was a bright room with a magnificent view over the estate and contained a black-board on one wall, an enormous desk for me with a multitude of drawers, and two smaller ones for the children to sit at side by side.

"How many girls did you teach at your school in London?" Isabella asked me one morning, seated behind her desk and dressed immaculately as always, her pencils laid out in a neat line before her.

"My classroom held about thirty," I said.

"And were they my age or Eustace's age?"

"Closer to Eustace's," I said, a remark which made him look up and smile. He had a lovely face, I thought then. Where his expression was usually guarded and almost frightened, when he smiled, all those things disappeared entirely and he seemed like a different boy. "A little younger, in fact. They were known as the small girls."

"And were they trouble?" she continued.

"Trouble?"

"Did you ever have to discipline them?"

"Occasionally," I said. "But very rarely. You must understand, Isabella, that the school I was employed in was not something out of a fiction. The teachers did not seek any opportunity to flog their unfortunate charges or to make them wander the courtyards carrying a board that said, *Take care of him: he bites*. Nor were there any Mr. Brocklehursts at our establishment. No, we treated our girls with kindness and in return they showed us respect and interest in their work. Most of the time."

"I should like to go to a school with other girls," said Isabella thoughtfully. "But Father said that we must attend to our studies here."

"Private tuition is the privilege of every wealthy family," I explained. "It is only the poorer classes who must be educated together. The truth is that most of my small girls would have left our school by the time they turned twelve or thirteen."

"And what would happen to them then?" asked Eustace. "Would they get married?"

"Oh dear me, no," I said, laughing a little. "Don't you think that would be a little young? Could you imagine Isabella getting married?"

Eustace snorted a little and his sister silenced him with a look. She turned to me with a dark expression and I could see that she had taken my light-hearted remark badly.

"I call that a very rude remark," she said in a low voice. "Do you think that no one would want me?"

"Oh really, Isabella," I said, hoping to lighten the mood. "I didn't mean anything of the sort. I only meant that it would be rather unusual for a girl of your age to find a suitor, don't you agree? In time, of course, there will be any number of young men vying for your hand."

"And what about you, Eliza Caine," she asked, leaning forward and picking up one of her pencils before pressing the finely pared point down slowly into the top of her left hand. "You're not married, are you?"

I hesitated, nervous that she might injure herself. "No," I said. "No, I'm not."

"But you're quite old. What age are you, anyway?"

"What age do you think I am?" I asked, wishing that she would not pursue this topic any further.

"Sixty-seven," said Eustace.

"I'm twenty-one, you cheeky boy," I said, smiling at him.

"Twenty-one and unmarried," said Isabella. "Don't you worry about being left on the shelf?"

"It's not something I give much thought to," I replied, a lie.

"What, never?"

"No. I have my position, after all. Here at Gaudlin Hall. And I'm very content with it."

"But would you choose us over a husband?" she asked.

"Well, I don't know," I said, uncertainty creeping into my voice.

"Don't you want children of your own? Isn't it tiresome to be taking care of someone else's?"

"I should very much like to have children," I said. "One day, hopefully, that might happen."

"But if you married, then you wouldn't be able to work, would you?" she continued, her voice growing more intense as she spoke, her argument being driven home to me, the pencil tip pressing deeper against her skin until I became agitated that she might pierce it entirely and draw blood.

"Why wouldn't I?" I asked.

"Well, who would look after your children? You couldn't let another woman bring them up, could you?"

"Isabella!" whispered Eustace, poking her in the side with an unhappy expression on his face, a mixture of fear and horror that she was making these apparently innocuous remarks.

"I suppose not," I said. "I expect my husband would be working and I would devote my time to looking after the children. That is the way of the world, after all. But really, Isabella, these are hypotheticals and—"

"Children are a mother's responsibility, are they not?" she continued. "And no other woman should attempt to take a mother's place."

"Well, I suppose so," I said, uncertain what she was getting at.

"You wouldn't allow it, would you?" she asked. "If someone asked you to marry them, I mean. And if you said yes. And if you had children. You wouldn't allow another woman to bring them up?"

"No," I said. "That would be my job."

"Then you understand," she said, leaning back, returning the pencil to the groove at the top of her desk, apparently satisfied now.

"Understand what?" I asked, for no matter how hard I thought about it, I had no idea of the point she was trying to make.

"Everything," she said with a deep sigh and turned her head away, looking out the window. I watched her for what felt like the longest time; she seemed to be in a daze of some sort, a daze which left me in the same state, and it was only when Eustace spoke that we both snapped out of it.

"Miss Caine," he said quietly, almost in a whisper, and I spun round.

"Yes," I said. "To work, children. We can't sit around gossiping all day, can we? I thought today that we should look at the Kings and Queens of England. There's so much to learn about history there and I think you'll find the stories fascinating."

"We know something about Kings and Queens," he remarked. "A King stayed here at Gaudlin Hall once."

I laughed. "Can that be true?" I asked, wondering whether he was inventing some story for mischief's sake.

"It is true, actually," said Isabella, turning back to look at me, her piercing blue eyes meeting my own. "Father told us all about it. It was a long time ago, of course. More than a hundred years. 1737, to be precise. When Great-Grandfather was master of Gaudlin."

"1737," I said, running through the lists in my head. "So the king would have been—"

"George II," she replied. "I told you he wasn't making it up. I wouldn't be so quick with that if he was, would I?"

"No, of course not," I said. "Really, Eustace, I wasn't doubting you," I added, looking at her brother, who smiled brightly back at me. "I was just surprised, that's all. The sovereign here at Gaudlin Hall! How exciting it must have been for everyone."

"I daresay it was," said Isabella. "But the Queen, Caroline of Ansbach, took ill after a turn in the gardens. She was bled and purged in the room next to your own, Eliza Caine, but it didn't do her much good. The doctor was a fool, you see. He didn't know how to treat her, that was the problem. Provincial doctors often don't. One is often better served to leave nature to take care of the body than to trust a Norfolk physician. His attentions would have been better suited to the horses in the stable or Heckling's dog, Pepper." I stared at her, both amused and perplexed by the way she talked; it was obvious that this was a speech that she had heard many times before—perhaps the words came directly from her father as he recounted the tale to friends over the dinner table—but hearing such adult syntax emerging from the mouth of one so young was disconcerting and not a little unsettling. "In the end, they took her back to London," she continued. "But her bowel ruptured and she died. The King was distraught. He loved his Queen very much, you see. He never took another wife despite living for almost a quarter-century afterwards. That's quite honourable, don't you think? But he took against Great-Grandfather on account of the association. He didn't invite him to appear at court any more. It was a source of enormous disappointment to Great-Grandfather, who was a supporter of the Crown. Our family always has been, since the Restoration. We were on the wrong side during the Wars of the Roses but that's going back a long way. And we were forgiven for it, in time. Anyway, a thing like that lingers, wouldn't you agree? A death in a household?"

"But you said the Queen didn't die here," I pointed out.

"I wasn't talking about the Queen," she said, waving a hand in front of her face and dismissing my remark, which, to her, was apparently a very stupid one. "So should we learn about King George II today, Eliza Caine, or were you planning on going further back in time? To the Lancasters and the Yorks, perhaps, since I brought them up?"

"Further back," I said, opening my book and turning to the chapter I had marked. I felt a slight breeze in the room and wished I had brought my cardigan but had no desire to wander through this empty house in search of it, passing the room where Caroline of Ansbach had been bled, poor woman. "I thought we might commence with the capture of Edmund Tudor and the beginnings of that triumphant but bloody dynasty."

I glanced towards the window and sighed. One of the children must have written in the condensation while I wasn't looking. Something so vulgar I refused even to draw attention to it.

Chapter Eleven

ON SUNDAYS, THE children and I attended services in the village church and, during those first weeks, I felt a little like an animal on display in a zoo whenever we entered and made our way along the nave towards the family pew in the front row. Every head would turn in that terribly subtle way where no one would actually make it obvious that they were watching us but their eyes burned through me nevertheless. At first, I thought it was because the children were always so beautifully turned out but gradually I began to suspect that it was me they were interested in, a sensation that was new to me, as I was not accustomed to turning heads.

At peace within the stone walls of the church, my spirits often lifted by the choir who were almost invisible in the balcony behind us, I found that I looked forward greatly to Sunday mornings and the solace the service offered me. Reverend Deacons always gave a thoughtful sermon and, unlike some of the services I had heard in London, his words did not sound as though they had been regurgitated time and again for a fresh congregation, but then he was a young man and filled with enthusiasm for his calling. As he spoke of love and kindness towards our fellow man, I would often find my thoughts drifting back to Father, and sometimes I struggled with my emotions. I had settled in well to Norfolk, or so I believed, but the abruptness of my departure from London so soon after his sudden death had left me emotionally raw, and now that things were more stable, I found my thoughts turning back to him more frequently whenever I was alone or in church. I missed him terribly, that was the truth of it. I missed our conversations; I even missed the insect books and regretted not keeping one for myself instead of delivering them all to the custody of Mr. Heston and the British Museum. "I will always look after you," he had told me after my return from Cornwall. "I will keep you safe." Now that he was gone, who would look after me? Who would protect me? Who would keep me safe if trouble came my way?

After one particularly moving homily, when I was close to tears at recalling how happy we had been together, I told the children that I wanted to remain behind and say a last few private prayers, and we arranged to meet in a few minutes' time at the village pump, where the road led back towards Gaudlin Hall. The rest of the congregation departed as usual and I sank to my knees, my head in my hands as I said prayers to God for the safe repose of Father's soul, and prayed that he was looking down at me and protecting me still. When I lifted my head again I found that I had been crying and, to my embarrassment, Reverend Deacons was clearing some of his effects from the altar and staring at me. I sat back on the pew as he walked towards me and attempted a smile.

"Are you all right?" he asked.

"Fine, thank you," I said, blushing a little. "You'll have to forgive me, I didn't mean to make a fool of myself."

He shook his head and came towards me, sitting down in the row in front of mine but turning his body so that he was looking directly at me. He had a kindly face and I liked him for it. "There's nothing to forgive," he said with a shrug. "It's Miss Caine, isn't it?" he said.

"Yes, that's right."

"The new governess over at the Hall?" I nodded again and he turned his head slightly, his expression becoming a little more troubled. "I think I owe you an apology, Miss Caine."

I raised an eyebrow, uncertain what he could mean. "Whatever for?" I asked.

"You've been here a couple of weeks now. I've seen you in the village and here, at church service, but I haven't been out to see you. To introduce myself, so to speak. I hope you don't think ill of me for it."

"Not at all," I said, shaking my head, and in truth the idea had never crossed my mind that he would make an expedition to meet me. What was I, after all? Nothing more than a paid employee. A governess. I was not mistress of Gaudlin Hall even if I was the only woman in residence. "I expect you're a very busy man."

"I am, I am," he said, nodding slowly. "But that's no excuse. I should have made the time. I told myself I should speak with you, but . . ." He shivered slightly, a ghost walking over his grave, and I got the impression there was something about the place that disturbed him. "Well, I'm sorry, anyway," he said after a moment, shaking his head to dismiss whatever thoughts were lingering there. "How are you getting on?"

"Quite well," I said. "The children are a delight."

"They're unusual children, I think," said Reverend Deacons, considering this. "Their hearts are good, of course, but they have suffered so much. Isabella is an extraordinarily intelligent girl. I wonder whether she might one day be the wife of a brilliant man. Eustace shows great promise too."

I frowned, only noticing one word in that statement. "Suffered?" I asked. "Suffered how?"

He hesitated. "We all suffer, don't we, Miss Caine?" he said. "Life is suffering. Until the great day of judgement, when peace and equanimity may be restored for those who are pure of heart and deed."

I raised an eyebrow. I did not know Reverend Deacons, of course, but I felt this remark was somehow beneath him. "But you said they suffered," I insisted. "It sounded as if you meant that they had suffered in some way other than the general. Might I ask what you meant?"

"They have seen great upheaval in their lives," he said, looking down and examining the cover of his prayer book, which, I noticed, was inscribed with the letters *AD*. "Why, over the last twelve months you are . . . what must it be . . . the sixth governess at Gaudlin Hall?"

I stared in surprise. This was most certainly news to me. "The sixth?" I asked. "But you must be mistaken, I'm only the second. Miss Bennet was governess before me. Surely she was here for some time?"

"Oh dear me, no," said Reverend Deacons. "No, Miss Bennet had only been here a month. If even that."

"A month?" I asked. "But I don't understand. Why did she leave so soon? And if you are correct, then where are the other four? They can't have stayed much longer if I'm the sixth governess in twelve months."

The vicar appeared uncomfortable, as if he regretted having ever begun this conversation. He looked as if he would prefer to be safely back in his vicarage, awaiting the pleasures of his Sunday lunch and an afternoon stroll with his puppy. "Mr. Raisin," he said. "He really is the person who should be discussing these matters with you. He has responsibility for the estate, after all."

Mr. Raisin! That man again! To my embarrassment, I blushed at the name. Perhaps he had been in my thoughts a little in recent days.

"I have tried to meet with Mr. Raisin," I said, growing irritated with my own silliness, a note of displeasure evident in my tone. "Several times, in fact. But he is a difficult man to get hold of. His assistant, Mr. Cratchett, keeps a close grip on his appointment book. I wonder if it might not be easier to gain access to the Kingdom of Heaven than to Mr. Raisin's private office."

Reverend Deacons raised an eyebrow and I turned away, wondering whether this had been a sacrilegious remark. "I'm sorry," I said after a moment. "Only it's so frustrating. I can't get any answers anywhere. I feel quite alone sometimes."

"You should be more insistent," he said in a gentle voice. "Don't let Cratchett tell you what you can and can't do, who you can and can't see. You have the right to know, after all," he added in a more forceful tone, a tone that sent a shiver down my spine. "A woman in your position, why you're little more than a girl. You have the right to know!"

A series of questions appeared in my head but I hesitated, trying to select the right one. I suspected that if I pushed Reverend Deacons too far, he would close up entirely and repeat that I should speak only with Mr. Raisin, but I also felt that there were things that he would tell me, things that he wanted to tell me, if only I could find the right way to ask.

"You say I am the sixth governess in a year," I said quietly, trying to keep any suggestion of hectoring out of my tone. "The children's parents have been gone that long then?"

"Yes," he agreed. "Just over a year, in fact."

I frowned. What kind of parents abandoned their children for such a protracted period? Yes, of course they were moneyed and travel was so much easier these days. Why, they could take a boat from Southampton to France and be in Rome in a matter of weeks if they put their mind to it and didn't dawdle along the way. And this was how the wealthy classes lived, wasn't it? Or so I believed, from my reading. They went on grand European tours. They rented villas in Italy and houses in Mesopotamia. They took cruises down the Nile and spent evenings drinking cocktails on the Bosphorus. They were not like me, condemned to a life lived in one place, with no possibility of change. But to leave their children at such a young age? Why, Eustace would have turned eight since they left. It was outrageous. It made a farce of their believing themselves to be the upper class when they cared so little for their young. Wolf spiders ate their own.

"And the other four governesses," I continued. "They were like Miss Bennet? They worked for a short period of time and then advertised for their replacement? Are the gentlemen from the *Morning Post* expecting my notice to be placed with them any day now?"

Reverend Deacons frowned and looked deeply troubled. "Only Miss Bennet placed her own advertisement," he said. "Mr. Raisin placed the others."

"Well, that's something, I suppose. But these other four. What were their motives for leaving? They didn't like the house? How is it possible when it's so beautiful! They didn't care for the children? I can't believe it when they're so . . ." I searched for the word. Lovable was entirely wrong. Warm? Certainly not. A joy to be around? Not quite. In the end, I settled for the word he himself had used to describe them. "Intelligent," I said. "And interesting."

"It had nothing to do with the house, nothing to do with the children," he replied, his words emerging from his mouth in a great hurry now, and I could see that I was putting him under tremendous pressure but I had no desire to stop.

"Then what was it? Why would they leave?"

"They didn't leave," he said, his voice rising, almost shouting at me now, and it rang around the church, bouncing off the strong stone walls and echoing in the chamber. "They died."

I stared at him. I was glad to be seated for I felt a little light-headed at the words. "They died?" I said finally, my voice emerging from my mouth in a near whisper. "All of them? How?"

"No, not all," he replied, turning away from me, desperate to go now. "The first, Miss Tomlin, yes, she died. In such terrible circumstances. And the other three. Miss Golding, Miss Williams and Miss Harkness. They all died too. But Miss Bennet, your predecessor, she survived. There was that awful incident, of course, which precipitated her departure, but she survived it."

"What incident?" I asked, leaning forward. "Please, I know nothing of these things. I beg you to tell me."

He stood up and shook his head. "I have said too much already," he replied. "There are certain things which . . . there are confidences, Miss Caine. Can't you understand that? I have asked you to speak to Mr. Raisin about these matters and I implore you to do so. If you have questions, ask them of him. If you have concerns, ask him to alleviate them. If you have spiritual problems, then yes, do come to me, but not in matters relating to the affairs of the last twelve months at Gaudlin Hall. I have buried too many of your predecessors and have no desire to bury another. Now I do apologize, I have behaved badly I fear, I have left you with more questions than answers, but I must leave you now."

I nodded; it was clear that he was going to tell me no more and I stood up and shook his hand and made my way down the aisle towards the bright, sunny day. As I reached the door I looked back and saw Reverend Deacons moving to the front pew and seating himself heavily in it, his face in his hands, and I watched him for only a moment before turning away.

On the street outside, I looked around for the children but could not see them. I did, however, see Dr. and Mrs. Toxley, the couple who had rescued me on my first night in Norfolk when I had almost stepped out beneath the approaching train.

"Miss Caine," said Mrs. Toxley cheerfully as she saw me. "How are you?"

"Very well, thank you," I said. "I'm so glad I saw you. I wondered whether you might like to come to afternoon tea one day this week. Wednesday perhaps?"

I had been wondering no such thing, of course. The idea had just come to me on the spot. But I had no companions, no friends at all. And Mrs. Toxley was only a few years older than I. Why shouldn't I invite her to tea, after all? Yes, I was a mere governess and she a doctor's wife, but what of it? Her smile faded a little and I noticed her husband shifting uncomfortably in his stance.

"Well, of course," she replied, stuttering slightly, perhaps surprised by the absurd spontaneity of the invitation. "But why don't we meet at Mrs. Sutcliffe's tea shop here in the village? Wouldn't that be more convenient for you?"

"I'd love for you to come to Gaudlin Hall," I said.

"She makes the most excellent custard tarts. I think you'd enjoy—"

"Please," I insisted, reaching out and touching her on the elbow, an unusual gesture for me for I was not a tactile woman. "Please come to Gaudlin Hall. Shall we say Wednesday at three?"

She looked at her husband, who appeared deeply troubled, but then seemed to take some independent sense of purpose for she nodded, said not a word, and I smiled. "Thank you," I said. "I'll see you then. Now, please don't think me rude, but I've just seen Mr. Cratchett emerging from the public house and I need a word with him."

The Toxleys watched in surprise as I left them with almost the same sense of urgency as I had approached them, and I marched on in the direction of Mr. Raisin's assistant who, upon seeing me, raised an eyebrow, turned and walked in the opposite direction.

"Mr. Cratchett?" I called but he ignored me, so I shouted louder—"Mr. Cratchett! If you please!"—at such a volume that he had no choice but to turn, as did several other villagers passing, who looked at me as if I was an undesirable element.

"Ah, Miss Caine," he said. "What a delight."

"Let's not play games, Mr. Cratchett," I replied. "I wanted to let you know that I'll be coming in for an appointment with Mr. Raisin on Tuesday morning at eleven o'clock. I shall need about an hour and would prefer it if we were not disturbed during that time. I hope that he will be free at that hour but just so you both know, if he is not, then I am perfectly willing to sit in your office until he is free. I shall bring a book with me to pass the time. I shall bring two, if need be. I shall bring the complete works of Shakespeare if he insists on keeping me waiting interminably and those plays will get me through the long hours. But I will not leave until I have seen him, are we quite clear on that? Now, I wish you a very pleasant Sunday, Mr. Cratchett. Enjoy your lunch, won't you? Your breath smells of whisky."

And with that, I turned on my heels and walked away, no doubt leaving him completely astonished in the street, annoyed by my audacity, but feeling very pleased with myself for having managed to get through this unprepared speech without stumbling once. Tuesday at eleven o'clock. The time was now set and I would get some answers or I would be damned. I looked ahead, almost laughing out loud at my own strength of purpose, and was pleased to see Isabella and Eustace standing near the pump as instructed, playing some game with stick and ball.

"Come along, children," I said, marching straight past them, feeling like a new woman entirely. "Let's not dawdle. Lunch won't prepare itself, you know."

Chapter Twelve

MY MOOD OF well-being lasted through the dinner hour and into the early afternoon, at which point the strange mixture of emotions that I had experienced that morning—grief, confusion, frustration and euphoria—seemed to settle down into a sensation of melancholia and I strolled around the grounds, my mind troubled at the things I had learned, or failed to learn, since waking that day. The sixth governess in a year! It seemed extraordinary. The first four dead and the fifth running through Thorpe Station in such a rush that she almost knocked me over in her urgency to get away. What had happened to them all? What had driven them to such terrible ends?

Returning to the Hall and looking up towards my bedroom window on the third floor, I felt a distinct sense of unease and wrapped my arms around my body, rubbing them up and down a little to bring some warmth to my bones. I wondered whether each of the previous governesses had used the same bedroom that I used—there were at least a dozen, after all, in the Hall, so it was entirely possible that they hadn't—but felt quite chilled at the idea that it was the same one. It had occurred to me before, after all, how well appointed my room was, not the usual type (I imagined) that an employee would be offered. It was so large and the view over the grounds was exceptional. Were it not for the fact that the windows had been sealed shut, then it would have been almost perfect. I looked up at that window now and sighed. But perhaps the children had given me a new room since it would not have bad memories attached to it?

As I looked, however, I was surprised to see a figure standing behind the curtains, leaning in a little, looking down at me. It was difficult to make out who it was as the white lace separated the glass from the person, and I frowned, certain that it must be Isabella. (Eustace did not strike me as the kind of boy who was interested in going through someone else's belongings.) This was exactly why I didn't leave my door open, I thought. I wanted this small piece of privacy to be maintained for myself. Staring at the figure, I noticed it move and then slip away from the window, and I marched through the front door of the house, preparing to be firm with the girl when, to my astonishment, I noticed Isabella in the parlour to my left, seated on the couch with her legs stretched out, engaged with one of her storybooks. I was surprised to say the least and even a little disappointed. So it *had* been Eustace! Perhaps I had misread his character. I did not like the idea of scolding him, for in truth I thought him a dear boy, but there would be no way around it; we would have to have words. I started to move towards the staircase to go up to my bedroom but, before I could do so, Eustace emerged from his sister's left, where he had been previously out of sight to me, followed by Pepper, Heckling's dog, who was looking up at the ceiling and growling in a low, throaty voice, one of his hind paws stamping urgently on the floor, as if he was preparing to attack.

Feeling no fear, I ascended the staircase, turned to my left, ascended the larger staircase to the second floor and made my way down the corridor to my room, flinging open the door and staring around, ready to confront my intruder.

To my astonishment there was no one there. I looked around, utterly confused. It had been less than a minute since I had seen the figure behind the curtains and there was no way that anyone could have left the room and gone downstairs without passing me in the meantime. I opened the wardrobe, looked under the bed, but the room was empty. I almost laughed. Had I imagined the whole thing? Had the events of the day so far played games with my mind and my imagination? I sighed. It was the only possible explanation. But I had been so certain!

I made my way to the window and pulled the curtains apart, placing my two hands against the enormous sealed glass, standing in the same position where I had imagined the figure to be, and, exhausted now, closed my eyes and relaxed my body against it. What happened next took no more than ten seconds, perhaps fifteen at the very most, but I can recall it now as if I am still in the throes of it and I swear that it felt like an hour.

The window, impossible to open, sealed shut at its lock with boiling tar, flew open wide, the two doors splitting outwards, and a rush of air blew into the room as a pair of hands—I felt them! I felt those two hands!—pushed sharply against my back, lifting me off the floor with as much vengeance as that terrible wind had on the afternoon I journeyed back to Gaudlin Hall. They pushed with as much determination as the unseen force that had tried to cast me under the train upon my arrival at Thorpe, and my body fell forwards through the window now and, in the split second when I exited my room, my eyes opening wide at the fifty-foot fall to the ground below which I knew would certainly kill me, another set of hands, another invisible pairing, larger hands though, these ones, stronger ones, pushed me again from the front, thrust into my stomach as if I was being punched, winding me, forcing me back into my bedroom. The wind outside roared and I gasped, those few seconds so shocking that I could not understand what was happening or even yet feel fear, but it was not over yet for the hands behind thrust forward again, and out I went once more, the floor gone from beneath me, the ground visible before me, my death place, where my body would be smashed to pieces, but once again before I could fall those second hands pushed me back, even harder this time, so forcibly that I had never felt such pain, and I fell back into the room, tumbling to the floor, scrambling back against the wall, my back hitting it so hard that I cried out and, as I did so, the windows slammed shut, the wind immediately silenced, and I was left there, terrified and weeping, my entire body racked with pain, uncertain what had just taken place.

I must have lain there for half an hour, unable to move, fearful of what would take place if I attempted to right myself, but finally I sensed that the room was at peace and slowly, carefully, I lifted myself to my feet. I opened my dress and looked at my stomach. It was deeply bruised, a great red mark tender to the touch, one that I knew would change in colour and sensation over the days that followed. Had I been able to see my own back I had no doubt there would be similar markings there. Determined to fight my fear, I made my way back towards the window and slowly reached out to the handles, nervous of touching them but somehow sure that my ordeal was over. I tried to twist them but they would not give. They were sealed as tightly as ever. It was as if they had never been opened at all.

I fell back on to the bed and felt a great cry of fear lift from my throat and put a hand across my mouth to stop myself from screaming out. What had happened in those fifteen seconds? How had such a thing taken place? I had not imagined it, for my bruises were real. There was a presence in this house, something unholy; an idea that I had previously dismissed as fancy took hold of me and told me it was true. Only there was something else, something I hadn't imagined before.

There were two of them.

Chapter Thirteen

I F MR. CRATCHETT HAD been desperate to get away from me on Sunday afternoon, he seemed resigned to my appearance when I arrived at Mr. Raisin's office shortly before eleven o'clock the following Tuesday morning. I had walked to the village from Gaudlin Hall, a walk that took almost an hour but was infinitely preferable to taking the dandy-horse. The bruises on my chest and back had deepened and grown variegated, the discoloration unpleasant to the eye, the tenderness distressing to the touch, and somehow I felt that walking might reduce the pressure of my injuries. Besides, I welcomed the stroll, for my spirits had grown so low that I hoped some fresh air would prove a fillip.

Naturally, I had slept badly on Sunday night after the terrifying incident. Unwilling to go downstairs and discuss what had happened with the children, I found myself in the unhappy position of having no one to confide in. No friend, no relative, no confidante of any sort could come to my aid. How I wished I had been blessed with an older brother, someone who might take on my trials as his own, or that my younger sister, Mary, had survived to be my companion. But there was no one, of course. I was alone.

I considered switching my room for one of the many empty bedrooms on the second or third floor of the Hall, but whatever spirit was feeling such animosity towards my presence would not, I believed, be put off by so simple a change. After all, it had tried to prevent me from entering the house when it forced me off the dandy-horse; now it was trying to eject me from it by more forceful means. I considered writing to my former employer, Mrs. Farnsworth, to ask her advice, but hesitated, knowing that to commit such thoughts to words would make me sound like a lunatic. She would have said that I was imagining things, or privately told the teachers at St. Elizabeth's that I had taken to drink to relieve the pain of my grief. But even if others might doubt me, I could not doubt myself, for the bruises on my body were proof enough of the assault; these were injuries that could not have been self-inflicted nor invented as the fantasies of a disturbed mind.

And so I resolved to stay where I was. Of course, I was frightened. My life, like the lives of the previous governesses, was in danger and, in the small hours of the morning when fear and anxiety were threatening to overwhelm me, I thought about packing a bag and stealing Heckling's horse and carriage, making my way back to Thorpe Station and onwards to London or Cardiff or Edinburgh, I cared not where. But there was one thing, or rather two, which prevented me from taking such drastic action: Isabella and Eustace. I could not leave them alone with this presence in the house; if it injured me, a grown woman, what injuries might it inflict on two defenceless children? I did not feel brave but I had sense enough to know that I could not leave Norfolk with the weight of their injury on my conscience. Even Miss Bennet had felt that responsibility. By morning time, I was resolved to see this experience through, to understand it and, if necessary, to win.

"Miss Caine," said Mr. Cratchett, standing up when I entered and offering me an obsequious smile. "How charming." He must have hurried with his shave that morning for two spots of dried blood remained on his face, one above his lip, the other beneath his chin, and it was a most unedifying sight.

"Good morning, Mr. Cratchett," I said, smiling at him. I did not feel quite the same sense of unwavering purpose that I had when I tackled him after the church service; I was once again ready to be overwhelmed by the fact that here were two men of the world, men of business and property, while I was nothing more than a governess, reliant on my position for food and board. "I hope you did not think me too forward on Sunday," I added, wishing to make amends with him. "But Mr. Raisin has proved a formidable man to arrange an appointment with."

"Oh, think nothing of it, dear lady," he replied, waving his hands in the air in an absurd fashion. "You have nothing to apologize for, I assure you."

"You're very kind," I replied, stopping myself from pointing out that I had offered no apology, merely an explanation.

"Miss Caine, Mrs. Cratchett and I have been married some three years now. If there is one condition I am familiar with, it is the tendency of the gentler sex to suffer nervous anxiety."

He offered a polite bow and I considered picking up the large paperweight on his desk, designed for some reason in the shape of Ireland, and bringing it down upon his skull. Would any jury in the land convict me?

"Yes," I said, looking away and trying to keep my irritation at bay. "But I trust Mr. Raisin was able to find time in his diary for me?"

"It was not without some difficulty," he replied, determined to let me know that he was still in charge around here. "But fortunately I was able to do a little—how shall I put this?—adjustment of the pieces on the chessboard. An appointment from here moved over there; one from this afternoon diverted to later in the week." He shuffled his hands in the air before me as if he was actually engaged in the process of physical movement. "In short, what needed to be done was done. And I am happy to say that Mr. Raisin has cleared some time for you."

"Thank you," I said, relieved. "Shall I . . . ?" I nodded in the direction of the other office, wondering whether I should just go in, but he shook his head and shuffled me over to a freshly installed armchair.

"He'll be out shortly," said Mr. Cratchett. "Please take a seat until he's ready. I'm afraid I don't have any reading material for ladies here. The only periodical we take is the daily issue of *The Times*. I'm sure you would find it very boring. It's all politics, crime and matters to do with the economy."

"Well, I'll just look through it and see if there is any information about the new style in hats," I said, smiling at him. "Or perhaps there'll be a nice recipe or a knitting pattern."

He sighed and reached for the paper, handed it to me and went back behind his desk, where he placed his pince-nez on his nose and returned to transcribing. A moment later the door opened behind him and, without its owner emerging into the front office, a voice called Mr. Cratchett's name, and he in turn informed me that I might go inside.

"Miss Caine," said Mr. Raisin when I stepped inside. He was seated behind his desk in his shirt, tie and waistcoat, lighting a pipe, attempting to inflame the ball of tobacco in the chamber, which seemed to be proving difficult for him. After a moment, the match went out and he lit another, drawing on the lip until it finally caught.

"My tobacco has dried out," he said by way of explanation, indicating the couch that ran along the wall, and I made my way over to sit down as he took his jacket from a hanger, put it on and sat in an armchair facing me. To my surprise, I felt an extraordinary comfort to be in his presence again. "It's my own fault, of course. I left it in my front parlour last night and forgot to replace the lid. Whenever I do that, I have this very problem."

"My father was a great pipe smoker," I told him, although the scent of the smoke coming from Mr. Raisin's pipe was not quite the same as the one Father had enjoyed, for which I was grateful, as I was sure that the memory that would have been triggered by smelling Father's distinctive smoke would have overwhelmed me.

"It's the most wonderful relaxant," he said, smiling at me. "Sir Walter Raleigh was a capital fellow." I stared at him, confused, and then recalled that it had, of course, been the explorer who had first brought the tobacco plant back from the New World. "Did you know," he asked, removing the pipe from his mouth and pointing the stem in my direction, "that after his execution, Sir Walter's widow carried his head with her everywhere she went in a velvet handbag?"

"I didn't," I said, raising an eyebrow in surprise.

"Don't you think that's an extraordinary thing to do?"

"She must have loved him very much," I said with a shrug that provoked a burst of laughter from Mr. Raisin.

"I'm damned fond of my wife, Miss Caine," he told me. "Damned fond of her. But I promise you that if her head was lopped off in Old Palace Yard on charges of treason, I'd bury it with the rest of her body and not carry it around with me. I call it macabre, don't you? It's taking heartache to a ridiculous place."

"Grief can bring on strange reactions in a person," I said quietly, running my finger along the smooth wood on the table top that separated us. For some reason, my stomach had turned over slightly during his last remarks and I felt an extraordinary urge to run from the room, as far from him as possible, despite the number of questions I had for him. "We are, none of us, accountable for what we do at such times."

"Hmm," said Mr. Raisin, considering this but appearing unconvinced. "What did your father smoke anyway? Was he an Old Familiar man like myself?"

"Johnson's Original," I told him, shaking my head, feeling utterly distracted. "Do you know it?"

"Yes. It's not my blend though. I prefer something with a sweeter flavour."

"Father's pipe always reminded me of cinnamon and chestnuts," I said. "A strange combination, I know, but whenever he lit up in the evening, as he was reading by the fireplace, the pipe was in his hand and the aroma of cinnamon and chestnuts filled the room. It gave me a sense of great comfort."

Mr. Raisin nodded. "His death was unexpected?" he asked me.

"It was a rather sudden illness," I replied, looking away and down at the carpet. "Brought on by exposure to the cold and rain."

"He was an elderly gentleman?"

"Not especially, no," I said. "But his health had not been good for some time. I rather blame myself for allowing him out that night when the weather was so bad, but he insisted. We were going to hear Charles Dickens, you see. He was reading from one of his ghost stories in London, quite close to where we lived."

"Ah yes," said Mr. Raisin, breaking into a smile which completely illuminated his already handsome features. "Which among us is not an admirer of Mr. Dickens? Did you read his latest? *Our Mutual Friend*? It was a bit fantastical in my opinion. I hope his next will be an improvement."

"I didn't, sir, no," I said. "We don't receive periodicals at Gaudlin Hall."

Mr. Raisin sighed. "Then things have changed a good deal since the glory days of that house," he said. "Mr. Westerley received all the popular papers. And *Household Words*, of course. The *Illustrated Times*. *All the Year Round*. Everything that you might expect. He was a great reader, you see, and liked to be kept informed of events. As did his father before him. Of course, the thing about old Mr. Westerley was that he—"

It occurred to me that Mr. Raisin was making small talk to eat up our time. The more he talked about my late father, about Charles Dickens or the variety of periodicals available to those who could afford them, the less time he had to answer any of my questions. The minutes would simply tick away. The hands on the clock would move closer towards noon and before I knew it his capable assistant would no doubt be upon us, ushering me out, insisting that there were a lot more appointments scheduled for the day and that my time was now up.

"Mr. Raisin," I said forcefully, and he stared at me, his eyes opening wide, offering me the astonished countenance of one who is unaccustomed to being interrupted, particularly by a woman. He appeared quite uncertain how to handle it. "I do apologize, but I wonder if we could get down to business. There are a number of things I wish to discuss with you."

"Of course, Miss Caine, of course," he said, recovering himself. "Everything is in order, isn't it? There isn't any problem with your wages? You're not having difficulties with Heckling, are you?"

"My wages are being paid promptly," I said. "And my relationship with Mr. Heckling is, I think, as good as anyone's could be. The truth is I felt that our previous meeting, our only meeting for that matter, was rather unsatisfactory in its conclusions."

"Oh?" he asked. "How so?"

"Mr. Raisin, when I arrived in Norfolk, I was happy to have a job, happy to have a home. Happy to make a fresh start after losing my father. I see now that I accepted the position without giving it due thought or consideration. I should have asked more questions and, indeed, questions should have been asked of me. But there we are, we cannot change the past. And now that I have been here for a few weeks, now that I have settled in, I must admit that I have grown more . . ." I struggled to find the correct word.

"Curious?" he suggested. "Inquisitive?"

"Concerned," I said. "There have been a number of unusual incidents and, to be frank, I am uncertain how to explain them without having you doubt my sanity. But, if I may, I will put them to one side for a moment and concern myself with more concrete matters. Mr. Raisin, I should like to ask you a direct question and I would be most grateful if you would give me a direct answer."

The lawyer nodded his head slowly and an anxious expression coloured his features. Perhaps he had come to realize that there was nothing to be gained by dissembling any further. He opened his arms a little and used the thumb and forefinger of his right hand to remove a fleck of tobacco from between his front teeth before replacing the pipe in his mouth. A cloud of grey smoke camouflaged his face for a moment. "Ask your question, Miss Caine," he said in a resigned tone. "I cannot guarantee that I will answer. You must understand that I am forced to maintain a degree of confidentiality towards my clients." He sighed a little and seemed to relent. "But please ask. If I can answer, then I promise I will."

"Mr. and Mrs. Westerley," I said. "The children's parents. Where are they?"

He nodded and turned away. I had the distinct impression that he was not surprised by what I had asked, that he had been expecting this very question.

"You've been in this village for several weeks now," he stated in a flat tone.

"That's correct."

"Then it strikes me as rather curious that you need to ask me that question at all. I've lived in Gaudlin all my life, you see, and have always found the gossips here to be first-rate. I'd trust them to get information to a recipient quicker than the Royal Mail."

"I've brought up the matter of Isabella and Eustace's parents with several people, in fact," I told him. "But each time I do I am met with hostility and a refusal to answer. I say 'the Westerleys' and everyone changes the subject. Suddenly we're on to discussing the weather or the price of grain or whether or not Mr. Disraeli has any chance of becoming Prime Minister. Everyone from the girl in the café to the vicar in the church gives me the same answer."

"Which is?"

"Ask Mr. Raisin."

He laughed. "And so here you are."

"Yes. Here I am. Asking Mr. Raisin."

He exhaled loudly and stood up, walking over to the window and looking out on to the back courtyard where, I could see, the leaves of a wild maple tree were turning to flame-red in a corner. There were some very fine rose bushes lined up along one side and I wondered whether it was he or Mr. Cratchett who tended to them. I decided not to interrupt his thoughts, however; at that moment I believed that he was deciding whether or not to tell me the truth, and if I rushed him in his decision, then I would discover nothing. Finally, after a lengthy pause, he turned round with such a serious expression on his face that I felt what it must be like to be an accused person in this office and to have that countenance turned upon me.

"What I am prepared to tell you, Miss Caine," he began, "is a matter of public record so there can be no question of confidence-breaking. In all honesty, I am surprised that you do not know it already for it was a matter of some scandal in the newspapers a little over a year ago."

I frowned. The truth was, for all my fine talk, I never looked at the newspapers. I kept up with a few bits of politics, of course. I could name the Prime Minister and the Home Secretary. I knew a little about the war in Prussia and the assassination attempt in Kiev, for these were subjects that had been discussed in the teachers' room at St. Elizabeth's. But other than this, I suppose I was rather ignorant of contemporary news stories.

"The children's parents," he began. "Well, I suppose I should start with Mr. Westerley. I knew him since he was a boy, you see. We were schooled together. We were like brothers growing up. My mother died when I was just a child so my father brought me up alone. And as he worked exclusively for old Mr. Westerley, James and I were thrown into each other's company from an early age."

"Your story is similar to my own," I told him. "My mother died when I was nine."

He nodded and I could see that he warmed to me a little then. "Well then you know something of what it is like to grow up with just your father's company. Anyway, James was a mischievous boy but he grew into an exceptionally kind-hearted and thoughtful young man, well read, popular in the village. His father, old Mr. Westerley, was something of a tartar but there's nothing wrong with that. When one has money and responsibilities, one cannot go around being friendly to everyone. He had plans for James to marry a girl from Ipswich, the daughter of a local landowner there, but that wasn't to be. These weren't feudal times, after all. James wasn't going to be told whom he might and might not marry. In the end, of course, he didn't even marry an Englishwoman."

"Isabella mentioned that to me," I told him. "She said her mother was Spanish."

"Yes, that's right. James went to Madrid for six months—this must be fourteen years ago now, I suppose—and he fell in love with a girl he met over there. She wasn't anybody, of course. Her family had nothing. There had been a scandal of some sort, it's rather indelicate to talk of, but James didn't care about her family's past. He wanted Santina, that was the girl's name, and it seemed as if she wanted him too. Anyway, the point is that he came back to Norfolk with this girl and brought her to see his father. Needless to say there was a great commotion, the old man said that they could not marry, but the deed had already been done. The ring was on the girl's finger. Awfully upsetting for everyone, of course, but old Mr. Westerley, tough as he was, decided not to break with his son over it and, in time, forgave him and showed a certain amount of courtesy towards his daughter-in-law."

"There was no estrangement then?" I asked.

"There was," he conceded. "But only for a brief period. Everyone was reconciled once tempers abated. Truthfully, Santina made a genuine effort with everyone. She treated old Mr. Westerley with great respect; she made friends with the villagers. She contributed to life here. For those first few years there was really nothing too extraordinary about their situation at all. Despite being a foreigner, she grew to be accepted by everyone and all was well."

I nodded, thinking about this. A stranger, a foreigner, in a place like this. Set up in the big house. I imagined things couldn't have been easy for the new Mrs. Westerley.

"You make it sound like a perfect idyll," I said. "Why do I feel you're about to destroy it?"

"You're quite perceptive, Miss Caine. A year or so later, Mr. Westerley passed away and James inherited everything. Santina was with child at the time and when she gave birth a few months later to a little girl, Isabella, everything changed. It was an extraordinary thing. I remember seeing her at Gaudlin a few days before the child was born and then when Isabella was a week old, and I swear that it was like looking at a different woman."

"In what way?" I asked, sitting forward.

He frowned and considered it; I could see that these were memories that caused him great distress and that he wanted to be precise with his words. "My wife purchased a gift to welcome the child into the world," he said, sitting down again and looking directly at me, his face etched with pain. "A small toy. Nothing out of the ordinary. We went over to Gaudlin to see the Westerleys and when we got there, Santina was in her bedroom, indisposed, and James went upstairs to fetch her, leaving my wife and me alone with the child. Charlotte went next door to the powder room and, a moment later, Isabella woke and, hungry I expect, started to cry. You must understand, Miss Caine, that I have children of my own. I am accustomed to dealing with infants and pride myself on the fact that, unlike most of my gender, I am quite happy to soothe a crying baby. The child was distraught and so naturally I reached down to pick her up. The moment I did so, the moment I lifted her, Santina appeared in the doorway and, seeing what I was doing, began to scream. Fearful, it was! A sound unlike any that I had ever heard before. I didn't know what was wrong and simply stood there, rooted to the spot, shocked. Even Isabella stopped crying, so loud and appalling was the sound issuing from her mother's mouth. In a moment, James was in the room, looking back and forth between us, wondering what on earth was going on, and I replaced Isabella in her cradle and left, making my way to the front of the house, where Charlotte discovered me a few moments later and we called for Heckling to bring our carriage round. The whole thing had been terribly disconcerting. I had done something to upset Santina—but what? I couldn't make sense of it."

I stared at him. "And all you did was pick the child up?" I asked.

"I swear, that was all."

"So why was she so upset?"

Mr. Raisin laughed bitterly. "Upset? She wasn't upset, Miss Caine. She was demented. She lost all control of herself. A few minutes later James came out and he was equally flustered. He apologized and I apologized and, fools that we were, we kept on insisting that it was our own fault until I suggested that Charlotte and I should really be getting along and he waved us off. My wife and I made our way home, terribly upset by the whole business, but I tried to put the entire thing out of my mind."

I thought about this. "Mrs. Westerley and you," I said after a moment, "had you been friends before this? You say that Mr. Westerley and you had grown up almost as brothers. Was she jealous of your attachment perhaps?"

"I don't think so," he said, shaking his head. "Charlotte and I had been very welcoming to Santina when she first arrived in England and she had told me on more than one occasion how grateful she was to me for that. I always thought we rather liked each other, if I'm honest. We certainly had never exchanged a cross word, nor had there ever been an uncomfortable moment between us until then."

He took his pipe out of his mouth now and settled it on the table next to him. I could see a slight shake in his hands, a nervousness at the recounting of this story, and a moment later he stood up and walked over to the right-hand side of the room where a small cabinet of drinks stood. "It's early, I know," he said, pouring himself a whisky. "But I feel I need this. I haven't talked about these matters in a long time."

"It's quite all right," I said.

"Would you like one?"

I shook my head and he nodded, set the decanter back and took a sip from his glass. "After that," he continued, "everything at Gaudlin Hall changed. Santina became a different woman entirely. She could not bear to be away from her daughter for even a minute; she did not trust anyone else to take care of her.

Naturally, James wanted to employ a nanny, for that was the way things had always been done in the Westerley family, but Santina would hear none of it. She said she would take care of the child herself."

"But it's quite natural, surely," I said, speaking in my ignorance of things I did not fully understand. "She was devoted to her daughter. She is to be admired for such dedication."

"No, that's not it, Miss Caine," he said, shaking his head. "I have seen devotion. My own wife is utterly devoted to our children. Most women I know are. Most men too, even though they try to hide it under bluster and bluff. But this was not devotion. This was something obsessive. She simply would not allow anyone else to be near Isabella. To touch her, to hold her. To take care of her. Not even James. Once, on a night when I confess we might have imbibed too much of this good Scotch whisky, my friend confided in me that—excuse me, Miss Caine, but I must speak plain if I am to speak true—that they no longer shared a marital bed."

I looked away and felt a sudden distress that I had come to Mr. Raisin's office at all. What business was any of this of mine? Why did I feel I had the right to know the workings of a marriage whose participants I had never even met? I felt an urge to get up, to leave, to run away. I didn't want to know anything more. But, like Pandora opening her box to let loose all the evil in the world, I had asked Mr. Raisin where the children's parents were, and this was what he was now doing; the box could not be sealed again until the answer was delivered.

"Do you wish for me to stop, Miss Caine?" he asked. "You look distressed."

"Please go on," I said, swallowing, anxious for where this story might lead. "Tell me what else you know."

"Naturally, relations between the couple became strained," he continued. "So you can imagine my surprise when, a few years later, Santina found herself with child once again. With Eustace. James confided in me that there had been a brief rapprochement, that he had demanded his rights as a husband, and the result was the second child. This time, things went much the same way. If anything, they were worse. Her obsession with her children became almost pathological. She stayed with them twenty-four hours a day and woe betide anyone who tried to step between them. She was quite ill, of course. There was something not right, I believe, in her head. She needed medical attention. Perhaps it was something from her own childhood that haunted her and damaged her, I don't know. I mentioned about the scurrilous rumours I heard but there is no way of knowing whether there is anything in them."

"A scandal, you said," I replied. "What kind of scandal?"

"Really, Miss Caine. It's quite wicked. I don't believe we should discuss it."

"I should like to know."

He stared at me and for a moment I thought I could see tears in his eyes. "James spoke of it to me once," he said finally in a quiet voice. "He told me what Santina had told him. Or rather he hinted at it. I think even he could not find the words to describe such cruel and depraved behaviour."

"You'll have to speak more plainly, Mr. Raisin."

"Santina's father and uncle," he said, clearing his throat. "They were base fellows. It seems that they behaved . . . how shall I put this . . . in a deeply inappropriate manner towards her when she was a child. They took the most despicable liberties. Not just criminal ones but ones that run counter to the law of nature. Must I be clearer, Miss Caine, or do you understand me?"

I nodded, feeling the gorge rise inside me. "I understand you perfectly, sir," I said, surprised that my voice did not waver. "The poor girl must have suffered terribly."

"It's hard to imagine it," he replied. "To think that a father could do such a thing. And an uncle. I don't understand it, that's the truth of it. Are we all animals under the skin, Miss Caine? Do we mask our baser instincts with fine words and clothes and decent behaviour? They say that if we were to give way to our true desires we would, all of us, set upon each other with a lust for blood that has no equal in history."

What Mr. Raisin described might have been outside the experience of most young women of my age but of course I knew only too well a little about such behaviour from the events that had taken place at St. Elizabeth's the previous year. My young friend, Mr. Covan, had been given responsibility for the middle girls, who were aged around ten years old. One of those girls, a quiet, pretty little thing whose name I shall not record, went from being a well-behaved student to a troublemaker over the course of a few months and no one could get to the bottom of it. She grew quite violent in class one day and attempted to assault Mr. Covan. The girl had to be restrained and was in danger of expulsion, only she revealed a set of circumstances to Mrs. Farnsworth after much questioning which led to the police being called and Mr. Covan being escorted from the grounds that very day. A trial was avoided when the young man took his own life, but it was a shocking episode, one which caused great distress to all the teachers and particular upset to me, who had nurtured affectionate feelings towards him and who felt betrayed and frightened by the revelation of his true nature. But of course this was as naught compared to the harm inflicted on the girl herself, who, by the time I left the school, had still not returned to her old self but seemed intent on causing as much chaos around her as possible.

"I find human nature to be a very disturbing thing," I told Mr. Raisin. "People can be capable of the most despicable cruelties. If Mrs. Westerley suffered at the hands of her own family, perhaps it was only natural that she wanted to keep her children close to her. That she did not want anyone to harm them."

"I can understand her desire to protect them, Miss Caine," he replied. "But damn it all, she would barely let their own father lift them or play with them, let alone anyone else. It was a situation that could not be allowed to continue. And yet it did. It continued for several years and we all simply grew accustomed to the fact that there was a madwoman living at Gaudlin Hall. We became complacent, I suppose. We thought that it was not our problem. James and Santina's relationship became utterly fraught and he aged before my eyes. The poor man didn't know how to fix things. It might have gone on interminably but matters came to a head some eighteen months ago when a regrettable incident took place. Santina was in a park with Isabella and Eustace and, when she had her back turned for only a moment, another lady invited them both to join her own two children in a game of chase. For a few seconds, they were lost to Santina and she went . . . well, I have used the word 'mad' already but really, Miss Caine, that is the only way to explain it. She lost her reason entirely."

I sat there, wide-eyed. "What did she do?" I asked.

"She lifted part of a fallen branch off the ground. A heavy, substantial piece of wood. And she beat the woman. She beat this good woman badly. She might have killed her had others not intervened. It was a terrible thing. A truly terrible thing." He had grown quite pale by now. "The police were called, of course, but somehow James managed to prevent her from being charged. You'll find, Miss Caine, that in a place like this, money and position can buy you a lot of favours. The truth is that it would have been better for all had she been arrested and imprisoned that day. If she had, then the rest might never have happened." He ran a hand across his eyes and sighed, taking another drink from his glass, a longer draught this time. "I'm afraid my story becomes rather distressing from here on, Miss Caine. I shall have to ask you to prepare yourself."

"It's already distressing," I said. "I can scarcely imagine worse."

He laughed bitterly. "Try," he replied. "Whatever deal James made with the constabulary, whatever conversation he had with his wife in the wake of this attack, it must have lifted the veil of so many years from his eyes because he could see at last how unhealthy the attachment between Santina and her children had grown. How love had been stretched beyond its natural boundary to a place where it had been transformed into obsession and cruelty. You've seen Isabella's curious nature, after all. The maturity combined with childishness. That has its roots in her intimate relationship with her mother. Anyway, James insisted that a new relationship needed to be established. That Santina could not spend all her time with the children. That they needed other influences. And so, over her objections, he hired a governess. The first governess. Miss

Tomlin. A nice girl. A little older than you, rather pretty in her way. We all liked her. She spoke French fluently but nobody minded that. I saw her occasionally in the village with the children and I took to playing a ridiculous game with myself: where was Santina? For if I looked around I knew that I would be able to discover her somewhere, hiding, watching, fretting. But still I thought that this was healthier than what had gone before. I felt that she was learning to loosen the cord that connected her to Isabella and Eustace. And I genuinely believed— I genuinely believed this, Miss Caine—that this would be for the best in the long run. After all, one day the children would grow up, would marry, and would move away from Gaudlin Hall. And Santina would need to be ready for that. But of course I was entirely wrong, for she simply could not live with the idea that her children were in the care of another. That, for a few hours of each day, they were, to her way of thinking, in danger.

"One night, a little over a year ago, she came into the living room at Gaudlin Hall while the children were upstairs to discover her husband and the governess in conversation. She was quite relaxed, quite composed. She waited for them both to turn away from her and then she reached for the poker from the fire, the heavy iron poker that had been there for generations, and she set about them both, catching them off guard, with as much fury as she had attacked that unfortunate lady in the park. Only this time there was no one to intervene and a poker, Miss Caine, is a more deadly weapon than a fallen branch." He bowed his head and became silent.

"Murder?" I asked, whispering the dreaded word, and he nodded his head.

"I'm afraid so, Miss Caine," he said quietly. "Cold-blooded murder. When I think of that lovely Miss Tomlin, her youth, her beauty, her life taken away from her. The scene at Gaudlin Hall that night was shocking. As the family lawyer, as a lifelong friend, the officers who discovered the carnage summoned me and I promise you, Miss Caine, that I will never forget what I saw. No one should ever have to witness such butchery. No one ever could and sleep soundly again."

I looked away. I felt sick to the pit of my stomach. I wished I did not know this story. Was I little more than a fearsome gossip, wanting to know these intimate secrets when truly they did not concern me? But we had got this far. We might as well finish.

"And Mrs. Westerley," I said. "Santina. She was not released this time, I presume."

"She was hanged, Miss Caine," he replied. "The judge showed no mercy, and why should he have, after all? She was hanged from the neck until dead."

I nodded and put a hand to my chest, feeling the bruises that were still tender.

"And the other governesses?" I asked.

Mr. Raisin shook his head. "Not today, Miss Caine," he said, glancing at the grandfather clock. "I'm afraid I must stop there. I have to be in Norwich soon and I feel that I may need a few moments to allow my emotions to settle before I leave. Can we talk again another time?"

I nodded. "Of course," I said, standing up and retrieving my coat. "You've been very generous. I feel I should apologize, Mr. Raisin," I said. "I can see how distressed you are. I think I have only added to your pain."

"You had a right to know," he said with a shrug. "And you have a right to know the rest too. Only . . . not today, if you please."

I nodded again and turned for the door, hesitating as I reached for the handle before turning back to him.

"It's shocking though, isn't it?" I said, trying to imagine how far love could be perverted so that the natural bond of mother and child should descend into something so obsessive. "To commit two murders simply to prevent anyone else from becoming close to your children. It doesn't bear thinking about."

Mr. Raisin looked back at me and frowned. "Two murders, Miss Caine?" he asked.

"Yes," I said. "Mr. Westerley and Miss Tomlin. It's shocking."

The lawyer shook his head. "I'm sorry," he said. "I fear that I haven't been entirely clear. Mrs. Westerley was not a double murderer. Miss Tomlin was the only fatality on that terrible night. Oh, she wanted to kill them both of course. And she damn near succeeded, if you'll excuse my language. But no, Mr. Westerley, James, did not die. Although considering the life he has now and the condition in which that woman left him, it might have been better for him if he had."

I stared at him. "Mr. Westerley is alive?" I asked, astonished.

"Yes."

"Then I return to my original question of an hour ago," I said. "I asked where the children's parents are. I know where Mrs. Westerley is, of course. But Mr. Westerley? Where is he?"

He stared at me as if I was quite mad. "You don't know?" he asked.

"Of course not," I said, growing more frustrated now. "If I knew, then why would I ask? Has he left Norfolk? Abandoned his own children?"

"Miss Caine, James Westerley would no more abandon his children than I would mine. And he has not left Norfolk since the day he returned from that ill-fated voyage to Madrid. No, James is still here, with us. He never left. He's at Gaudlin Hall. He's in the house with you. He's been there since you arrived."

Chapter Fourteen

I NEVER NEEDED AN alarm to wake in the morning nor, as a child, did I ever require Father to knock on my door to rouse me for school. When Aunt Hermione took me to Cornwall for the summer after Mother's death, she proclaimed herself astonished that I always appeared downstairs for breakfast at precisely the time that she had told me the night before. She called me an unnatural child but seemed impressed by my punctuality. All my life, when I have known that I must wake at a particular time, I always wake.

And so when I told myself to rise at four o'clock the morning after my appointment with Mr. Raisin, I knew that I would not fail, and sure enough my eyes opened at that hour to a darkened bedroom. I roused myself and parted the curtains, looking across the grounds of Gaudlin Hall while keeping back from the window, although I did not fear it entirely for the spirit that haunted that place seemed uninterested in repeating its tricks. The fear grew from never knowing when it might strike next. Or how.

A fog had descended across the gardens, a pea-souper that reminded me of the "London Particular." It was difficult to make anything out and I dressed quickly, making my way downstairs to the kitchen. Sitting in a position where I might keep a close eye on anyone who walked round this side of the house, I made some tea and waited. Four thirty came and went, five o'clock appeared and with it a faint splinter of light on the horizon. I could feel my eyes starting to fail and, after almost nodding off, stepped quickly towards the library to find a book that might keep me awake. While I was selecting one I heard movement from the room beyond, and I stood at the kitchen door, looking in, pleased but a little frightened that I had finally trapped my prey.

"Mrs. Livermore."

The lady jumped, startled, uttering an oath, and spun round, her hand pressed against her chest in surprise. "Whatever do you think you're doing?" she asked, the first words she had ever spoken to me, despite the fact that we had been in this house, or around it, together for several weeks. "Creeping up on a person like that? You might have given me a turn."

"How else would I get to meet you?" I asked, not standing on ceremony. "It's not easy to make your acquaintance."

"Aye," she replied, nodding and staring at me with a contemptuous expression before turning back to the cooker where she had set a pan of water to boil. "Them as lies in bed all morning are likely to miss me. You need to get up early, Governess, if it's conversation you're after."

"Would I have got any?" I asked. "I suspect that you would have denied me any discourse."

She sighed and looked at me with an exhausted expression. She was a stout woman, perhaps closer to fifty years of age than forty, and wore her greying hair in a tight bun behind her head. Her eyes were bright, however, and I suspected that she did not suffer fools lightly. "You may speak plain with me," she said in a low voice. "I'm not an educated woman."

I nodded and felt slightly embarrassed. Was "discourse" a word only used among the learned classes?

"Well, perhaps you're right anyhow," she added after a moment, relenting slightly, and turned back to the range. "I were making tea," she said.

"May I join you?"

"I don't suppose I should get any peace if I said no, should I?" she asked. "Sit down in there, I'll bring the tea in, you can say what needs to be said and then I can get on with my work. Are we agreed?"

I nodded, and turned to make my way back towards the parlour, a room that I had not spent much time in hitherto. Before leaving the kitchen, however, I noticed a grey mark on my hand—I must have collected some dust on the banisters as I had made my way downstairs—and went over to the sink to wash it off. I gave a slight gasp as the water hit my hands, and Mrs. Livermore turned to me.

"What's the matter with you now, girl?"

"It's just the water," I said, flushing a little. "It's so cold."

"Well, of course it's cold," she replied. "Where do you think you are, Buckingham Palace?" I moved away, rubbing my hands together to warm them. The water was always freezing cold, of course; if we wanted hot water at Gaudlin Hall it had to be heated on the range.

"Tea," said Mrs. Livermore a few minutes later, entering the room with a tray carrying two cups, the teapot, a jug of milk and a bowl of sugar. "I've no fancies, so don't be asking for any. You can make your own breakfast later."

"That's quite all right," I said, my tone less combative now. "And I'm sorry about startling you earlier. I really didn't intend to give you a fright."

"Aye," she replied, looking away. "Well just think on, Governess. Because next time you might get a ladle to the head." I smiled and reached for the pot but she brushed my hand away. "Let it brew," she said. "Let the goodness take."

She reached into the pockets of her pinafore, removed a small cigarette and lit it. I stared at her, startled. I had never seen a woman smoking before, and certainly not a neat little roll-your-own like this. I had heard that it had become the fashion among the London ladies, of course. That was their privilege. But for a domestic to do so within a house like this was quite extraordinary.

"I've not got a second," she said, noticing my interest in the cigarette. "So don't ask."

"I had no intention of asking," I replied, wanting no part of the malodorous thing anyway. I glanced at the pot again and she nodded, indicating that I might pour. The tea came out thick and steaming and I added milk and sugar and took a sip to warm me.

"Well, go on," said Mrs. Livermore. "Spit it out." I stared at her, unsure what she meant. Had she poisoned it perhaps? "Not the tea, you daft mare," she said, almost smiling. "You've got summat to say, Governess, so best that you get it off your chest before you explode."

"I saw Mr. Raisin yesterday," I replied, keeping my tone steady; she would not bully me. "The solicitor in the village."

"I know who Mr. Raisin is," she said, sneering at me. "I've

not been collecting my wages every week for the last year from Farmer Haddock's prize goat."

"Yes, well," I said. "I made an appointment with him and we had a conversation. There were certain things I wanted to know and he was good enough to tell me."

"Good enough to tell you what exactly?" she asked, narrowing her eyes as she leaned forward to lift her cup.

"That Mr. Westerley is still here. At Gaudlin Hall. Residing in this house."

She snorted a laugh and shook her head, taking another deep drag from her cigarette before washing the taste down with a good mouthful of tea. "How long have you been here now, Governess?" she asked.

"Three weeks."

"The girl before you, Miss Bennet she called herself, she had all that figured out in half that time. And poor Miss Harkness before her, may the Good Lord have mercy on her penitent soul"—she blessed herself, twice—"she put it all together within two days. But then she were a nosy sort and something of an hysteric. I shouldn't speak ill of the dead but I speak as I find, Miss—" She stared at me, a rather startled expression on her face. "I don't know your name, do I?"

"Eliza Caine," I told her.

She smoked some more and sized me up. "Eliza were my mother's name," she said finally. "I've always liked it. I said to my Henry, if we had a girl we should call her Eliza. Only we had a flurry of boys, didn't we? Great lumps, all of them. One as bad as the next. You a London girl?" I nodded. "I went there once," she told me. "When I were young, around your age. Couldn't stand it. All that noise! I don't know how anyone puts up with it. I should lose my reason. I don't know how they don't all go mad up there. Do you think London folk are a bit touched in the head, Governess?"

"Not especially," I said. "Although I know it's a common generalization. Much like saying that all country people are uneducated and even a little stupid."

She blew a smoke ring out of her mouth—disgusting—and her expression told me that she rather liked what I had just said, admired it even. "My point being," she said finally, leaning forward and speaking in a much more refined tone to impress this fact upon me. "My point being that you've been here three weeks and you're only coming to learn these things now. Bright as a button, you, aren't you? Sure that you don't have some country blood in you somewhere?"

"The truth is that I wouldn't have known any of it at all if Mr. Raisin hadn't told me," I said. "And really, I do think someone might have mentioned it before now. My own employer here in the house and we have yet to speak face to face. I haven't seen him with his children. He doesn't join us for meals. When does he come and go? Where does he eat? Is he a ghost or does he take human form?"

"Oh, he exists all right," said Mrs. Livermore. "He's no ghost. He's here in the house right now. But if Mr. Raisin told you that much, then why didn't you ask these other questions of him? It's not my place to tell you things."

"There was no more time," I explained. "He had other appointments. And he was rather emotional after telling me about the episode that took place here at Gaudlin Hall."

"The episode?" she asked, frowning.

"When Mrs. Westerley . . ." I hesitated; it was very early in the day for such terrible stories. "When she set about her husband and the first governess, Miss Tomlin."

"Hark at you," said Mrs. Livermore, laughing bitterly. "Pleasant language for a nasty deed. Set about them, you say? When she beat one into the grave and tried to do the same to the other, you mean."

"Yes," I said, nodding. "Exactly that."

"Episode my eye."

"Mr. Raisin said that I should meet Mr. Westerley."

"Oh he did, did he?"

"That's right," I said, holding her gaze. "He said that you would introduce me."

She looked away, her brow creasing. "He's not said 'owt to me about that."

"I assure you it's quite true."

"Mr. Westerley usually sees only me."

"And the children, of course," I said.

"He hasn't laid eyes on his children since the episode, as you call it."

I stared at her. "But that's impossible," I said. "Why ever not?"

"If you saw him, you'd understand. But I don't believe it's in your interests that you do."

"It seems to me to be the most extraordinary thing," I cried in frustration, throwing my hands in the air. "The master of this estate, the father of those children, keeps himself hidden away and entertains no company other than, well, forgive me, you, Mrs. Livermore—"

"There's worse fates."

"Please don't be sarcastic. All I want is to understand. We are both employed here, after all, can we not share confidences? I as governess and you as Mr. Westerley's cook or maid or whatever it is that you do."

She took a long drag on her cigarillo now in a manner

reminiscent of Mr. Raisin himself. For a long time she remained quite silent, as if she was considering this. Finally, in a quieter voice, she spoke. "A cook, you say. Or a maid."

"Well, yes. I mean if that is what you are, after all. I don't mean it in a disrespectful fashion."

"I should hope not, Governess," she said, stressing my own position. "There's plenty would be pleased with the position of cook or maid at Gaudlin Hall. It's a good job for the right girl. Or a widow woman. And back in old Mr. Westerley's day there were plenty of staff here. Not like now. The place is falling down about our ears owing to the lack of them. It's in disrepair, haven't you noticed? That roof will come down on top of us one day soon if no one sees fit to mend it. But you're wrong if you think that I'm a cook or a maid. It's true that I prepare Mr. Westerley's food," she added. "But then you've prepared food too, Governess, haven't you?" she asked me. "You know how to put together a stew or a lamb hotpot?"

"Of course," I said. "When I was living with Father in London I prepared all our meals."

"Don't make you the cook though, does it?" she asked.

"Well, no, of course not," I said. "I'm sorry, Mrs. Livermore. I didn't mean to offend you. Although I really don't see why it should be offensive."

She laughed and shook her head. "You'd have to get up a lot earlier than this to offend me," she said. "I'm made of tough stuff. Have to be, the life I've lived. No, I'm not a cook. That's not where my training lies."

"Mrs. Livermore, you're talking in riddles," I said, exhaustion beginning to overtake me. "Can we not just be clear with each other?"

"All right then," she said, pressing the remains of her cigarette out and standing up, smoothing down her pinafore, which, now that I looked at it, did not resemble a cook's outfit as much as I had earlier imagined. "You say Mr. Raisin says you're to meet the master; all right then, I'll take you at your word." She walked towards the door, stopped and turned round. "Well?" she asked. "Are you coming or not?"

"Right now?" I asked, standing up. "But it's so early? Won't he be angry to be awakened at this hour?"

"Don't you worry about that," she said. "Come along if you're coming." And with that she made her way quickly through the kitchen and I followed behind, almost having to break into a run to keep up with her. Where was she going to take me? My mind raced with the possibilities. I had, in my idle moments, visited most of the rooms in the house and they were for the most part quite empty. There were no signs of life. Surely the master of Gaudlin would have a suite of rooms for himself? A bedroom, a library, a study, a private bathroom?

We made our way through the house to the main staircase, ascending and turning on to the landing where the children's rooms were situated, and Mrs. Livermore hesitated for a moment.

"Here?" I asked and she shook her head.

"They're not awake yet," she said. "Come on. Up again."

We ascended once again to the floor on which my own bedroom and six empty bedrooms lay. But he couldn't be here, I was sure of it; I had looked inside each one and they were quite empty. To my surprise, Mrs. Livermore went to the room at the furthest end of the corridor and opened it. I followed her in but there was nothing to be seen. The room was stark and empty, a four-poster bed, stripped of its sheets, in the centre of the room. She looked at me and I stared back.

"I don't understand," I said.

"This way," she replied, turning round and pressing on a panel in the wall, where I now saw that a door was hidden, painted in keeping with the rest of the wall so that one would not know it was there unless one looked quite closely. I gasped in surprise when she pushed it open to reveal a set of stone steps beyond, and I followed her through, lifting my skirt to prevent it dragging along the dust on the stone floor.

"Where are we?" I asked in a hushed tone.

"All these great houses have secrets like this," she told me as she climbed the steep steps. "Think of when they were built, after all. They served as battlements, as defending posts. You think that's the only door like that in the house? It isn't. I don't usually use it, of course. I come in from outside the house."

I thought about the two occasions when I had followed her round the corner of the house only for her to vanish out of sight altogether. As if reading my mind, she turned to me and smiled.

"You want to take a look at that wall, Governess. The door's perfectly visible if you only look. See it once and you'll never miss it again. It's the first time that's the difficulty."

"You knew I was following you then?" I asked.

"I have ears," she grunted, climbing again. "I'm not daft."

We found ourselves near the top of Gaudlin Hall, at a point where another staircase met our own position and returned downwards to the opposite side of the house. "That'll lead you back out," she told me. "That's how I usually come in."

A large door stood before us and I felt a distinct chill run through my body. He couldn't be close to here, could he? Mrs. Livermore reached into the front pocket of her pinafore for a large and sturdy key. I hesitated; I had a curious worry that it might lead to the roof and that she was going to throw me off for my insolence, but as we went through I was presented with two staircases, leading in two different directions.

"That way's the roof," said Mrs. Livermore, nodding towards the left. "This way's the master."

We ascended again, a short flight, and turned at the top, where we were met by another solid oak door. She stopped in front of it and turned round, her expression softening slightly. "How old are you, Governess?" she asked.

"Twenty-one," I replied, uncertain why she would ask.

"You look to me like a girl who hasn't seen much unpleasantness in her life, would I be right on that?"

I thought about it and finally nodded. "You would," I said.

She pointed at the door. "If Mr. Raisin says you can meet the master, then I'm not going to stand in the way of that," she said. "But you don't have to, you know. You can turn round and walk away right now. You can go back down those stairs and we can lock the door behind us and you can return to looking after them children and I can go back to doing what I do and you might sleep better of a night. It's your decision. So speak now as there'll be no turning back afterwards."

I swallowed hard. I was desperate to know what was on the other side of that door but her warning was sufficiently serious for me to reconsider. It was true that I wanted to meet Mr. Westerley, I had a right to after all, but had he turned into a monster of some sort after his wife's terrible actions? Would he be as likely to strike me down as converse with me? And I could not get past the fact that it was still so early; might he not be sleeping?

"Speak, Governess," said Mrs. Livermore. "I've not all day to stand here."

I opened my mouth, almost prepared to say no, that I had changed my mind, but something in her previous speech suddenly struck a chord in my mind and I stared at her. "You can go back to doing what you do," I said. "That's what you just said to me. And downstairs, you insisted that you're not a cook and you're not a maid."

"Aye," she said, frowning. "And what of it?"

"What is it you do then, Mrs. Livermore?" I asked. "What is your position here?"

She hesitated for a moment and then her face relaxed, a half-smile appearing on it, and she reached a hand out, tenderly, and pressed it to my arm. For a moment I saw that beneath all her bluff there was a kind woman locked inside. And that she was not trying to prevent me from learning what I wanted to know but was simply uncertain whether it was in my interests.

"Don't you know, child?" she asked me. "Haven't you figured it out yet?"

I shook my head. "Tell me," I said. "Tell me please."

Mrs. Livermore smiled and took her hand away. "I'm a nurse," she said. "I'm Mr. Westerley's nurse."

For a moment I would have sworn that there was someone behind me, breathing on my neck, the presence again, the spirit, or something like it. But it was a comforting presence this time, not the one that had forced me off my dandy-horse or tried to push me from the window. Perhaps it was the one who had saved me on that occasion. Or perhaps I was imagining it entirely.

I nodded and looked at the door, determined now. "Please open it, Mrs. Livermore," I said. "I wish to meet my employer."

Chapter Fifteen

B Y LUNCHTIME, I had almost recovered.

The children were delighted not to have any classroom studies that morning; I had no choice but to cancel our class as there was certainly no possibility that I could have concentrated on Shakespeare's sonnets or the difference between a peninsula and an inlet after such a traumatic and upsetting experience.

After Mrs. Livermore had gone for the day—or rather, had retired to her small cottage hidden behind the trees that ran along the rear of the stables; the cottage to which she would go back and forth throughout the day, mostly unnoticed by me—I wandered around the house feeling lost and disconsolate. Isabella and Eustace were outside playing but I could neither bring myself to read nor to sew nor to practise on the small piano that I had lately taken to attempting. Instead I prayed for night to fall so that I could retire to my bed, to sleep, for what Coleridge had called "the wide blessing," and to wake again the following day refreshed and ready to begin anew. I wondered whether I would feel that ghastly presence in the house that seemed to come and go of its own will, but all was still until the ringing of the doorbell, which jolted me and made me cry aloud.

Afternoon had fallen. It was growing dark early now and the fog had returned. I could not hear the children or see them from the window.

I walked down the hallway nervously, uncertain of what might be awaiting me on the other side, and opened the door only a little at first, carefully, but then upon seeing who it was I relaxed immediately.

"Mrs. Toxley," I said, surprised at first to see her but then recalling that I had invited her on Sunday to call over this afternoon, an appointment I had entirely forgotten until that moment.

"You look surprised to see me," she said, remaining outside, her eyes looking around the front of the house nervously. "We did say today, didn't we?"

"We did, we did," I agreed. "I'm so sorry. Can I be entirely honest with you and say that it slipped my mind? There have been a number of upsetting incidents here and I forgot our arrangement."

"I could always come back another day if it's more convenient?" she suggested, stepping back with a certain relieved expression on her face, but I shook my head and ushered her in.

"You must think terribly of me," I said. "What kind of person invites another over for tea and then forgets? I can only apologize." I peered out into the fog. A shadow passed between the trees; I blinked, it vanished. "You didn't see the children as you came up the driveway, did you?"

"I saw Isabella," she said. "She was marching around with a ball in her hands, looking very cross. And I heard Eustace shouting after her but didn't see him. Is everything all right?"

I glanced at the grandfather clock in the hallway. There was time enough for them to stay outdoors yet. "Everything's fine," I said.

"You look tired, Miss Caine," she replied, a concerned expression on her face. "Have you been sleeping?"

"I have," I said. "Only I was up quite early this morning, so perhaps my appearance is a little drawn."

"There's nothing worse than someone telling you that you look tired, is there?" she asked, smiling at me, putting me at my ease. "I always think it's terribly rude. I shouldn't have said anything."

"Let's go into the kitchen," I said. "I'll put some water on for tea."

She followed me in and I took her hat, coat and gloves and she handed me a charming, neatly packaged box. "A small gift," she said.

I was touched by such an unexpected kindness and opened it. Immediately an explosion of powerful odours emerged from the box. Mrs. Toxley had brought pear cakes infused with cinnamon and I felt a weakness overtake me.

"I bought them at Mrs. Sutcliffe's tea shop in the village," she explained. "I would have made the cakes myself only Alex said that I should stay away from the oven if I didn't want to poison anyone. I'm a frightful cook. Miss Caine, are you quite all right?"

I nodded and sank into a chair, burying my face in my hands. Before I knew it, the tears were forming in my eyes and began to fall.

"My dear," she said, sitting next to me and putting her arm around me. "Whatever's the matter?"

"I'm so sorry," I replied, trying to smile and wipe the tears away at the same time. "I didn't mean to embarrass you. It's just that I associate the scent of cinnamon entirely with my late father. He died only a month ago and he has been very much on my mind lately. Particularly now, when things are growing so difficult here."

"It's my fault," she said, shaking her head. "I shouldn't have brought the cake."

"You weren't to know," I replied, drying my face and taking a deep breath before smiling at her. "There," I said. "All my silliness over, I think. I was going to make tea, wasn't I?"

I went across to the sink and turned the water on, letting it run for a minute to take away any sediment left in the pipes. I ran my fingers under it and pulled them away immediately. It was just as icy cold as it had been that morning.

"How have you been settling in?" asked Mrs. Toxley, who instructed me to call her Madge when we were seated again and drinking our tea. I wasted no time eating my pear cake in order to allow the scent of the spice to dissipate from the kitchen more quickly.

"Well, at first," I replied. "But it seems as if every day brings fresh challenges."

"You know about Mr. Westerley, don't you?" she said, reading my expression, and I nodded.

"I only learned yesterday. Mr. Raisin told me about the traumatic relationship he had with his wife. I saw him earlier."

"Mr. Raisin?"

"No, Mr. Westerley."

She opened her eyes wide in surprise. "You saw him? I'm astonished. I didn't think . . . well, I didn't think anyone was allowed."

I shrugged my shoulders. "I'm not sure that I was allowed, if I'm being honest," I told her. "I rather insisted upon it."

"And how was he?" asked Madge. I shook my head and she sighed. "He's upstairs somewhere, isn't he? It makes me so sad to think of it," she continued. "Alex and I, we were great friends of the Westerleys, you see. We dined together quite often. Alex and James went shooting together. We had some very happy times."

"You knew his wife well then?" I asked.

"Santina? Oh yes. I knew her for years. I was something of a friend to her when James first brought her back from Spain. Old Mr. Westerley was up in arms, of course, that a foreigner, particularly a foreigner of no note, should be brought into the family, but I thought she was rather sweet. And so beautiful! But there were suspicions that she was after the money."

"And was she?"

Madge laughed and shook her head. "There was never a woman who cared less for money than Santina Westerley. Oh, she wasn't opposed to having some, of course not. Why should she be? But no, she did not marry James for his money."

"She married for love then?"

Madge considered this. "I'm not sure," she said. "She was fond of him certainly in those early days. No, I think she married him because he offered her an escape. Still, old Mr. Westerley refused her an allowance at first. He was convinced that she was a gold-digger. But she was not particularly interested in material things. She didn't go looking for new gowns constantly, for example, she seemed content with the ones she had. She wasn't interested in jewellery. James bought her some at the start, of course, but she had the sort of neckline that was best unadorned. Perhaps the occasional pendant, that was all. No, even old Mr. Westerley agreed in the end that she had not married James for financial gain."

"And did he love her?" I asked.

"Oh yes. I should say so. Of course, they were both so young when James came back from Spain with his new bride. But they seemed very happy with each other then. It wasn't until much later that she became, well, troubled."

"Troubled how?" I asked.

She shook her head and frowned, as if she wanted to find the precise words to explain what she meant. "Something had happened to her, that much was obvious," she said. "When she was a girl, I mean."

"Mr. Raisin made mention of it," I told her, leaning forward, feeling a degree of distress that any adult would injure a child in the way that he had implied. "It's an abomination."

"Yes, but I thought she had put those days behind her, if such a thing is possible. I truly believed that she and James would find peace together. I was a great supporter of their union. And they were happy for a time. No one will ever convince me differently."

We said nothing for a while, sipping at our tea, both of us lost in our reflections. I was thinking of the girl Santina, of what might have happened to her to produce such a damaging psychosis. Madge was no doubt recalling happier times between the two couples.

"You have been married a long time?" I asked after a lengthy silence and she smiled and nodded.

"Nine years," she said. "Alex and I met when my brother brought him home from the Varsity for a weekend. They were studying together and had chummed up from the start. Of course I was only sixteen when I first laid eyes on him and he was three years older so naturally—"

"You fell quickly in love," I said, smiling at her.

"No, I hated him," she replied, bursting out laughing. "Oh don't look so shocked, Eliza, the feeling didn't last long. He teased me terribly that first weekend, you see. He said the most frightful things and I think I responded in kind. Mother thought we would have to be separated at dinner one night for the number of insults that we were throwing in each other's direction. It was all a mask, of course. He wrote to me soon after, you see. Apologized for being such a brute."

"And did he explain it?"

"He said that when he first laid eyes on me he knew that he would be incapable of spending the weekend trying to do what he really wanted to do—which was to make me fall in love with him—and so settled on the next best thing, making me despise him instead. Naturally I wrote back and told him that I had never met such a vulgar, pompous, despicable, unpleasant, rude, discourteous beast in all my life and that should he find himself down with us for another weekend I would refuse to have anything to do with him. He came the following weekend and brought me flowers and a copy of Keats' *Poems* and I told him that my letter had been a lie and that I had spent every hour thinking of him."

It surprised me how open she was, how willing to tell me the story of her courtship, but I could see that she enjoyed the memory of it.

"We were married within the year," she added after a moment. "I was terribly lucky. He's a fine man. But what about you, Eliza? Any sweethearts waiting for you back in London?"

I blushed and shook my head. "I don't think I am exactly what a young man is looking for," I said, and to her credit, Madge Toxley did not dispute this, for the evidence was there for all to see. She was a beauty who could make a man like Alex Toxley fall for her in a heartbeat; I was not.

"Well," she said, shifting a little uncomfortably in her chair, "who knows what the future might bring. How is he, anyway?"

she asked, changing the subject abruptly. "James, I mean. Is he well?"

"No," I said.

"No, of course not," she said, reddening slightly. "Of course he's not well. I meant . . . how is he coping? He won't see us, you see. Either of us. Alex was terribly upset last year. He tried time and again after James was released from the hospital but it was to no avail. He wrote letters, spoke to the doctors. When Mrs. Livermore came to tend to him he spoke to her and she promised that she would do what she could but it seems that James is adamant. He does not want visitors."

"My dear," I said, reaching across and laying my hand on top of hers. "The truth is that I don't believe he would even know if you were there."

She stared at me and shook her head. "What do you mean?" she asked.

"The man I saw this morning," I began. "I use the term 'man' with great caution for there is little of the man left. He is . . . how he survived his attack, I do not know. His face is . . . I'm sorry, Madge, I don't wish to distress you, but his face is a jumble. He's scarcely recognizable as human."

She put a hand to her mouth, but I did not regret my choice of words. I had deserved to know the truth about Mr. Westerley and I was a complete stranger to him. She and her husband were old friends of his. If she thought he was sitting up in bed issuing orders about whom he might or might not see, and was hurt by the exclusion, then she deserved the truth as well.

"Shall I stop or continue?" I asked her. "Is this too upsetting?"

"It is but I'd rather know," she said. "And so, I daresay, would Alex. Please tell me everything."

I sighed. "He lies there," I said, "a shell of a man. The skin half ripped from his face. There is bone and cartilage on display. Mrs. Livermore changes the dressings, she tells me, three times a day, otherwise there is the chance of infection setting in. His teeth are gone. His mouth lies open, gasping for breath. A horrendous sound, Madge. Like a dog dying in the street. And the rest of him . . . well, I did not see his body of course, that lies beneath the sheets. But he will never walk again, I am certain of that. He can barely move his arms. He is a man who seems dead to me, were it not for the fact that his heart continues to beat. It's a blasphemy, I know, but that poor man would have been better dying in the attack and not surviving it. Surviving it!" I repeated, laughing a little in bitterness at the word. "As if that is survival."

I glanced across at Mrs. Toxley, who had grown quite pale now. I could see that she was close to tears but she had a strength to her, a resilience that I had recognized on the first day when I saw her on the platform, and she simply breathed deeply now and nodded.

"I don't know what to say, Eliza," she said eventually. "Truly I don't. It still astonishes me that Santina could have done such a thing."

"Were you there the night it happened?" I asked.

"A little afterwards, yes. I didn't see Miss Tomlin's body, nor did I see James. Alex was attending to him. But I saw Santina. The police were taking her away. There was . . . there was blood on her face. And across the front of her dress. It was quite dreadful."

"Did you speak to her?"

"A little," she said. "Of course, at the time I didn't know what had happened. I assumed there had been a break-in of some sort. I thought perhaps the Westerleys had disturbed a burglar and the scene had ended in violence, that only Santina had escaped unscathed. It never occurred to me for a moment that she could have been the aggressor."

"And how did she seem?" I asked, leaning forward.

Madge thought about it, concentrating hard. "Composed," she replied eventually. "Quite relaxed. Like someone who has finally succeeded in doing something she has been planning for a long time. There was an other-worldliness to her, if you understand what I mean. She seemed more like a spirit than a woman. She seemed unreal."

"And did you see her again?"

"Several times," she replied. "At the trial, of course. I was called as a witness, as was Alex, to express my opinion of her character and of her rather unusual activities in the time leading up to the crime. And then again at the sentencing. And then once more, on the morning she was hanged. I didn't tell Alex that I was going to see her then. He wouldn't have understood. But you have to realize, Eliza, that it was a traumatic time for all of us. We are none of us the better for it yet. I believe the entire village is still suffering from the trauma. But I needed to see her. If I tell you what happened, will you respect my confidence? Will you tell no one else?"

"I swear it," I said. "I need to know, you see. Because the truth is, I sense her here. In this house."

Madge stared at me. "What do you mean?" she asked, sitting back a little.

"Do you believe in the afterlife?" I asked.

"I believe in God, if that's what you mean. I believe in the day of judgement."

"And you believe in heaven and hell?"

"Of course."

"And what if," I began, able to hear how ludicrous my words sounded but needing to hear them said aloud, "what if a soul departs this life but is neither in heaven nor hell? What if they remain?" She stared at me and swallowed, uncertain how to respond. I shook my head, dismissing this. "You said you saw her one last time," I said. "Where was it? At the prison?"

"Yes. On the morning she was to hang. I felt that, despite everything that had happened, she should see a familiar face that day. And so I went to her. I told no one. I lied to Alex, a thing I have never done before or since."

"And what happened?" I asked. "What did she do? What did she say?"

"I'll never forget it," she replied, looking away. "I still wake at night sometimes with the memory of it. I was brought to a solitary room where—"

"Eliza Caine."

I half jumped from my chair and Madge startled too and we both turned round to see Isabella and Eustace standing at the doorway.

"Children," I shouted, furious to find them eavesdropping. How long had they been standing there? How much had they heard? "What are you doing here?"

"Eustace hurt himself," said Isabella, and the boy stepped forward and I saw a large gash along his kneecap, the wound looking not too deep but the blood seeping from it nevertheless. "He fell over on the gravel."

"I didn't fall," said Eustace, his chin trembling as he tried not to give in to tears. "I got a surprise, that's all. The old man surprised me; I'd never seen him outside before."

"Sit down, Eustace," I said, and Madge stood up and settled him on her chair. "I'll have to wash the wound out. You'll be a brave boy, won't you?"

"I'll try," he said, snuffling a little.

Madge sat next to him and put an arm around his shoulders and he seemed comforted to have her there. I supposed that he had known her all his life. I went to the sink, put the plug in and turned on the tap, letting it fill while I went to the pantry for a clean cloth. I found one without much difficulty and returned to the kitchen, turned the tap off and plunged both my hands, the cloth between them, into the base of the sink, intending to soak it through in order to clean Eustace's leg with the fresh, cold water. I plunged them into the water deeply, the level above my wrists, and I can recall the curious sensation even now. For a moment, a split second, I sensed that something was wrong, something felt unusual, the water was not as icy as I had expected. This thought could only have been there for a fraction of a thousandth of a second, however, for then I screamed, a hideous yell, pulled my hands from the water and fell backwards, holding my scalded hands in the air before me, the skin already turning red, preparing to blister, the nails completely white against the scarlet skin. The water had been at boiling point; the tap that never produced anything but icy-cold water had filled the sink with enough boiling water to almost rip the skin from my hands before I could tend to Eustace's wound. I screamed and fell backwards and the sound of my screams was terrifying even to me as I looked across and saw Isabella with her hands over her ears, Eustace staring at me with his eyes and mouth wide open, and Madge lifting herself bodily from her chair and rushing towards me.

And yet, despite the agonizing pain that I was suffering, and the awareness that it was only going to get worse and worse over the next few hours and days, there was one small part of my brain that disassociated itself from this terrible agony and focused on a single line of Eustace's, a simple phrase that repeated itself over and over and made me wonder what he could possibly have meant by it.

The old man surprised me; I'd never seen him outside before.

Chapter Sixteen

I DECIDED THAT WE, the children and I, should get away from Gaudlin Hall for a day. I was suffocating under the weight of so many secrets being withheld and only revealed to me when I forced them out of one of the residents of the village. I quite understood now why the previous governess, Miss Bennet, had used such underhand tactics to find a replacement. I assumed that she too had learned of the fate of her four unfortunate predecessors and could not bear to stay any longer. Whether she had suffered as many "accidents" as had befallen me, I did not know. At my lowest moments, it occurred to me that I might do exactly as she had done: place an advertisement in a newspaper, pretend by the use of my initial instead of my Christian name that I was master of this place and find someone to take my burden away from me. It was likely, after all, that there were any number of young women seeking a change in their circumstances. Like Miss Bennet, I could be away from Gaudlin within the week if luck was on my side.

Only one thing prevented me from undertaking such a course of action: the children. Or, more precisely, Eustace. From the moment I arrived to discover that the Westerley offspring had been left to fend entirely for themselves, I had felt a compunction to take care of them. This had grown as I had got to know them, and in Eustace's case I was already feeling something approaching love, for he was a dear boy, always ready with a smile or a precocious comment, a child who was quite clearly troubled by the things that were taking place around him, things that he understood as little as I did. Isabella was a more difficult study. She was friendly towards me, always polite, but the distrust was obvious. She would not let her guard down—perhaps she had done so in the past and been disappointed—and so I did not feel as close to her as I did her brother. It made for some tense moments between us.

At times like this I wondered how different my life might have been had my sister Mary not died so soon after her birth. Was my protectiveness towards the children, not just the Westerleys but also the small girls who had been entrusted to me at St. Elizabeth's, a result of losing a sister before she could even be conscious of my existence? This was not something I liked to dwell on but it was there, occasionally, at the back of my mind. A whisper of neediness on my part that would not be muted.

My hands began to heal and Mrs. Livermore—Nurse Livermore, I suppose I should call her—helped me to remove the heavy bandages a week after Dr. Toxley had applied them. As the gauze was stripped away, my heart was filled with trepidation, so nervous was I at what might be discovered underneath. I watched her face and, although she tried to disguise it, a grimace crossed her features, an expression that suggested she had seen some unpleasant things before but this was in line with the worst of them.

"How does it look?" I asked, afraid to throw my glance down, but she was not one for delicacy.

"You have eyes, Governess," she growled. "See for yourself."

I closed them for a moment, breathed in deeply, then looked down. The skin was raw and tender after a week of being tightly wrapped, and yellow with the detritus of the cooling balm the doctor had applied between the flesh and the fabric, and I knew that in time some of this would go away, but the scars that remained, those raw and inflamed grooves of scarlet, would, I knew, never fade. The burns had been too severe. They would serve as my Gaudlin scars. The presence, for that was how I defined it now, that strange presence that was opposed to my being at Gaudlin Hall had scalded me so badly that I would bear these disfigurements for ever. I tried to flex my fingers and, to my relief, I could do so, although not without a great deal of pain. At least sensation remained. I would rather have that than not.

"Leave them be for now," said Mrs. Livermore, walking over to the sink and washing away the filth from the bandages. "Let the air at them. They'll soon lose their temper."

Naturally, I was by now quite frightened of the presence. It had blown me off my dandy-horse, thrown me from the windows of my bedroom, turned the ice-cold water to a scald. I also believed that it had been responsible for my almost falling under the passing train on the day I arrived in Norfolk. It knew who I was. Perhaps it had followed Miss Bennet to the station, and recognized me as her replacement and thought to get rid of me before I could even arrive at the Hall. Yes, I admit that I was frightened of it, but I felt a strength and resilience nonetheless and was determined not to be beaten.

And I would never allow it to harm the children, although that did not seem to be its intention anyway.

Dr. Toxley had delivered a jar of a thick white ointment to the Hall with instructions that I should ease it gently into the skin of my hands every six hours for a week, and I was grateful for his consideration, for it helped to soothe the burning pains which threatened to strike up every few minutes. It was a day or two later, when I felt sufficiently recovered from my ordeal, that I settled upon the idea of a day trip.

"We're not supposed to leave here," said Isabella as the children finished their breakfast that morning and I told them of my plan. She had brought a copy of Bunyan's *Pilgrim's Progress* to the table and I thought it an extraordinary book for one so young to be reading. I had tried it myself a year before and found it a frightful bore. "We're meant to stay. In the house."

"Well, I never heard such nonsense," I exclaimed, drinking the last of my tea but not turning to look at her as I spoke. "Whoever said such a thing?"

She didn't answer, simply turned her head away and continued to chew reflectively on a piece of toast. Outside, I could hear Heckling's dog, Pepper, scratching at the door, whimpering for a moment, then running off.

"It's not healthy to be stuck inside these walls all day," I added. "A little fresh air can do wonders for the spirits."

"We go outside and play," protested Eustace.

"Yes, of course you do," I said. "But always here in the grounds. Wouldn't you like a change of scenery?"

"No," said Isabella and "I would, rather," replied Eustace at the same time, incurring a furious look from his sister that made him shrink in the seat a little. "Well, I would," he muttered to no one in particular.

"We'll have no classes today," I said firmly, determined that my voice would be the one that would carry the argument. "We'll have a field trip. That can be just as educational, don't you agree? In London, at the end of the school year, I always brought my small girls to the House of Commons for an afternoon's education, and once we were even permitted into the Strangers' Gallery."

"A field trip to where?" asked Isabella suspiciously.

"Into the village, I expect," said Eustace, a bored expression crossing his face now.

"Goodness me, no," I replied, shaking my head. "Why, we see the village all the time. How about I ask Mr. Heckling to take us in the coach to Norwich? We could be there in less than two hours and spend the afternoon enjoying the city."

"What's in Norwich?" asked Eustace.

"A lot, I'm sure," I said. I had never been to Norwich, of course, except for my brief experience passing through it when my train arrived in the station on that first night. "There will be shops and playgrounds. Perhaps a museum or two. There's a great cathedral in the city. I was reading about it in a book I discovered in your father's library." Isabella's head turned to me as I made reference to her father and her eyes narrowed a little. I felt immediately self-conscious that I had said this; perhaps she didn't want me to use the library. Perhaps she didn't like to hear mention of her father. But then he was another of the reasons I was desperate to get away for a day. As much sympathy as I felt for the poor man, who surely deserved the respite of a quiet death to the horrific incarceration he endured at the top of the house, I nevertheless felt repulsed knowing that he was nearby, gasping for breath, struggling to eat, having his every need, both personal and impersonal, taken care of by Mrs. Livermore. It was callous of me, perhaps, but I was young. I would have preferred to see him in a hospital than living in the same house as me, even if it was his house in the first place. It felt abnormal that four of us were living here but only three of us ever met.

"There's a castle too," I continued. "William the Conqueror saw to its construction in the eleventh century. We could lark around it and call it a history lesson. You'd enjoy that, wouldn't you, Eustace?"

He considered this. "I would," he said finally, nodding his head. "Very much."

"Then it's settled."

"We're supposed to stay here," repeated Isabella.

"Well, we're not going to," I insisted, standing up and clearing away the breakfast things. "So how about you both get yourselves ready to leave and I'll speak to Heckling."

I could feel Isabella glaring at me from the table but resolved not to turn and look at her. Instead, I looked out the window towards the garden, where a fox emerged from behind one of the trees, glanced around him and sidled away into one of the bushes. Behind me, I could feel the presence looming, a weight beginning to press itself against my back, very gently at first, then with more pressure, like knuckles kneading away on my muscles, and when I spun round it immediately subsided. I swallowed and looked at the children, trying to smile, trying to pretend that nothing had happened. "So there we are," I said.

"If we have to go anywhere," said Isabella, "I would like to go to Great Yarmouth. If we have to, that is," she added.

"Great Yarmouth?" I asked, surprised by her sudden declaration of interest. "Why there particularly?"

She shrugged her shoulders. "It has beaches. We could make sandcastles. I've always wanted to see it but never have. Miss Bennet said she'd take us there but she never did. She lied to us."

I thought about it; in fact, Great Yarmouth had been one of the places I had considered for our day trip, but I had discounted it in favour of Norwich as I thought the children might enjoy looking at the shop windows in the city. But now that Isabella was showing an interest I thought it only fair to meet her half-way and nodded my head.

"All right then," I said. "It's as good a place as anywhere, I suppose."

"But the castle," protested Eustace, his lower lip turning down in disappointment.

"Another day, another day," I said. "We have so much time in front of us. We'll go to Norwich next week perhaps. Today let's take Isabella's suggestion and visit Great Yarmouth."

And so we went. Heckling took us in the carriage to Thorpe Station and from there we boarded a train for a short journey of no more than forty minutes, passing through Brundall and Lingwood along the way, the green of the fields moving past us at such a speed that I found the whole experience entirely relaxing. A young mother with two small children joined our carriage at Acle and I felt pleased that I might have some adult conversation for a change, but no sooner had the doors closed than the two, a little boy and girl, twins I thought, began to cry for no apparent reason. Isabella and Eustace stared at them as their mother tried to console them but only when she rose and left the carriage did their tears dry. With the return of silence, I felt happy to see them go.

It was pleasant to sit back and stare out the window, not having to make conversation with anyone. We had the carriage to ourselves now and the children entertained themselves with a pocket game they had brought with them while I watched outside and occasionally dipped in and out of *The Life & Strange Surprising Adventures of Robinson Crusoe* by Mr. Defoe which, risking Isabella's disapprobation, I had borrowed once again from her father's library.

It was a bright, sunny day; indeed the more distance we put between Gaudlin and ourselves, the more temperate the day became. When we disembarked the train on to the platform at Great Yarmouth I breathed in deeply, filling my lungs with fresh air. I hadn't realized quite how stuffy Gaudlin was until I was away from it, and resolved to ask Heckling, upon our return, to enter the house and open some windows during the day from now on. (I was rather nervous of opening windows ever since the incident in my own bedroom and had stayed clear of them.) The children appeared pleased by the change of scenery too and I noticed that Isabella's mood had visibly lightened. She was chattering away now without any self-consciousness, while Eustace, staring across towards the sand and sea, looked as if he wanted nothing more than to run and run until he exhausted himself, much like a dog who is only accustomed to his home and the lead and is suddenly released to the freedom of the mountain, the thrill of clambering up and down rocks, the joy of liberation.

"We have you to thank for this, Isabella," I remarked as we walked towards the beach, climbing over a small wooden fence and making our way across the dunes. "Who needs stuffy old Norwich when you can have this?"

"Ann Williams always said good things about Great Yarmouth," she replied, taking off her shoes and letting her toes sink into the sand. Eustace followed a moment later and I picked up his shoes and stockings and placed them inside my holdall. "She had a very happy childhood, Ann Williams. Or so she told us. Happy childhoods seem to be things one reads about in books, don't you think? They don't seem to be the stuff of real life."

"Ann Williams?" I asked; this name was new to me. "And who might she be? A friend of yours?"

"No, I don't have any friends. Surely you can see that, Eliza Caine." I looked away, uncertain how to respond to this. "Ann Williams was the third governess, after Miss Golding but before Miss Harkness."

"Ah," I said. "I see."

"I liked Ann Williams," remarked Isabella, looking out to the sea. "Doesn't it look blue!" she added, staring across at the sea, her face lighting up with pleasure for once. "And the waves are so inviting. I think I should like to swim."

"Miss Williams would play hide and seek with me," whispered Eustace, tugging at my sleeve. "She would cover her eyes, count to fifty and then come looking for me. She never found me, of course. I'm a very good hider."

"I don't doubt it," I said, eager to move on from this subject. The business of the previous governesses was one that I had yet to get to the bottom of. I thought it would take another appointment with Mr. Raisin in order to do that but, unlike my eagerness of a couple of weeks earlier, I had put this off, uncertain that I wanted to know the full story, even though I felt that I should.

"I brought my swimming costume with me," said Isabella, turning to me. "Can I go in?"

"I don't see why not," I said. "What about you, Eustace? Do you feel like a swim?"

He shook his head and clung close to me.

"Eustace doesn't care for the water," said Isabella. "But I've always liked it. Mother used to say that I might have been a mermaid in a different time."

I stared at her and noticed her pale a little; this was a child who never made reference to either of her parents and yet here was this remark. She swallowed and looked away, certain I have no doubt that I was looking directly at her, and unwilling to catch my eye.

"I'll change in the dunes," she said, running away from us both. "I won't be long."

Eustace and I walked a little further on in order to offer her some privacy and we found a nice stretch of clean white sand to settle ourselves upon to watch her swim. It was a perfect paradise sitting there with the sun on my face and the sensation of honest sea air filling my lungs. If only we could live here, I thought. We could come to the beach every day, regardless of the weather. Wash away the taint of Gaudlin Hall.

A few moments later, Isabella went dashing past us in her swimsuit and I had a vision of how she would look a decade from now, when she was the same age as me. She would be very different, of course, for she was turning into a beauty while I was no such thing. She would be much sought after by young men and would, I suspected, break several hearts before she found one that she wished to cherish. It would have to be a very special young man, I was certain, who would capture her affections and hold on to them.

"It's nice here, isn't it?" I said and Eustace nodded. "Haven't you ever gone swimming?"

"Once, when I was little," he replied. "I couldn't do it. I got frightened whenever the ground went from under me."

"It's not so very difficult," I told him. "It just takes confidence, that's all. We're naturally buoyant, you know." He turned his face to look at me, his expression crinkled up with lack of comprehension. "We naturally float," I explained. "Of course, there are many adults who claim not to know how to swim, but do you know, if you threw a baby into the sea, it would swim without any difficulty."

"Why would anyone throw a baby into the sea?" he asked, sounding rather horrified by the notion.

"Well, I'm not advocating it," I said. "I just mean that before we learn to feel afraid of things, our bodies know how to do them anyway. It's one of the more disappointing aspects of growing older. We fear more so we can do less."

He thought about this but shook his head, as if it was all too confusing. Reaching down, he picked up handfuls of sand and let them pour slowly over his bare legs and feet, waiting until they were covered entirely before slowly lifting them and allowing them to emerge, like monsters from a swamp. He seemed to enjoy doing this for it made him smile every time.

"I'm glad we have this time together, Eustace," I said after a while. "There was something I wanted to talk to you about."

He didn't turn his head or cease his game but I could tell that he was listening. I thought about how to phrase this; it had been on my mind for some days and I had been waiting for an opportunity to broach it.

"Do you remember the day I burned my hands?" I asked. He didn't say anything but I took his silence as assent. "You made a remark that afternoon," I continued. "About an old man."

"Did I?" he said innocently.

"Yes, Eustace. You did. It was when you came into the house after you hurt your leg."

"I fell over," he replied, remembering it, and lifting his right leg now to examine where the wound had been, but it had been fairly insignificant, if a little bloody, at the time, and had entirely healed now.

"That's right. You fell over. Because you saw an old man."

He sighed deeply, the sound of his breath exhaling through his nose so loud that it rather startled me. I hesitated. If he did not wish to discuss this, perhaps I was wrong to challenge him on it. But no, I decided, I was there to take care of the children, to look after their well-being, and I needed to know if something had happened to upset him.

"Eustace," I said. "Are you listening to me?"

"Yes," he replied quietly.

"Tell me about the old man," I said. "Where did you see him?"

"He was standing in the driveway," he replied. "At the opening between the two tall oaks."

"He'd walked into the estate from beyond the trees then?" I said.

"No, I don't think so. I think he was just there. In the driveway."

I frowned. "And did you recognize him?"

"No," said Eustace. "Well, yes, I'd seen him before, I mean, but I don't know who he is."

"He's not from the village then?"

"He might be," he replied, shrugging his shoulders. "I don't know."

"Perhaps he's a friend of Mr. Heckling's?"

"Perhaps," said Eustace.

"And what did he say to you?" I continued. "This old man. Did he say something to upset you?"

Eustace shook his head. "He didn't say anything," he replied. "He was just watching me, that's all. At least I thought he was watching me. But when I looked at him I realized—oh look! Isabella's waving at us."

I turned my head to the sea and, sure enough, Isabella could be seen waving in our direction. I waved back. I should really be watching her more closely, I thought. But observing her as she pulled her hand down and dived deeper into the surf and swam in a perfect groove, I could tell that she was a strong swimmer—perhaps her mother had been right about her—and that she would not come to any difficulty out there.

"What happened when you looked at him, Eustace?" I asked, turning back to the boy now, and he stood up, brushing all the sand from his legs and turning to look at me with an expression of alarm on his face.

"I don't want to talk about it," he said.

"Why not?"

He breathed heavily again and, as much as I could see this was a subject that disturbed him, I felt it imperative that I should press him on it.

"If he wasn't looking at you," I continued, "who was he looking at? Was he staring at the house? Perhaps he was a potential burglar."

"It was nothing like that," insisted Eustace. "I told you, he was an old man."

"Well, what kind of an old man? What did he look like?"

"He looked like every other old man," he said. "Not very tall. A little stooped over. He had a beard."

I sighed. That was a description that could have suited almost every old man I had ever seen in my life. "Eustace," I said, placing a hand on his shoulders, and he looked up at me, his pale face trembling a little, and I could see tears forming in his eyes. "Who was he looking at?"

"There wasn't anyone else there," he said finally. "Just Isabella and I. But he was looking behind us and saying that she should leave."

"That who should leave?"

"I don't know!" cried Eustace, raising his voice now. "He just said that she should leave. That she wasn't needed here."

I frowned. I could feel a thousand different thoughts and explanations running through my head, but what seemed most curious of all was the idea that the old man, whoever he was, might be addressing the presence. That he could see the spirit in physical form. But if he could, then why could I not?

"Eustace," I said firmly. "If you see this old man again, or if you feel surrounded by . . . how shall I put this . . . someone or something you don't recognize, then I want you to—"

"Look," said Eustace, raising his hand and pointing to the distance, where a black shape appeared to be making its way towards us. I glanced back at the sea and could make out Isabella still swimming, although closer to the shoreline now, and then turned back, following Eustace's gaze towards whatever it was that was approaching us.

"It's a dog," said Eustace quietly after a moment. "It means us harm."

I raised an eyebrow and watched and it was true that the dog was running towards us at an accelerated rate. I turned round, thinking perhaps that its master was on the beach behind us, summoning him, but no, we were alone. As it came closer I began to feel nervous and wanted to turn and make my way back to the path, but I knew of course that to run from a charging dog would serve only to encourage it. We would do better to befriend it, to make it know that we did not mean to injure it in any way.

Closer it came and I could make out its face now, and it was the stuff of nightmares. A dark black dog, as black as night, with a bright-pink tongue emerging from its mouth. It began to bark as it approached us, to bark so ferociously that my heart beat faster in my chest and I could feel my very breath being taken away from me.

"Don't run, Eustace," I said quietly, placing an arm around his shoulder protectively. "Whatever you do, don't run. It won't harm you if you stay very still."

"It doesn't intend to harm me," he replied in a calm voice, and I looked down at him, but he was staring at the dog and not looking at me at all. I glanced over towards the sea again and now Isabella was emerging from the depths, smoothing her swimsuit down and watching us and the dog.

Now it arrived. It stopped before us and rooted itself in the sand, a low, throaty growl emerging from somewhere deep inside its body. Stalactites of drool slipped from the corners of its mouth.

"Good boy," I said in a conciliatory tone. "Good dog."

I reached out to pat it, thinking this might persuade it to relax, but as I did so it barked so angrily that I pulled my unfortunate scorched hand back and wrapped my arm around Eustace even more tightly. This, however, served only to infuriate the beast for it began to drool and whine, then bark with such ferocity that a panic started to rise in me. It darted forward, not pouncing on me yet, but with such a sudden speed that Eustace and I were separated, the dog standing between us, ignoring the boy entirely, turning its dark rage completely on me.

"Please," I said, knowing how ludicrous it was to try to reason with a dog that appeared to have lost control of its senses, but then what else could I do but beg, beg it to spare me? "Please."

I saw it drag its hind left paw on the sand a few times, then sink its body into a crouch, its head lowering as it kept its eyes fixed firmly on me, and I knew that the moment was upon me. I had but a matter of seconds before he would jump, and when he did I would have no choice. I would have to kill or be killed. I said a silent prayer and positioned myself, ready to defend my life.

"Go away!" came a voice as if from nowhere and, to my astonishment, Isabella had appeared and placed herself between the two of us. "Go away," she insisted. "Do you hear me? Be gone."

The dog retreated a little, beginning to whine in protest, but the child was not to be disputed with. "Leave us," she cried. "Do you hear me?"

It did not need to be told again. It turned on its heel and, defeated, trotted away, the very picture now of a kind, obedient pet. I sank to the sand, amazed by what I had witnessed, as Isabella turned back to me, looking down at me with a mixture of disapproval and contempt.

"You're not afraid of dogs, are you?" she asked. "They just need to know who's in charge, that's all."

Chapter Seventeen

I T WASN'T UNTIL after lunch that I began to recover my equilibrium. I had been badly shaken by the encounter with the animal but the children appeared to have already forgotten it. Eustace, who of course had been there throughout, did not seem to be in the least concerned by what had happened, and when I questioned him about it, all he could say was, "It was just a dog. It didn't mean me any harm."

And on that point, I believed he was absolutely right. The dog had not meant him any harm at all. It was me he wanted.

The children, however, seemed to be enjoying their day thoroughly. Isabella was quite refreshed from her swim and her spirits were higher than I think I had ever seen them.

"We should come here again," she said, dancing around me on the street, appearing like a little girl for once rather than the young adult she often seemed to be. "It's a splendid place."

"Perhaps," I said. "Although there are other wonderful places in Norfolk, I'm sure. We wouldn't have to come here all the time. But you're right. It is good to get away for a day."

"Thank you for taking us," she replied, dazzling me with a rare smile. "Eustace," she added, turning to her brother, "tell Eliza Caine how appreciative you are."

"Very," said Eustace, who seemed lost in thought now, tired perhaps after all the exertions of the day.

"You look sleepy, Eustace," I said, putting a hand to his head and brushing the hair from his eyes. "It's the sea air, I expect. Not to mention that fish lunch. We shall all sleep well tonight, I daresay." I glanced at my watch. "Perhaps we should make our way back to the train station," I suggested. "I told Heckling we'd be back at Thorpe by five."

"Oh must we?" cried Isabella. "Can't we stay a little longer?"

"A little longer, if you like," I said. "But not too long. What shall we do next then? Take a stroll?"

"I want to see the church," she declared, pointing towards a small steeple in the distance, and I raised an eyebrow, rather surprised by this.

"I thought you didn't like churches," I said.

"I don't like attending them," she replied. "But I quite like visiting them. If they're empty, I mean. If there's no religious instruction going on. And you like them too, don't you, Eliza Caine? After all, you wanted to visit the cathedral in Norwich."

"Yes, I do," I admitted. "All right then, let's go across and take a look. We won't stay long though. If we're to catch the four o'clock train we can't dawdle."

Isabella nodded and we wandered down the path in silence, all three of us, happy to be left quietly with our thoughts. It was true that I had always liked churches. Father had been a religious man, after a fashion, and had brought me to Mass every Sunday when I was growing up, but occasionally he would take me outside our parish to a church that he had heard was particularly ornate, or provided excellent acoustics for the choir, or had some extraordinary architecture or wall friezes. I had enjoyed these expeditions enormously as a girl; there was a feeling of peace within the walls of a church, a sense of mystery that appealed greatly to me. The church in Great Yarmouth was no exception. It must have been two hundred years old but was in good repair, a masterful construction of stonework with high ceilings and carefully carved wooden pews. At the nave, I turned and looked up to see a fine representation on the ceiling of the Lord in his heaven, surrounded by angels, each of whom turned to stare at him with awe and wonder. To his side, watching all of this with a curious expression on her face, an expression that suggested dominance rather than love, was his mother Mary. I stared at her, wondering what the artist had been thinking, for this was not how she was typically represented. I didn't like it; I turned away.

The children were nowhere to be seen but I could hear their voices outside, loud at first but then fading slightly as they walked further from the door, and I made my way down the aisle, imagining myself for a moment as a bride turning on the arm of her handsome new husband, smiling at a congregation of friends and family as I emerged from my solitary state to a union of equals. And, embarrassing even to myself, the face I saw beside me was none other than Alfred Raisin's. Foolish girl! I smiled at my own simplicity but, in truth, I wondered whether one such as I might ever know a contentment such as that, and thought it unlikely.

Emerging into the bright afternoon sun, I shaded my eyes and looked around me. The streets were mostly empty but Isabella and Eustace had not made their way outside; neither were they to be seen on the road that ran in the direction of the train station. Instead they were some thirty feet away from me, standing in the church graveyard, examining the stones. I smiled; there were times when they reminded me of myself for I, too, on those expeditions with Father, had always enjoyed reading the gravestones, imagining stories in my head of how their occupants had passed from this world to the next. I was particularly intrigued by the graves of children and infants, I suppose because I had been a child myself at the time. They scared me but attracted me at the same time. They reminded me that I was mortal.

"Are we ready, children?" I asked, approaching them now, but neither turned their head to look at me. "Children?" I said again, louder this time, but it was as if they had been turned to statues. "Oh come along, do," I insisted, and they turned a little, stepping out of the way to allow me to see the grave they were examining with such serious intent. I read the name and dates. They meant nothing to me at first. And then I remembered.

"Ann Williams" was the name inscribed in the stone. *Beloved daughter and sister. Born 15th July 1846. Died 7th April 1867. She will be missed.*

"She loved Great Yarmouth," said Isabella in a reflective voice. "I'm sure she's glad to be back here."

Later that night, back at Gaudlin Hall, after a light supper the children retired for the night. Eustace was particularly exhausted, poor boy, but I waited until he had been upstairs for about five minutes before going up and entering his bedroom.

He was lying in bed in his nightshirt, his eyes half closed, but he turned to look at me and smiled.

"Are you coming to say goodnight?" he asked and I nodded, smiling at him.

"Did you enjoy today?" I asked, sitting on the side of the bed and stroking his hair a little.

"Yes, thank you," he said sleepily.

"Such an interesting story you told me about that old man," I added, hoping to catch him off guard now. "But there was one thing I forgot to ask."

"Hmm?" he said, already half asleep.

"You said that you'd seen him once before," I said. "That he'd spoken to you before the day when you fell over and hurt your knee. What did he say, Eustace? Can you remember?"

"He asked me whether I liked my new governess," he replied, yawning and turning over in the bed, away from me.

"And what did you tell him?" I asked.

"I said that I did. Very much," said Eustace. "And he said that was good. And that I wasn't to worry because he wouldn't let anything happen to her. He said he had come to protect you."

Chapter Eighteen

I BEGAN TO TAKE long walks around the estate in the afternoons. My daily routine had settled down to classes with the children in the morning followed by a simple lunch shortly after noon, when Isabella and Eustace would chat about whatever was capturing their attention that day while I sat quietly, tense, certain that every sound or movement in the house would lead to some unexpected trauma for me. I was not sleeping well and the exhaustion was mirrored on my face, which had grown pale and drawn. Heavy, dark bags lingered beneath my eyes and by late afternoon I felt great difficulty in keeping them open. And yet by nightfall, exhausted as I was, I could manage no more than a few unsettled hours of sleep, so certain was I that the presence would return to cause me harm. After lunch, I would allow the children time to engage in their own pursuits before we completed our lessons in the late afternoon. During their free hours, I would take my coat and shawl and step into the woods of the Gaudlin estate, the fresh air invigorating my drooping spirits, the closely packed trees offering something approaching security.

It did my soul some good to wander freely, to allow the Hall to disappear between the foliage, and as I stepped out into the clear spaces beyond the wood and towards the lake that sat near the end of the property, I could imagine myself in London again, strolling along the banks of the Serpentine in Hyde Park, with nothing more to worry about than what I would cook Father for his supper that evening or what exercises I might set my small girls the following day.

In truth, much as I had grown to care for Isabella and Eustace, I felt a longing for those I had left behind. My small girls had been an important part of my life. I enjoyed seeing their faces in the mornings, even the ones who were more troublesome than others. I took pride in the lessons and took care to ensure that each girl felt that she had a place in the classroom and that she would not be bullied by the others. And I believe they cared for me too.

There was one girl who came back to my mind more and more often as I walked the grounds of Gaudlin Hall. A girl by the name of Clara Sharpe, who had been five years old when she had first entered my classroom, a bright and mischievous child, but not a naughty one, given to high levels of energy in the mornings and long periods of sullenness in the afternoons. (I took this to be related to the breakfasts she ate before leaving her house and the lunches she was provided with before the midday session; I suspected they had a negative effect on her mood.)

For all her ways, I liked Clara a great deal and took an interest in her development, particularly when I realized what a gift she had for mathematics. Unlike most of the other girls, for whom numbers seemed to present little more than an endless series of Greek hieroglyphs, Clara had the sort of brain that could organize and rationalize without difficulty and, as young as she was, I rather thought that she might in time follow me into the pedagogical profession. I even spoke to Mrs. Farnsworth about her on several occasions, and she suggested that with her mathematical skills, Clara might someday have a future as a secretary for a bank manager. I recall the incident specifically because I made a remark, intended as a joke, that perhaps she could even *be* the bank manager one day, whereupon Mrs. Farnsworth removed her glasses and looked at me aghast and accused me of being a revolutionary, a charge I denied.

"You're not a modern, are you, Eliza?" she asked, standing to her full height and looking down at me, filling me with as much trepidation as she had when *I* was a small girl and she my teacher. "I won't stand for moderns at St. Elizabeth's. And neither will the Board of Governors."

"No, of course not," I replied, blushing furiously. "I was being facetious, that's all."

"Hmm," she said, unsatisfied. "I hope so. Clara Sharpe the manager of a bank! The very idea!"

And yet, although I did not consider myself to be a modern at all, I found her level of offence to be, in itself, offensive. Why should the girl *not* strive for higher things, after all? Why should we all not?

So intent was Mrs. Farnsworth on scolding me that I rather suspected she would have liked to call Father in to discuss the matter with him, and perhaps she might have done so had she not finally realized that there was a distinction to be made between the small girls and their teachers, and that she could call on parental authority to discipline the former but it was entirely her responsibility to control the latter.

I thought of Clara now because she ended up in a rather distressed condition. Her father was a drunkard, while her mother did all she could to keep the family home together, despite the pittance her husband brought in for the upkeep of his wife and daughter. What little money the man earned was more likely to be spent on porter than on food or clothing, and there was more than one morning when Clara arrived in the classroom, her face bruised, and I longed to live in a decent civilized society where I might make enquiries about who had done the bruising and why. Not that I had any doubts as to the answer to that question. On such days, I dreaded to imagine what Clara's mother looked like, for I suspected her father of mistreating his wife just as badly as he did his daughter. I considered going to the police but of course they would have laughed at me and said that what an Englishman did in the privacy of his own home was his own business.

But the man must have gone too far one night and attacked Mrs. Sharpe when her ire was drawn, for she took a roasting pot from the oven, turned on her heel and hit him so sharply across the head with it that he fell to the ground, dead. The poor woman, a victim of unanswered violence for so long, was immediately arrested—for naturally, an assault upon a husband was a crime, whereas an assault upon a wife fell into the realm of marital privilege. Unlike Santina Westerley, however, who was clearly an unbalanced creature, Mrs. Sharpe was not sentenced to death. The judge, a modern sort—Mrs. Farnsworth would not have approved of him—believed that she deserved some leniency and commuted her sentence to life imprisonment without any possibility of parole, a sentence which, in the same position, I would have liked infinitely less than a week of nervous anticipation, a few seconds of extraordinary pain, and an eternity of peace ever after, the reward offered by the rope.

Clara, having no other family to take her in, ended up in the workhouse, after which I rather lost touch with her. But she returned to my thoughts on one of those mornings as I considered the murder of Miss Tomlin by Santina Westerley and her violent assault upon her husband, which had left him in such a horrendous condition. And I wondered about the minds of women who committed these acts. Mrs. Sharpe, after all, had been abused and beaten; Santina Westerley, I had no doubt of it, had been loved and offered the security of a home, wealth, position and a family. Placed alongside each other, I found that motivation was a curious thing.

It was while thinking this that I turned the corner of the estate and found myself back in front of Heckling's cottage, only to discover that difficult man standing outside, a pile of logs on the ground beside him, which he was cleaving in two with an axe. Upon seeing me, he put the axe down and wiped his brow with his handkerchief, offering me a nod as the dog, Pepper, ran towards me and scampered about my feet.

"Governess," said Heckling, licking his lips in a repellent fashion.

"Mr. Heckling," I replied. "No rest for the wicked, is there?"

"Aye, well, if I don't do it there's no one else as will," he muttered. The man was nothing if not a burst of sunshine on a gloomy day.

I glanced round and noticed the door at the side of the house, almost hidden, through which Mrs. Livermore made her daily journeys up and down the staircase to Mr. Westerley's rooms. I hadn't noticed it at all until the day she pointed it out to me, but now that I saw it I wondered why the original builders had sought to make it such a secret.

"Have you always worked alone, Mr. Heckling?" I asked, turning back to look at him, and he raised an eyebrow at the question.

"How's that?" he asked.

"I wondered whether it had always been just you on the estate. Fixing things, chopping logs, driving the carriage and whatnot. I would imagine, in past days, there was a lot more to do."

"Aye, there was that," he said, apparently reluctant to say too much about the past. "There were others, under me that is, but there's no need for them now so they were let go. I were kept on account of the grounds needing one caretaker at least. And I were born here, of course."

"You were born here?" I asked, surprised.

"In yon cottage," he replied, nodding at his dwelling. "My father were the caretaker before me, you see. And his before him. I'm the last of them though." He gave a sigh and looked away and for the first time I could see that beneath all his bluster there lay a rather lonely figure.

"You've no children of your own then?"

He chewed something at the side of his mouth. "None as are still living."

"I'm sorry," I said. Of course; we all had stories.

"Aye."

He reached down and gripped the handle of the axe in his hands before settling it against the stump and reaching into his pocket for a rolled cigarette.

"You watch everything, I expect, Mr. Heckling?" I said after a pause.

"How's that?"

"You keep your eyes open."

"'Cept when I'm sleeping."

"Have you ever noticed any intruders?"

He narrowed his eyes and took a long drag on the cigarette as he stared at me. "Intruders?" he said. "Now why would you ask such a thing, Governess? Has there been someone about?"

I shook my head. "Eustace mentioned something," I replied. "About an elderly gentleman who has been spotted on the grounds. They've been in conversation."

"Ain't no elderly gentleman around here," said Heckling, shaking his head. "Else I would have noticed him. Or Pepper here would, and that would have gone worse for him."

"Perhaps he was mistaken," I said.

"Happen he were. Boys invent things. You must know that as well as anyone."

"Eustace doesn't tell lies," I replied, surprising myself by how defensive I sounded.

"Then he'd be the first lad of his age who didn't. When I were a lad, lying came second nature to me. My father used to beat me for it regular-like."

"I'm very sorry to hear it."

His expression changed to one of confusion. "Why?" he asked.

"Well . . . that must have been unpleasant for you."

He shrugged. "I daresay I deserved it," he said. "That boy might need a beating if he lies about things he's seen and things he hasn't."

"I won't be beating Eustace," I said in a firm tone.

"Well, it's a father's job, I expect," he said, looking away with a sigh. "And Mr. Westerley ain't exactly in a position to do anything about the lad, is he?"

I didn't know whether he was being deliberately offensive or simply stating the facts as they were; he was right, after all.

It was a father's job to discipline his son and Eustace's father could certainly never do so again. I shook my head; all of this was neither here nor there, for I did not believe that Eustace was being deceitful.

"If you did see such a gentleman," I said finally, "an elderly gentleman, or any stranger who does not belong in these grounds, perhaps you'd be good enough to let me know."

"Or I might just shoot him," said Heckling. "On account of his being a trespasser and that."

"Yes, well," I said, turning away, "that would be another option, I suppose."

A sound made me turn back round and to my amazement I saw none other than Mr. Raisin, the solicitor, emerging from behind Heckling's cottage. He broke into a delighted smile before coughing and allowing his features to return to normal, whereupon he offered me a polite bow. "Miss Caine," he said. "How nice to see you."

"And you, Mr. Raisin," I said, reddening slightly for I know not what reason. "Quite a surprise."

"Yes, well, I had some business with Heckling here and was caught rather short, if you'll excuse me. Thank you, Heckling," he added, nodding in the man's direction. "Our business is concluded for today, I think?"

"Aye," said Heckling, picking up his axe again and taking a step back, waiting for us to depart so that he might begin chopping again. Taking the hint, Mr. Raisin and I stepped in line with each other and began walking in the direction of the house, where I saw his carriage was standing.

"A matter of some invoices," he stated as we walked along. "Heckling is a reliable man and honest as the day is long, but when he needs something he thinks nothing of simply ordering it from one of the village shops and telling them to send the invoice directly to me. I don't begrudge him this, of course, I know he would never take anything for his own benefit, but I do like to go through the invoices with him from time to time so we're both clear about the estate's expenses."

"I imagine it must be a complicated business," I said.

"It can be," he admitted. "But Gaudlin Hall is not the most byzantine of my clients. I know people with less property and far less money who tie it up in the most elaborate tangles. Unravelling the knots would take the skill of a lifelong sailor. Anyway, Mr. Cratchett takes care of most of the daily business for me. I'm simply on hand for anything more complicated. And it's nothing compared to the old days, of course. Certainly, when my father was lawyer for James's father—"

"Goodness me," I exclaimed. "Must everyone in this county follow their father's profession? And take up their father's duties when their time comes? Heckling was just telling me the same thing about his own family."

"It's the natural order of things, Miss Caine," he said, sounding a little offended, and I rather regretted the tone in which I had spoken. "And the law is a respectable business, you know. As is being a general caretaker, if that is the class into which one is born. As, for that matter, is being a governess."

"Of course, Mr. Raisin," I said apologetically. "I didn't mean to imply otherwise."

"Might I ask what line your father was in?" he asked.

"He worked in the Department of Entomology at the British Museum."

"And that was his lifelong career, was it?"

"Well, no," I admitted. "When he was my age, he was briefly a teacher. In a school for small boys."

"And before you came to join us here at Norfolk? Remind me what you did again?"

I smiled. For the first time in a long time, I felt like laughing. "I was a teacher," I said.

"In a school for small girls, no doubt?"

"Quite so."

"Well then, Miss Caine," he said, stopping before the carriage and raising himself to his full height, his chest puffed out and with an expression of pure satisfaction on his face, "it seems that what's good for us in the country is good enough for those in the blessed capital too."

I stared into his face, those bright blue eyes, and we smiled at each other. Our gaze held and his expression became confused. His lips parted; he looked at me as if he wanted to say something but could not find the words.

"Yes, yes," I said finally, willing to let him have his little victory. "I stand rightly chastised. But now, Mr. Raisin, you're not leaving us so quickly, are you?"

"Would you have me stay?"

I had no answer to this question. Finally, he sighed and patted his horse. "I have given myself a half-day's holiday, Miss Caine," he told me. "I thought I would sort out the issue of the invoices with Heckling and then retire to my home with a glass of claret and *Oliver Twist*, which I am reading for the first time since its original publication. It's such a wonderful story. I could let you have the back numbers if you'd care to take a look?"

"That's kind of you," I said.

"Kindness has nothing to do with it," he replied. "I understand it must get a little . . . how shall I put this? . . . boring out here at Gaudlin Hall from time to time. With such a dearth of adult company. A little reading might provide a welcome escape?"

I smiled and considered that there were three other adults almost permanently present at the Hall: Heckling, Mrs. Livermore and Mr. Westerley. One of whom didn't like to speak to me, one of whom didn't want to speak to me and one of whom simply couldn't speak to me. And yet, despite all that, "boring" was the last word I would have used to describe life on this estate.

"Perhaps," I said. "But, Mr. Raisin, before you go, could I trouble you for a few minutes of your time?"

His face turned slightly pained; I suspect that he guessed the subject on which I wanted to speak and he felt disinclined. "I would love to, Miss Caine. Truly, there is nothing I would like more. But work calls."

"You said you have a half-day's holiday."

"Ah yes," he replied, frowning. "I meant . . . that is to say . . ."

"Mr. Raisin, I won't keep you long, I promise. Just a few minutes. There are some questions I have for you."

He sighed and nodded, aware perhaps that there was no proper way out of this, and I indicated a bench at the front of the lawns and we walked towards it, sitting down. He kept a safe distance from me; Isabella and Eustace could easily have taken their places between us and none of us would yet have touched. I looked down at his left hand resting on his lap. The golden band on the fourth finger. He followed my eye but did not stir.

"You're not going to ask me more about the Westerleys, are you?" he asked. "I feel that I have told you as much as I know about them. From their first meeting to their last."

"No, it's not that," I said, shaking my head. "And if I may say so, Mr. Raisin, you were very generous with your time with me that day. I could see that it was a distressing subject for you. It was obvious by the end of our conversation how deeply affected you had been by the events that took place here."

He nodded and looked out towards the lawns. "It is not a time that any of us associated with it will ever forget," he admitted. "But before you ask me anything further, Miss Caine, will you permit me to ask a question of you?" I nodded, surprised that he would want to know anything about me. "Did you speak to Mrs. Livermore after our conversation?" he asked me. "Have you met your employer at last?"

"I have seen him, yes," I replied.

He turned away and his expression turned to one of resignation mixed with sorrow. "I would have advised against that. He is not a sight for delicate sensibilities."

"Fortunately, Mr. Raisin, I am made of stern stuff."

"I'm aware of that. I could tell the first day I met you. I admire that aspect of your character greatly, Miss Caine. Nevertheless, I hope the experience wasn't too upsetting for you."

"Is it wrong to say that I feel the poor man would welcome a release from his pain?"

Mr. Raisin shuddered a little, as if my remark had been a blasphemy. "I understand, of course," he said. "But we must not say these things. It is not man's right to decide when another should be released into the afterlife. Only God can make that judgement. After all, it was breaking that natural law which led Santina Westerley to the gallows and James Westerley to his living death."

"We were in Great Yarmouth the other day," I said, changing tack.

"We?"

"The children and I."

He nodded and seemed pleased by this. "Capital idea," he said. "I imagine that it does the children good to get some fresh air, away from this place. Whenever I see the boy, Eustace, I always think he's terribly pale. Isabella has a darker complexion, of course; that comes from her mother's side, I suppose. But Eustace is a Westerley through and through."

"I think they enjoyed it," I agreed. "It was certainly an interesting day."

"As it happens, my mother was a Great Yarmouth girl," continued Mr. Raisin, warming to his subject. "As a boy, we used to take a weekend's holiday there occasionally. My grandparents kept a very happy home." He smiled and then laughed a little, no doubt recalling some pleasant memory from childhood. "My brothers and sisters and I, we had some very wonderful times then." He slapped a hand down on his knee and shook his head. "Simpler times," he added in a resigned tone. "I fear that modern life places rather too many demands on us, don't you, Miss Caine? There are days when I rather detest living in the year 1867. Every thing moves so quickly. Change is happening at such a pace. I preferred the way of life thirty years ago when I was a boy."

"We visited a church," I said, interrupting him, not wishing to get sidetracked into a discussion on how the modern world was a disappointment to him. "Isabella seemed particularly keen to go there. It turns out that there was a grave she wished to visit."

Mr. Raisin frowned. "Isabella?" he asked. "And what possible grave could she wish to see in Great Yarmouth? She has no family there."

"The grave of Ann Williams."

His face fell. "Ah," he said, nodding. He understood perfectly. "Miss Williams. Of course. I had forgotten that she, too, was a Great Yarmouth girl."

"Born in 1846, died in 1867," I recited, recalling the inscription on the gravestone. "She died at the same age I hold now. Twenty-one." He turned and looked at me in some surprise and for a moment I thought he was going to be so ungallant as to suggest that he thought me older than my years. But no, he remained silent. "Miss Williams, I am told, was the third governess here at Gaudlin Hall?"

He considered this for a moment and then nodded. "That's correct," he said. "She wasn't here very long, of course. Six or seven weeks, if I recall. I'd have to check back at my office but I don't think it could have been much more than that."

"And Miss Tomlin, Mrs. Westerley's unfortunate victim, was the first governess."

"Yes, that's right."

"Miss Tomlin the first. Miss Williams the third. Miss Bennet, of course, who advertised her own position, was the fifth, my immediate predecessor. And I think you mentioned that day in your office a Miss Golding and a Miss Harkness."

"Yes, the second and fourth governesses respectively," he replied, swallowing and looking down at the ground. "Very fine ladies, both of them. Miss Harkness was the only child of an old friend of mine from the Liverpool assizes. He took her loss very badly, poor man."

"Miss Tomlin, Miss Golding, Miss Williams, Miss Harkness, Miss Bennet and I, Miss Caine. I have the order correct?"

"You do."

"Six governesses in a year. Don't you think that an extraordinary number?"

He looked me directly in the eye. "Only a fool would not think so, Miss Caine," he said. "But as I explained, there were so many unfortunate accidents—"

"Accidents!" I said, bursting out laughing as I looked away from him. I turned my gaze to the trees, their leaves strewn about their roots, their dark branches cold and uninviting. In the midst of their cluster I thought I could see the quick movement of a man, a flash of white beard, and I gasped, leaned forward and stared, but nothing further appeared and the landscape settled into serenity once again. "You are a believer in coincidence then, sir," I remarked bitterly.

"I am a believer in bad luck, Miss Caine. I am a believer in the fact that a man may be taken at a hundred years of age and a child may be brought back to God before he has even reached his first birthday. I believe that the world is a mysterious place and that we cannot expect to understand it."

"Of the six governesses," I said, determined not to allow his speechifying to overwhelm me; we were not in a courtroom here, "you yourself told me that only two live. Miss Bennet and I. Don't you recognize that there are strange forces at play here?"

"Strange forces?" he asked. "In what way?"

"A malevolent presence," I explained. "A ghost."

Mr. Raisin leapt to his feet, his face reddening. "What would you have of me?" he asked. "What do you want me to say to this?"

"Tell me what happened to them!"

"The governesses? No! It's too horrible. I have lived through all their deaths, not you. You cannot ask me to relive them."

"But I am their successor!" I cried, looking up, refusing to appear weak before him. If I was to survive this place it was imperative that I showed nothing but strength. "I deserve to know."

"I don't think it would do any good," he protested. "It will distress you for no purpose."

"I have a right to hear their stories, surely you agree?"

"I'm not sure that I do," he insisted. "You never knew any of these ladies, after all. They are strangers to you."

"But I hold their position. Unlike you, unlike Mr. Heckling, unlike the Queen herself, I have not inherited this position from a relative who has passed. I am simply the latest claimant to a job that has proved fatal to so many of its occupants."

He sighed, exhausted, and sat down again, considering this, his head in his hands. A lengthy pause ensued between us and I swore that I would not speak first. "Very well," he said eventually. "But I assure you, Miss Caine, this will serve no good purpose. These are tragic stories, horrible coincidences, nothing more."

"I shall decide that for myself, Mr. Raisin," I said.

"I don't doubt it," he replied, arching an eyebrow, and I thought perhaps he was torn between admiring me and wishing that he had never come to Gaudlin Hall that morning. "Well, you know about Miss Tomlin, of course," he began. "The first governess. We have more than adequately described the fate of that unfortunate lady. Miss Golding was the next. After Santina, Mrs. Westerley that is, was arrested and Mr. Westerley was removed to hospital, I had no choice but to advertise for a governess for the children. Miss Golding was a local girl. Not from the village but from King's Lynn, which, as I'm sure you know, is not so very far away. She came from a good family. I interviewed her myself. I was concerned with there being so much notoriety attached to the estate at that time that the position might attract the wrong sort of person. And I was right, of course, it did. I had any number of ghoulish types show up at my door. It rather disgusted me. But when I met Miss Golding, I knew immediately that she was the right one. She was down to earth, you see. The no-nonsense type. I like that in a woman. I don't care for frills and fancies, never have. Give me a plain-spoken woman with her feet on the ground and I'm a contented man. And I admired the fact that Miss Golding was sympathetic towards recent events but not fascinated by them, as others were. Also, her primary concern, and she made this quite clear at the interview, was for the well-being of the children. I appreciated this greatly for, as you can imagine, Isabella and Eustace were quite traumatized by what had taken place. It was still barely a month since the terrible events."

"Of course," I said, realizing, with a slight sensation of guilt, that I had never given much thought to how the children had responded in the immediate aftermath of their governess's murder, their father's assault and their mother's arrest. "They must have been very upset."

"Isabella was reasonably calm," said Mr. Raisin, stroking his beard as he recalled those difficult days. "But then she's a calm girl most of the time, isn't she? A little too calm, I would say. And in truth, she was always much closer to her father than her mother. I would hear her cry at night and I knew then how badly she was taking it. But she hid it well. She has an ability to mask her true feelings, that girl. I'm not sure it's entirely healthy."

"You heard her?" I asked, surprised.

"Forgive me," he said. "I should have mentioned. My wife and I took the children in on the night of the attacks. There was no one else to look after them, you see. We kept them with us for a few weeks. Until Miss Golding was hired, at which point Isabella insisted on moving back into her home here at Gaudlin Hall, and I saw no reason to say no, particularly when they had a responsible adult present."

"And Eustace?" I asked. "How did he cope?"

"Through silence," said Mr. Raisin with a sorrowful smile. "Poor little Eustace never spoke a single word from the moment I took him away in my carriage that night until a few days after he returned here to Gaudlin. Gradually, after Miss Golding took him in hand, he began to talk again. But he's a terribly troubled little boy, Miss Caine. You can see that, can't you? I think sometimes that he has been the most badly affected by all of this, and all that came afterwards. I worry about him, I truly do. I worry for his future. The traumas of childhood can affect us badly when we're older."

I looked away and felt heartsick. Everything he was saying was true. And I felt desperately sorry for the boy, of whom I had grown so fond. And yet I also felt a sense that there was nothing I could do to help him. That I did not have the skills to return him to happiness. His innocence had been taken for ever.

"So Miss Golding took over as governess," I said, urging him on.

"Yes. And all was fine for a while. She proved as efficient as I had expected her to be. And meanwhile, Santina's trial went ahead. She was found guilty, of course, there could never have been any question of that. The murder of Miss Tomlin and the attempted murder of her own husband. There were some delays before the sentencing as the judge fell ill for a short time. And after that it took another week for the sentence to be carried out, for Mrs. Westerley to be . . . well, hanged. But throughout all of this, I thought that Miss Golding was doing a capital job. The children seemed as well as could be hoped for in the circumstances and she herself was a cheerful and efficient presence in the village. I felt that I had chosen well."

"And what happened to her?" I asked. "How did she die?"

"The timings were quite closely connected," he said. "It was such extraordinary bad luck. Santina was hanged on a Tuesday morning, on the stroke of noon. I was there to witness it, of course. I felt it my duty. I remember that morning very well. As she moved towards the gallows she looked in my direction and for a moment I saw the beautiful, carefree young woman she had once been, the girl who had dined at our table a hundred times, who had beaten me at whist and fives on any number of occasions. She looked to me and smiled a little, regretful, and I betrayed my oath by crying out to her that the children were fine, that I had made certain they would be cared for. I told her that I would look after them always and take care of them as if they were my own. I thought this would give her some consolation at the end, but it had the opposite effect for she grew furious and made to run at me and would, I think, have gone for my eyes had she not been restrained by her jailers. She had lost her senses, of course. It's the only explanation. Fear. The terror of the hangman's rope."

"And you were the only one there?" I asked. "From the village, I mean?"

"Yes, the only one. No, wait, I tell a lie. Mrs. Toxley was there. You know Madge Toxley, don't you?"

"I do."

"Not at the hanging, of course. But at the jail itself. I saw her departing as I arrived. I thought it a strange thing at the time but never thought of it again until just now. They were friends once, of course, but I considered it a strange thing that she should visit. Still, I put it out of my mind as I was there to witness a hanging, not to speculate about the friendships of others. And I had been to two hangings already in my lifetime,

Miss Caine, and they are not pleasant experiences. I dreaded it, if I'm to be honest."

I shuddered. I couldn't even imagine what it would be like to watch another person killed in such a fashion.

"I stayed at an inn in Norwich that night," he continued. "I had a restless sleep. And when I returned to Gaudlin the following morning, Mr. Cratchett told me the terrible news that Miss Golding had been killed the previous evening."

"How, Mr. Raisin?" I asked, leaning forward. "How did she die?"

"A terrible accident, but ghoulish in its symmetry. Miss Golding had rather a good imagination and could be quite useful with her hands. She was attempting to build a sort of swing for the children between two trees using a length of rope that she must have borrowed from Heckling or discovered in one of the sheds. Anyway, she was halfway up a tree, tying the second of the ropes in place, when she must have lost her footing and somehow found herself enveloped in the rope as she fell. It wrapped around her neck and choked her."

"She was hanged," I said, closing my eyes, breathing steadily. "Just like the children's mother."

"Effectively, yes."

"And Mrs. Westerley was already dead by the time this happened?"

"Yes, for about five hours I should think."

"I see." I considered it. I did not feel surprise. Had he told me that poor Miss Golding had died in the morning, I would not have believed it. I was sure that it could only have taken place after Santina Westerley's punishment had been carried out. "And Miss Williams," I continued, "the third governess whose grave I stood by in Great Yarmouth. What happened to her?"

"Poor girl," said Mr. Raisin, shaking his head. "She drowned in her bath. A lovely young woman but permanently tired. I think she stayed up too late most nights reading. *Should* women read, Miss Caine? There's a question for you. Does it excite them too much? Miss Williams was never without a book. She raided James's library as if it was pure oxygen to her. She told me once that she had always had trouble sleeping but that it had been exacerbated since arriving at Gaudlin Hall. Of course, she was quite an accident-prone girl too. She had endured several scrapes since her arrival. I told her that she needed to be more careful and, on one occasion, she grew rather hysterical about it, saying that these accidents were not her fault, that they were inflicted upon her by forces unseen. I believe that she was taking a bath at night, fell asleep, slid under the water and, sadly, she was lost to us."

"And Miss Harkness?" I asked. "The fourth governess?"

"It does seem rather odd, I know," said Mr. Raisin. "And I can understand why you would find the whole series of events startling and unsettling. But Miss Harkness was a clumsy woman. Why, she stepped out in front of me on the street in the village on two occasions and nearly fell under the hooves of my horses. She claimed it was the wind, but she wasn't looking where she was going, that's the truth of it. But my reflexes are good, I was able to steer quickly away from her both times. On a separate occasion, however, with poor Mr. Forster from Croakley, she was not so lucky and she was trampled to death in the street. It was awful. Really too horrible to describe. Shortly after that I hired Miss Bennet, who became the fifth governess. But in case you think that there is something sinister about all this, recall if you will, Miss Caine, that Miss Bennet thrives. She has, I believe, returned to London to her former position."

"Which was what?"

"A teacher. Like you. I forwarded her final week's pay to her father's account in Clapham, if you can believe it, because she wouldn't even stay long enough for the bank to open and for me to retrieve the notes."

"And Miss Bennet," I asked. "She was perfectly safe all the time she was here?"

"Of course," he said, then started to laugh a little and shake his head. "She was an hysteric though. I didn't care for her at all. She would come storming into my office talking all sorts of nonsense about Gaudlin Hall and the things that were going on here. Mr. Cratchett suggested that we have her committed and he may well have been right. She behaved as if she was a character in a ghost story."

"But she was perfectly safe?" I insisted. "Please, Mr. Raisin, I have to know."

"Yes, she was safe, of course she was. Well," he added, "she injured herself with a meat knife on one occasion; it was quite a serious cut and she would have bled to death had Mrs. Livermore not been on hand to help her. And there were a couple of other trivial incidents that she spoke of but—"

I stood up and walked away from him, uncertain whether or not to allow my thoughts to go where they were heading. I stared out over the grounds of Gaudlin. I felt an urge to run and run and run.

"Miss Caine, are you all right?" he asked, standing up now, too, and approaching me. I could feel his presence behind me, the warmth of his body, so different to that malevolent presence that had stalked me ever since my arrival. I wanted nothing more than to step backwards, to allow myself to fall into the security of his embrace. But of course I did not. I remained still.

"Quite all right, thank you," I said, stepping away now and smiling at him. "But it's getting late. And I've kept you long enough. You'll miss too much of your half-day's holiday if you're not careful and Mrs. Raisin will blame me."

"I assure you, Miss Caine," he said, taking a step towards me, "Mrs. Raisin will blame only me. She has a strong precedent in this regard."

I smiled and even laughed. "I'll see you to your carriage," I said.

As I watched Mr. Raisin disappear down the driveway I felt a great exhaustion overwhelm me, as if the events of the last month had finally taken their full toll on my spirits. I wanted to collapse on to the gravel beneath me, to bury my face in my hands, to cry aloud and be taken from this ghastly, ghostly place. My life had been so simple before, a daily routine of school and Father, our conversations by the fireplace, his books, my care for our house, even Jessie's ceaseless arthritic complaints, and now it was mysteries and unexplained deaths and a kind of brutality that made me question the very nature of existence. For a moment I felt ready to surrender myself to hysteria but the sound of laughter in the distance, that unexpected sound, made me look up and I caught sight of Isabella and Eustace throwing a ball to each other near the trees. I watched them for a few moments, considering joining them, before deciding against it and returning to the house. Closing the door behind me I stood in the centre of the hallway, looked around me and breathed as quietly as I could.

"Where are you?" I said in a low voice.

The curtain of the living room next to me began to move slightly and I watched it, rooted to the spot. There was no wind. The day was calm. "Where are you?" I repeated.

And it was then that I heard the voices. Two of them. A low conversation. An argument. The sounds were coming from inside the house. I knew it could not be the children for they were outdoors. And it could not be Mrs. Livermore and Mr. Westerley for their nursing room was too far removed from here to carry an echo, even if that unfortunate man could make himself heard beyond the distance of his bedpost. I listened carefully and judged that the voices were coming from upstairs, not the first landing but the second. I felt an unexpected sensation of calm within myself, no sense of fear whatsoever, as I ascended the staircase and listened while the voices grew louder but remained indecipherable. Were they even voices? It was hard to tell. Perhaps it was just the wind finding places to seep through the cracks.

I followed the sounds to a door at the end of the corridor and pressed my ear to it and my heart skipped a beat when I realized that I was not wrong. There were most certainly two voices, engaged in a bitter feud. A man and a woman. I could not hear a word they were saying, it was more a sort of low murmur, but I could tell the difference in their gender and I could identify the tone of their conversation, which was growing more violent by the minute.

I would not be intimidated any longer. I reached for the handle and twisted it, flinging the door open, marching inside without a care for my safety.

The room was empty. Some old toys were scattered in a corner, a dusty rocking-horse and a child's cot. But other than that it was devoid of ornament or, more importantly, of people.

"Where are you?" I cried out, my voice rising now, almost screaming in my frustration, fear and panic. My words must have echoed so far through the house that even the unfortunate Mr. Westerley, lying half dead in his bed near the rooftop, might have shifted slightly on his mattress and wondered.

"Where are you?"

But answer came there none.

Chapter Nineteen

STEPPING OFF THE train at Paddington Station, I felt as if I was walking back into my past. The commuters rushed to and fro, making their connections, almost none of them taking any notice of the young lady standing in the centre of the platform, looking around and breathing in the familiar, foul London air, something that had been lost to her for so long. Had anyone stopped to look at me they might have seen an expression of relief mingled with anxiety upon my face. I was home again, but this was no longer home.

The day was mercifully dry and I stepped outside on to Praed Street, taking note of the familiar flower sellers and tradesmen's stalls before making my way towards Gloucester Square, where stood the small house in which I had grown up. I felt the most curious feelings of apprehension as I approached it; I had feared that I might become emotional, that seeing it again would bring back so many happy memories that I would be overcome by them, but to my relief I did not feel any tears spring to my eyes. Through the front window I could see a middle-aged man handing a book to a young boy, and they examined it together as a woman, no doubt the man's wife and the boy's mother, entered the room with a vase of flowers, made some remark to her family and then laughed at something the boy said in reply. The front door opened and a girl of about seven stepped outside with a skipping rope, breaking her stride for a moment as she took me in.

"Hello," I said.

"Hello," she replied. "Were you looking for Mama?"

I smiled and shook my head. "I was just passing," I told her. "I used to live in this house. I spent all my life here."

"My name's Mary," said the girl. "I know all my letters and can recite the names of the books of the New Testament in order."

Mary. My dead sister's name. So a Mary would live in this house after all. "And the Old?" I asked, smiling at her again, and she scrunched up her face uncertainly.

"I'm not so very good at those," she replied. "Papa says I must study more. When did you live here?"

"Until quite recently. A couple of months ago."

"We've rented the house until our own is ready. Ours will be far grander than this."

"But will it be as comfortable?" I asked, feeling a sense of loyalty towards my family home; I didn't like to hear it insulted.

"I think so."

"Mary!" A voice from behind made the child turn as her mother, a pleasant-looking lady with an open expression, appeared in the doorway behind her. She hesitated for a moment but then smiled and greeted me. I replied politely but, not wishing to engage in any further conversation, said goodbye to Mary and continued on my way. I felt pleased that the house was once again occupied by a family. It had been a happy home once and might be again.

Madge Toxley had agreed to take care of Isabella and Eustace in her own home that day although, as she said herself, they scarcely needed minding as they were always so well behaved. Isabella was distressed at the notion of staying away from Gaudlin Hall for an entire day, insisting once again that "they weren't supposed to leave," but I put it to her that she had made no such strenuous objections when an afternoon's play on the beaches at Great Yarmouth had been on offer, an argument which silenced her a little.

Madge was surprised to see me when I arrived at her front door early that morning, sleepy children in tow behind me, and said that I had an emergency in London that I had to attend to and that she would be doing me the most tremendous favour if she could take care of them until later in the evening.

"But of course," she said, opening the door wide to let the children in, and as she did so I could see her husband, Alex, in the parlour beyond, looking out at me then disappearing out of sight. "There's nothing wrong, I hope?"

"No, just something I need to take care of, that's all. A person I need to speak to."

She nodded but appeared dissatisfied with my reply and I immediately recognized why.

"You have my word that I will return," I told her. "I would not abandon the children. I promise you that."

"Of course, Eliza," she said, blushing slightly. "I didn't think for a moment—"

"And if you had, it would have been perfectly understandable," I said, reaching out and placing a hand on her arm in an expression of trust and friendship. "No, I will be back this evening, no matter where the day takes me."

The presence, whatever it was, did not seem intent on causing either of the children harm. Its malevolence was directed solely towards me, but I did not want to take the risk. It set my mind somewhat at ease to know that they would not be alone.

In Paddington, the omnibus stop that I was seeking was a five-minute walk from my old terraced house and, when I arrived, I set my bag on the ground and stood next to an elderly lady, who turned to look me up and down with a rather disparaging expression on her face. I wasn't sure why particularly; I had made the effort to dress well for today, but for whatever reason I wasn't to her taste. I thought I recognized her as Mrs. Huntington, who had taken care of me occasionally as a child, but then I remembered that that good woman had lost her mind after her husband and son had been killed in an accident some years before and been committed to a home for the bewildered in Ealing, and so it could not have been her; she might have been her twin though, so alike was she. I prayed for the omnibus to arrive for the manner in which she stared at me both unsettled and aggravated me. When it finally came, I boarded, stated my destination, paid my halfpenny to the conductor, and sat down.

In the past I had never paid much attention to the streets of London. One never does perhaps when one lives in a city, but driving through them now I was struck by how dirty they appeared, how the fog never seemed to lift fully from the air but sat there, a miasma through which a person needed to fight for advancement, and I wondered why our capital city had become so polluted that one could scarcely see from one side of the street to the other. Norfolk had the advantage over London on that score; it was clean at least. One could breathe there. I could suffer a ghost for a little fresh air.

I had timed my journey so that I would arrive at the school shortly before lunchtime and the traffic was on my side, for when I saw the building coming into sight, I checked my watch and knew that there would be ten minutes to go before the boys in their classrooms were given the signal to take their hour's lunch break. Stepping down from the omnibus, I waited by the railings and watched. There was no need to rush; the moment would come soon enough.

Standing there, I couldn't help but recall my first morning teaching at St. Elizabeth's School, that transition I made from schoolgirl to schoolteacher, and the terror I felt when my small girls appeared before me, some nervous, some close to tears, watching and waiting to see what type of instructor they would have for the following twelve months. Naturally, I was the youngest teacher at my school and most of those who were seated behind desks in the adjoining classrooms had taught me only a few years before, so I knew only too well how cruel they could be at times. I had been beaten many times by these same ladies who had welcomed me that morning as if I was an old friend, their hypocrisy not lost on me for a moment, and I still felt intimidated shaking their hands or entering the teachers' private tea room, an area which had been always off limits to me as a student and had held the promise of nothing but terrifying times within.

I resolved that day never to frighten my small girls, never to intimidate or beat them; it was not necessary that they love me—in fact, it would be for the best if they did not—their respect was all that mattered and I would do my best to earn that. And during the three years of my employment at St. Elizabeth's I grew in confidence to the point where I both thoroughly enjoyed my job and believed that I had some skill at its execution.

Certain that my future did not hold the possibility of a husband or a family of my own, I imagined that I would spend my life within the four walls of my classroom, the decades would pass and I would grow older and greyer just as the portrait of the Queen and Prince Albert would never fade, but the small girls, my small girls, would never change, would remain the same age for ever, replaced on an annual basis by a fresh intake, many of whom would be the younger sisters of girls who had already sat before me. There was a part of me that looked forward to the day when a child would appear on the first day of school whose mother had attended before her. Then I would know that I had succeeded in my position.

The sound of a bell ringing from inside the school shook me from my reverie and I walked through the gates as the doors opened and the boys began to pour out on to the playing fields or took their places beneath the sycamore trees as they opened the tin cans that contained their meagre lunches. Some were running around already, chasing each other, trying to work off their natural exuberance after three hours of being seated studiously behind their desks. Two were engaged in a dispute of some sort which quickly descended into fisticuffs. I wondered for a moment whether I should intervene but to my relief a teacher appeared from one of the side doors, a tough-looking man, and the boys took fright and scarpered. I looked away from the fracas and entered the school through the front doors, staring around at this unfamiliar building as I chose a corridor at random and made my way along it.

The boys were still emerging, dawdlers perhaps, mischief makers, those who had been kept behind for a few minutes to be chastised for some malfeasance, and I glanced through the open doorway of each classroom, certain that I would recognize my prey when I discovered her. Most of the teachers were men, not unusual in a boys' school I realized; I had been surprised to discover that the woman I sought was even employed here and reasoned that this must be a progressive institution. After all, all but one of the teachers at St. Elizabeth's had been women; the only time this rule had been relaxed had been in the case of Arthur Covan and I did not imagine that a successor to him would be appointed any time soon. How nice it would have been, I daydreamed, if there had been more of a divide. It would have been agreeable to discuss classroom activities with a group of pleasant young men.

I reached the end of one corridor and was about to turn on my heel and return in the direction I had come from when I saw her. She was alone in a classroom, her back turned to me, using her eraser to clean the blackboard of the morning's lessons. I watched her and felt a mixture of relief that I had found her and resentment that she could be living her life here quite so brazenly while mine had descended into such trauma and constant danger. I stepped inside and glanced around; there were no boys present, which satisfied me, and I reached for the door handle, closing it firmly behind me.

She jumped, startled, and spun round, a hand to her breast. She appeared quite shocked and I wondered whether she always frightened so easily. When she saw me, though, and realized her foolishness, she laughed a little.

"I'm so sorry," she said. "I was in a world of my own. I nearly jumped out of my skin. I take fright easily these days. It was not always so."

"I didn't mean to creep up on you," I replied, although in truth that was exactly what I had meant to do. I had not written, after all, nor given her any notice of my intention to come to London. I did not want her to put me off or refuse to see me.

"It's quite all right," she replied, narrowing her eyes and looking at me more carefully. "I know you, don't I? It's Mrs. Jakes, isn't it? Cornelius's mother?"

I shook my head. "No," I said.

"Oh, I'm so sorry. I must be confusing you with someone. Did you need to see me or were you looking for someone else?"

"It's you I've come to see," I told her. "And if you have a few spare minutes, I would appreciate it."

"Of course," she said, sitting down behind her desk and offering me the seat opposite her. "I'm sorry," she added, "I didn't catch your name."

I smiled at her. Was she pretending or entirely serious? Did she take me for a fool? (Or rather, did she *still* take me for a fool?) "You don't recognize me?" I asked in a disbelieving tone.

She stared and looked a little uncomfortable, moving slightly in her seat. "If you could just tell me whose mother you are—"

"I am no one's mother, Miss Bennet," I replied in a steady voice. "And if you recognize me, it's because we met once, a little over a month ago. You brushed past me on the platform at Thorpe Station in Norwich. Our cases collided and dropped. You looked directly at me that day and I would swear that you knew then exactly who I was. So it rather surprises me that you pretend not to recognize me now."

I watched as the colour drained from her face and she swallowed, holding my gaze until she could look no longer and turned away. "Of course," she said. "It's Miss Caine, isn't it?"

"It is."

"This is . . . unexpected," she said.

"I can imagine." I could hear the chill in my tone and was surprised by it. I had not realized that I felt such anger towards this woman until I was seated directly opposite her. And now, separated from her by only the length of my arms, I could feel my blood beginning to boil. My suffering was her fault, my sleepless nights her responsibility. She could not look me in the eye now and so directed her gaze a little lower, towards my hands, which I separated and placed on the desk between us, the scars from my burns still clearly visible. I saw her expression turn to a grimace and she looked away.

"As you can see, I bear the scars of Gaudlin Hall," I told her. "But my damaged hands are the least of my concerns."

She forced a sentence out. "You have not been . . . you have not been happy there then?"

I laughed. I could scarcely believe that she was playing this so innocently. "Miss Bennet," I said. "Perhaps we might drop the charade? I need to talk to you about that place. I've travelled to London for no other reason than to discuss it with you and I don't have a lot of time. I have a train to catch back there in the afternoon and you, no doubt, have a classroom full of small boys who will be rushing back in here when their lunch hour is over."

"Rushing might be overstating the case a little," she replied, smiling at me, and I laughed. At the very least, it broke the tension.

"Yes, well," I said. "That's as it may be."

"I suppose I owe you an apology," she said. "For deceiving you as I did."

"It would have been kinder to be honest from the start. You might have met me, at the Hall for one thing. Not allowed me to arrive there that first night with no idea of what was going on. The confusion of that evening only added to my troubles."

"I couldn't," she said, shaking her head. "Don't you understand, Miss Caine, I couldn't stay another day! Another hour! But may I say this, with my hand on my heart, that I am very glad to see that you are well."

I laughed again, although this time my laugh was tinged with a little more bitterness. "Well?" I asked. "I'm alive, if that's what you mean. But I have been injured. Time and again. Threatened by a wild dog. Pushed from a window. My hands, as you can see, were nearly burned beyond recognition. And there have been other things. What I want to know, Miss Bennet, is quite simple. What happened to you while you were there? And how did you survive it?"

She stood up quickly and walked across to the window, looking out at the boys kicking a ball in the playground. "I know this isn't what you want to hear, Miss Caine," she said after a long hesitation, "but I really do not want to discuss it. I'm sorry. I appreciate that you came all this way but I simply cannot talk about that place. I still can't sleep, can't you understand that? I am constantly on edge. You saw that when you arrived here."

"But you got away," I said, raising my voice. "Which is more than can be said for Miss Tomlin. Or Miss Golding. Or Miss Williams. Or Miss Harkness. You survived Gaudlin Hall and none of your predecessors have been so lucky. And your successor might not either. So I ask again, what happened to you there? I believe you owe me an answer. An honest one. You can help me, don't you see that?"

She turned round and her expression was one of utter torment. "If you think I survived, Miss Caine, then you do not understand the state of my mind at all. I'm alive, that's true. I breathe. I come to work. I eat. I go home. But I am in a state of nervous anxiety all the time. I worry constantly that . . . that . . ."

"That what, Miss Bennet?"

"That she will find me."

I looked away, her phrase confirming for me at last that she too had felt the presence and been tormented by it.

"She," I said after a protracted silence. "You use the feminine pronoun."

"Don't you think of it as a she?" she asked.

"Yes," I admitted. "Of course I do. I think of it as being the late Mrs. Westerley."

She nodded and sat down on one of the boys' seats, picking up his slate in a distracted fashion and tapping it for a few moments before returning it to the desk. "I will say this much," she replied finally. "I am not a woman who is easily intimidated. Growing up, my mother said that I had more strength and courage than either of my older brothers. When I arrived in the village of Gaudlin and learned the story of the Westerleys and the governesses who preceded me, I thought it little more than a terrible coincidence. An unfortunate series of events that had made a group of superstitious provincial gossips say the place was haunted, that no good would come to anyone who lived there."

"Mr. Heckling is fine," I pointed out. "Mrs. Livermore is fine. Neither have suffered any attacks."

"But neither Mr. Heckling nor Mrs. Livermore have any responsibility for the children," she said quietly. "Nor do they take any interest in them."

I considered this. "That's true," I admitted. "But tell me, how long were you there before you felt something?" She shook her head and ran a hand across her eyes. "Please, Miss Bennet," I insisted. "Please tell me."

"A day," she said with an indifferent shrug. "A little less than a day actually. I arrived in the morning, you of course arrived at night. And I felt something before the day was over. There had been nothing unusual about that day at all and when I went to bed I was extremely tired. I remember climbing beneath the covers and thinking that I would certainly get a deep sleep after my long journey. I closed my eyes. I don't remember what I dreamed of, I never remember my dreams, or very rarely anyway, but I recall that it descended into some horrific sensation of being strangled. I could see a woman in my dream, a dark-skinned woman, with her hands around my throat, choking me. And I can recall . . . Miss Caine, have you ever found yourself in the middle of a dream and something inside you tells you that you need to wake up, that you need to escape it?"

"Yes," I said. "Yes, I've felt that sensation."

"Well, that's how I felt," she continued. "I forced myself to wake, thinking I could shake the woman off if I released myself from the dream. But to my horror, when I opened my eyes, the feeling was still there. There really *were* hands on my throat, I really *was* being strangled. Immediately, of course, I lifted my own hands from beneath the sheets to pull these stranger's hands away and, as I did so, I felt them, I felt the thin wrists and the strength of those fingers, but as my hands closed upon them, they dissipated and disappeared into nothingness. The choking ended, the presence evaporated. I leapt from the bed, fell into the corner of the room, choking and coughing, spitting on the floor. I didn't know what was happening, whether it had been some terrible nightmare that had manifested a delusion of the mind, but there was no chance that I had simply imagined the attack, for my throat was horribly sore. Indeed, the first thing that Isabella said to me the following morning was that I had a bruise on my neck."

"I felt those hands too," I said, looking her directly in the eyes. "On my first night in that bed."

"She tried to strangle you then also?"

"No, she pulled at my ankles. I felt as if I was being dragged down. I'm not certain what her intention was but it would surely have been malevolent."

"And did you think you were going mad?" she asked me.

"No," I said. "No, I didn't think that because I knew what I had felt. I can feel those hands still."

"As can I," said Miss Bennet. "Their memory still prevents me from sleeping through the night."

"And what else?" I asked, leaning forward. "What else happened to you? Come now, Miss Bennet, you've told me this much. You may as well tell me the rest."

"You've seen the condition of the roof?" she asked me and I shook my head.

"I've never been up there," I said.

"It's best that you never do," she said. "The house looks solid enough but in truth it's falling apart. The stonework does not sit together well. Fifty years from now, I promise you, Miss Caine, a wind will come that will knock that place down if they do not do any repairs. Earlier than that, perhaps."

"What were you doing on the roof?" I asked.

"I like to paint," she explained. "I'm not very good, of course, but it gives me pleasure. It's flat up there and the views over the Norfolk Broads are magnificent. It was a sunny day and I took my easel and paints to the roof. Two things happened that day. Despite the fact that the weather was so good, a strong wind appeared out of nowhere, lifted me from my chair and would have carried me over the side of the house had I not grabbed hold of a stone beam by the chimney and clung on to it until the wind finally subsided. When it did, I made my way down to the ground and was standing in the driveway, recovering my breath, when stones from the roof began to rain down. One missed me by no more than a couple of feet. Had it hit me, I would have been killed instantly. I ran, of course. On to the lawns. Only when I was at a safe distance did the stones stop falling."

I shook my head. I had not encountered any falling stones yet; was this a nightmare that awaited me upon my return? Did I need a suit of armour to prevent myself from being crushed to death?

"And then there was the incident with the knife," she said.

"The knife?"

"I was preparing lunch, chopping vegetables, and the knife I was holding . . . it sounds ridiculous, I know, but it seemed to take on a life of its own. It turned on me. I was holding it in my own hands but it was pushing me back towards the wall. As I stood there, pressed flat against the stone, my hands were getting closer to my throat, the point of the knife ready to slit me open."

"And how did you stop it?" I asked.

"I didn't," she said. "Isabella walked in. And she uttered just one word—"No"—and my hands were returned to my own control. I dropped the knife, fell to the floor, and when I looked up, Isabella was standing over me. *You should be more careful with knives*, she told me. *Mother never lets us play with them.*"

"*Lets* us? The present tense?"

"I noticed that too."

"And she wasn't frightened by what she had witnessed?"

Now it was Miss Bennet's turn to laugh. "Isabella Westerley?" she asked. "Frightened? You've met her, Miss Caine. You've spent this last month with her. Do you think that she's a child who feels those kinds of emotions? Do you think she's a child who feels any emotions at all?"

"She's very damaged," I said, defending her. "Think of all she's been through. The death of her mother, the ruination of her father's life. Not to mention all the governesses who have died. How she has kept her sanity at all is a mystery to me."

"You're assuming that she has," said Miss Bennet, shaking her head. "Anyway, I don't trust that girl. I never did. I would catch her spying on me, observing my every movement. She would creep up on me out of the blue and frighten me, that's the truth of it. A twelve-year-old girl and she frightened me greatly."

"And Eustace?" I asked, hoping that she would not cast any slur upon his character, for he was my favourite, he was my darling.

"Well, Eustace, of course . . ." she said, smiling a little at the memory of him. "He's a sweet boy. But, to use your own phrase, terribly damaged. I fear for his future, I truly do."

"Might I ask what it was that made you leave in the end?" I asked. "Was there some other incident? Something that pushed you too far?"

"I should think all that I have described would have been enough," she replied. "But yes, there was one more thing. Heckling's horse; you're familiar with the animal, I presume?"

"Yes," I said. "A placid creature. She should really be left to her retirement at this point."

"I would have said the same," she replied. "But she turned on me one day, when Heckling wasn't there to witness it, of course. I was taking a walk and had brought a small bag of sugar to give her as a treat; I did it most mornings and I thought she loved me for it. But on this particular day, when I reached for the bag, she reared up, her legs in the air, and had I not jumped out of the way they would have landed on top of me, pinning me to the ground. I was shocked, of course, and looked at the horse, begging it to take control of itself, but there was murder in her eyes, she was drooling, and I ran. I ran, Miss Caine, as fast as I could, and that old horse came after me with murderous intent. It was neighing and whinnying like the hounds of hell and had I not made it to the front door of the Hall and run inside before she could reach me I have no doubt that I would have been killed by her."

"It seems impossible," I said, thinking of that placid, worthy animal. "But something similar happened to me. With a dog. I was sure that it meant me harm. Were it not for Isabella, I believe it would have ripped my throat out."

"Her spirit is attracted to animals then," said Miss Bennet, shuddering slightly. "I wonder why. Anyway, for me that was the last straw. I drew up the advertisement, waited until I could see Heckling controlling the horse from a window—she was calm then, entirely her old self—and made my way to the village to telegraph the position of governess to the editor of the *Morning Star*. Which, I presume, is where you saw it."

"It was," I said, nodding. "But you didn't leave," I pointed out. "Despite everything that had happened. You waited until your replacement had been found."

She smiled at me. "Miss Caine," she said quietly, "I grant you that I do not come out of this adventure without a stain on my character. It was wrong of me to advertise the position under false pretences. I knew that it sounded as if I was master of Gaudlin Hall and not a mere governess. And I realize that if

I were a braver soul, then I should have waited for you to arrive and warned you of the things that were taking place there.
But I couldn't take that chance, you see. I couldn't risk your
turning on your heels and boarding the train back to London.
It was cowardly of me, of course. I know that very well. But,
you see, I had to get away. But the one thing that I wouldn't
do, the one act that I could not bring myself to commit, was
walking away from those children and leaving them to that
spirit. Leaving them without a protector. Until I knew that you
were coming, I could not leave." She hesitated and shook her
head. "No, that's not entirely accurate," she said, reconsider-
ing this. "I couldn't leave Eustace without a protector. Isabella,
I don't think she needs anyone to look after her. She can take
care of herself."

I stood up, pacing slowly around the classroom. A wall chart
listed the Kings and Queens of England, from the Battle of
Hastings to Victoria, and it distracted me for a moment, bringing me back to happier times. How I wished that I was simply
waiting for my small girls to run back in after their lunch break,
tired and yawning, ready for their afternoon's exercises.

"And you, Miss Caine," said Miss Bennet after a long silence.
"You have suffered badly?" I nodded and told her briefly about
the various incidents that had taken place since my residence at
the Hall began. "At least you have survived," she said.

"So far," I replied.

"But you're here," she said, smiling and coming over to me,
taking both my hands in hers. "You're here, after all. You got
away. Like me. Perhaps the spirit is losing her power."

I shook my head and pulled my hands away. "I think you misunderstand me," I said. "I may have survived, so far, but I have
not got away, as you put it. I am only here for the afternoon in

London. I told you already that I return to Norfolk by the afternoon train."

"You're going back to Gaudlin Hall?"

"But of course I am," I said. "Where else would I go? I have no other home."

"Go anywhere," she shouted, throwing her hands in the air, months of tension pouring out of her now in frustration. "Go anywhere at all. Go back to the school you used to teach in. Go to Cornwall or Edinburgh or Cardiff or London. Go to France or Italy. Travel into the heart of Russia, if you must, or live with those unfortunate women on the streets of the capital. But get away from that terrible place. If you have any sense, Miss Caine, get as far away from Gaudlin Hall as you possibly can."

I stared at her, shocked by her selfishness. "And then who," I asked her in an even tone, trying to control my growing temper, "who would take care of the children?"

"She would."

I shook my head. "I will not leave them to her," I said.

She shrugged. "Then she will come for you. Like she came for the others." She looked away, her tone suggesting that this much was both obvious and unavoidable. "She'll come; you'll die."

Her words were like a knife through me. "But why?" I asked, as much of myself as anyone else. "Why does she mean us harm? I seek nothing but to help those children. To take care of them. And what of the other presence? The old man? You have not spoken of him. What part does he play in this?"

Miss Bennet frowned and looked back at me, shaking her head as if she had not heard me correctly. "I beg your pardon?" she said.

"The other spirit," I said. "There are two of them, are there not? He prevented me from being pushed out the window on one occasion—I could feel his hands on me. Eustace has seen him, has spoken to him. He said that he was there to take care of me."

Miss Bennet wrapped her arms around herself and I could see that she had grown more frightened by what I said. "I'm sorry, Miss Caine. I have no idea what you're talking about."

"You never felt him?"

"No," she said. "Not once. Only the destructive spirit. Only her."

"Perhaps he was there and you never felt him? Perhaps he prevented those stones from falling on you, for example."

She considered this for a moment but shook her head. "I would have known," she said in a confident voice. "I am certain that I would have. I would have known if there was another. And there wasn't. I would swear to it."

I nodded. I had no choice but to believe her; she had no reason to lie. The bell rang and I could see the boys in the playground bringing their games to an end, gathering their lunch cans and making their way towards the doors.

"I should go," I said. "I suppose I must thank you, Miss Bennet, for your candour. You have confirmed a number of things for me. And, strange as it might sound, it is something of a relief to me to know that another has gone through what I am going through. It prevents me from thinking that I am going mad."

"But you are going mad," said Miss Bennet evenly. "You must be if you decide to go back there. Only a madwoman would return to that place."

"Then I am a madwoman," I replied. "And so be it. But the children will not leave while their father remains in the house,

I know that much for certain. They never speak of him, they never acknowledge his presence. But they are comforted to know that he is there. And I will never leave them alone to that malevolent spirit."

I reached for the door handle and heard her voice behind me, sorrowful now, regretful.

"You must think me a terrible woman," she said. "To have deserted them like I did."

I turned back to her and shook my head. "You did as your nature dictated," I said, smiling at her. "And I must do as my own nature dictates too. Goodbye, Miss Bennet."

"Goodbye, Miss Caine," she said. "And good luck."

It was late when I returned to Gaudlin Hall. The train had been delayed in London and then delayed a second time just outside Manningtree. It had been an uncomfortable journey. A middle-aged man in the carriage, seated opposite me, had begun an unwelcome flirtation, an experience which was entirely new to me and which, at another time, I might have rather enjoyed, but I could not enjoy it then and was forced to move to a dif ferent seat, where I had the misfortune to find myself next to an elderly lady who wanted nothing more than to regale me with stories of how cruel her daughter and son-in-law were to her, how they prevented her from seeing her grandchildren, and how neither of them were any better than they ought to be anyway and that they would find no place in her will.

Madge Toxley had brought the children home to their own beds and seemed relieved to see me, summoning her carriage immediately and making her way back down the driveway with extraordinary haste. As I ascended the staircase at Gaudlin Hall I prayed that I would be permitted to sleep through the night, to recover my energies for the following day, and be prepared to face whatever trauma might come next. I stopped on the landing before heading up to my own floor and was surprised to hear voices coming from Eustace's room. I glanced at the clock next to me; it was past midnight and far too late for either of the children to still be awake. I made my way down the corridor and stopped outside his room, pressing an ear to the door. It was difficult to make out what they were saying but after a moment my hearing adjusted and I could make out Eustace speaking in a quiet tone.

"But what if she doesn't come back?" he was asking.

"She will," came the reply, not Isabella's voice as I expected, but something older, something more mature, something masculine.

"I don't want her to leave us like the others did," said Eustace.

"She won't," said the second person, at which point I opened the door and stepped inside. There was no light in the room save for Eustace's candle which sat next to his bed on the table, illuminating him. His pale skin looked white as snow against his nightshirt. I looked around. He was entirely alone.

"Who were you talking to?" I asked, marching towards him, seizing him by the shoulders and raising my voice. "Who were you talking to, Eustace?"

He issued a short gasp of fright but, despite how much I loved him, I had had enough and was unwilling to release him from my grasp. "Who were you talking to?" I shouted, and now he relented.

"The old man," he said.

I could have wept in frustration. "But there is no old man," I cried, releasing him and turning round in a full circle before looking back at the boy. "There's no one else here."

"He's behind you," said Eustace and I spun round once again, my heart racing, but no, there was no one there.

"Why can't I see him?" I cried. "Why can't I see him too?"

"He's gone outside now," said Eustace quietly, sinking under the sheets. "But he's still in the house. He says he won't leave no matter how much she wants him to. He won't go where he's supposed to go, not while you're still here."

Chapter Twenty

"A GHOST?" ASKED Reverend Deacons, smiling at me, his expression such that he thought perhaps I was making fun of him.

"I know it sounds ridiculous," I said. "But I'm convinced of it."

He shook his head and indicated a pew on the left-hand side of the church, the Westerley family pew, the one where the children and I sat every Sunday. There was a brass plaque pinned to the corner, inscribed with the name of a Westerley antecedent, the dates of his birth and death. Seventeenth century. They went back that far at least then. "My dear girl," said the vicar, sitting at a small remove from me. "The idea is fanciful."

"Why must it be? What is it Shakespeare says, Reverend? There are more things in heaven and earth than are dreamt of in your philosophy."

"Shakespeare was in the business of entertaining an audience," he replied. "Shakespeare was nothing more than a simple writer. Yes, in one of his plays, a ghost might appear on the ramparts, naming his killer, demanding vengeance. Or attending a feast to haunt his own murderer. But these things exist to titillate and send a shiver down the spines of the paying crowd. In real life, Miss Caine, I'm afraid that ghosts are very much overrated. They are the stuff of fictions and of whimsical minds."

"It's not so long ago that men of your ilk believed in witches and superstition," I pointed out.

"Medieval times," he said, waving a hand in the air to dismiss the notion. "This is 1867. The Church has come a long way since then."

"Women were held underwater on suspicion of being witches," I stated bitterly "If they drowned, they were proven innocent but had lost their lives to the accusation. If they survived, then their guilt was proven and they were burned at the stake. Either way, they were killed. Women, of course. Not men. No one questioned such beliefs in those days. And now you call me fanciful. You do not see the irony?"

"Miss Caine, the modern Church cannot be held responsible for the superstitions of the past."

I sighed. It had probably been a poor decision on my part to come here but I was at my wits' end and had wondered whether a vicar might come to my assistance. In truth, I had never been a particularly religious person. I had observed, of course, and attended services on Sundays. But to my shame, I had always been one of those lost souls whose mind wandered a little during the homily and who paid scant attention during the reading of the lesson. What did it say of me that now, in a moment of such crisis, I turned to the Church for help? And what did it say of the Church that, when I sought consolation, it could do nothing but laugh in my face?

"We know so little of the world," I continued, determined not to allow myself to be treated like an hysterical woman. "We know not how we got here or where we will go after we leave. How can we be so convinced that there is no such thing as lost souls, half alive and half dead? How can you be so certain that it is a nonsense?"

"This is a product of living at Gaudlin Hall," he replied, shaking his head. "Your mind is open to delusion due to the unhappy history of that place."

"And what do you know of Gaudlin Hall?" I asked. "When did you last set foot there?"

"Your tone is combative, Miss Caine," he replied and I could sense that he was trying hard to keep the anger out of his. "Unnecessarily so, if I might say so. Perhaps you're not aware of this but I have visited Mr. Westerley." I raised an eyebrow in surprise and he nodded, sensing my scepticism. "It's quite true, I assure you," he continued. "Soon after he was brought back to the Hall. And on one or two occasions since then. The poor man is in such a terrible state that it's upsetting to see him at all. But perhaps you've seen him too?"

"I have," I admitted.

"Then isn't it possible, Miss Caine, that laying eyes on such an unfortunate specimen of humanity, and knowing the story of how he ended up in that position, has played with your imagination somewhat?"

"I don't believe so," I replied, unwilling to be patronized. "After all, if you see him as regularly as you say, and I have only laid eyes on him once, then why would I suffer these unhappy delusions when you do not?"

"Miss Caine, is it necessary for me to say?"

"It is."

He sighed. "I fear you will rebuke me for this, but is it not true to say that your sensibilities, as a woman—"

"Stop, please!" I insisted, raising my voice so that it echoed around the aisles. I closed my eyes for a moment, telling myself to control my temper, not to allow him to aggravate me so badly. "Do not say that I am more susceptible because of my sex."

"Then I will not say it," replied Reverend Deacons. "But you might find more answers in that suggestion than you like."

I wondered whether I should simply stand up and leave. What had brought me there anyway? It was a nonsense, all of it. This building, that altar, this ridiculous man with his vestments and sanctimonious airs. The living the parish afforded him while others starved. More fool me for thinking that he might ever offer me some solace. I gathered myself together, preparing to make a dignified departure, when a further thought occurred to me.

"I have a question," I said. "Not to do with the events at Gaudlin Hall. Perhaps you can provide me with an answer?"

"I can try."

"You believe in an afterlife, Father?" I asked him. "In the rewards of heaven and the damnation of hell?"

"Of course," he replied without hesitation, looking shocked that I would even dare to question his creed.

"You believe in these things without any proof whatsoever of the existence of either?"

"My dear girl, that is where faith comes in."

"Of course," I said. "But if you believe in these two forms of the afterlife, then why are you so opposed to considering a third?"

He frowned. "What do you mean by a third?" he asked. "What third exactly?"

"A third place," I explained. "A place where the souls of the dead can linger before being admitted to heaven or condemned to hell."

"You refer to purgatory, Miss Caine."

"A fourth place then," I said, almost laughing at the absurdity of the vast number of places where a soul could be located. "You believe in three but not four. A place where souls remain part of this world, still observing us and at times interacting with us. Hurting us or protecting us. Why should such a plane of existence seem so ridiculous to you when the others—heaven, hell and purgatory—do not?"

"Because there is no mention of such a place in the Bible," he said patiently, speaking to me as if I was a child, which caused me to throw my hands in the air in frustration.

"The Bible is written by men," I declared. "It has gone through so many changes, so many linguistic translations over the centuries that it adapts and re-creates itself in the form of the time in which the reader engages with it. Only a fool believes that the words of the Bible are the words delivered by Christ."

"Miss Caine, you are approaching blasphemy," he said, sitting back in the pew now and looking scandalized. I could see his hand trembling slightly as he spoke. I suspected that he was unaccustomed to being challenged so provocatively by anyone, let alone by a woman. His position, like so many of his ilk, was one of uncontested and unearned respect. "And if you continue to speak in this vein, I will not listen."

"I apologize," I said, not wishing to infuriate him or bring the roof of the church down on my head; there was enough possibility of that at Gaudlin Hall without it happening here too. "I don't mean to upset you. Truly I don't. But you must admit that there is so much that we don't know about the universe that it is entirely possible, indeed it is likely, it is *more* than likely, that there are mysteries whose revelation would surprise us. Shock us, even. Cause us to doubt the very foundations upon which we base our faith in this world."

He considered this, removed his spectacles and wiped them with his handkerchief before replacing them on his nose. "I am not a highly educated man, Miss Caine," he said after a lengthy pause. "I am a simple vicar. I have no aspirations towards a bishopric, nor do I expect that one would ever be offered to me. I seek no other earthly position than being a pastor to my flock. I read, of course. I have an enquiring mind. And I admit that over the course of my life, there have been times when I have had . . . questions about the nature and meaning of existence. I would not be human if I did not. The nature of spiritual belief is one of the eternal questions about the universe. But I reject your hypothesis on the grounds that it removes God from the equation. God chooses when we should enter this world and when we should leave it. He does not make half-decisions and leave souls lingering in crisis. He is decisive. He is no Hamlet, if you wish to speak in Shakespearean terms. Those would be the actions of a cruel and merciless Lord, not the loving one we read of in the Bible."

"You don't think God can be cruel and merciless?" I asked, trying not to laugh and provoke him even further. "Is your reading of the Bible so superficial that you do not recognize barbarity on every page?"

"Miss Caine!"

"Think not that I am unfamiliar with the testaments, Reverend. And it seems to me that the God of whom you speak has a great gift for brutality and malice. He is something of a specialist in the subject."

"You are disrespectful, madam. The God that I know would never treat one of his children in such a vindictive manner.

Leaving a soul to languish as you suggest—never! Not in this world!"

"But out of it?"

"No!"

"You know this for sure? He has told you?"

"Miss Caine, you must stop this. Think of where you are."

"I am in a building created of bricks and mortar. Put together by men."

"I cannot hear any more," he shouted, losing his temper with me at last. (Had I waited for this moment? Did I *want* to provoke a human, and not a spiritual, response in this impotent man?) "You will leave this place if you cannot speak with the respect that—"

I jumped up from the pew, staring down at him in frustration. "You are not there, Father," I cried. "I wake up at Gaudlin Hall, I spend most of my day there, I sleep there at night. And throughout it all there is but one thought running through my mind."

"And that is?"

"This house is haunted."

He groaned loudly in protest and looked away, his face a study of pain and anger. "I will not hear these words," he said.

"Of course you won't," I replied, walking away from him. "Because your mind is closed. As are the minds of all your type."

I marched down the aisle of the church, my shoes ringing on the tiles beneath my feet, and emerged into the daylight of a cold winter's morning, a great urge overwhelming me to scream aloud. Before me, I could make out the tradespeople of the village going about their business as if there was nothing amiss in the world. There was Molly Sutcliffe, emptying a bucket of soapy water into the road outside the tea shop. There was Alex

Toxley, making his way into his surgery. Over there, I could glimpse the shadow of Mr. Cratchett, sitting in the window of the solicitor's office, his great ledgers open before him, his eyes fixed on the pages as his pen scuttled across them, making its markings. There was Mr. Raisin's horse and carriage outside— so he was inside, at his desk—and a thought occurred to me. One question that needed an answer.

"Oh, Miss Caine," said Mr. Cratchett, looking up with a resigned expression on his face. "You are back to see us again. What joy. I wonder that I don't set up a special desk with your name on it."

"I know this is an inconvenience, Mr. Cratchett," I said. "And I don't want to take up any more of Mr. Raisin's valuable time. He has been more than generous to me already. But I have one question, just one, that I need to ask him. Would you speak to him and ask him whether he might have a moment to indulge me in this? I promise I will stay for no more than a minute or two."

Sensing that I might be as good as my word and that he might be rid of me all the quicker if he acquiesced, the clerk sighed, laid down his quill and repaired to the back office, returning a moment later, nodding wearily.

"Two minutes," he said, pointing at me and I nodded and strode past him. Inside the office, Mr. Raisin was seated behind his desk and, as he made a movement to rise, I ushered him down again and told him that he should stay where he was.

"I'm glad you came," he said. "Since we spoke the other day, you have been much on my mind. I—"

"I won't delay you," I said, interrupting him. "I know you're busy. I have just one question. If I was to leave, that is if we were to leave, together I mean, would the estate have any objections?"

He raised an eyebrow and stared at me. His mouth opened and closed several times in surprise. "If *we* were to leave, Miss Caine?" he asked. "You and I?"

"No, not you and I," I replied, almost bursting out laughing at the misunderstanding. "The children and I. If I were to take them back to London to live with me there. Or the continent. I have often felt a desire to live abroad. Would the estate approve of that? Would it support us? Or would we be pursued by constables and brought back to Gaudlin? Would I be detained for kidnap?"

He thought about it for a moment and shook his head. "It's out of the question," he said. "There are clear provisions in the estate that say that as long as Mr. Westerley is present at Gaudlin Hall, then the children may not leave for a protracted period of time. Even if they were in the care of a guardian such as yourself."

My mind raced ahead of me and I began to think in the most ludicrous terms. "And what if he left too?" I asked. "What if I took him with me?"

"James Westerley?"

"Yes. What if he, the children and I were all to move to London. Or Paris. Or the Americas, if necessary."

"Miss Caine, have you lost your reason?" he asked, standing up and raising himself to his full height. "You have seen the condition in which that poor man lies. He needs constant nursing."

"And what if I was to provide that?"

"Without any training? Without any medical qualifications? Do you think that would be fair to him, Miss Caine? No, it's out of the question."

"What if I learned?" I asked, aware now that I had far surpassed my allocated number of questions. "What if I underwent a nursing course and satisfied you that I knew what I was doing? Then would you let me take him? And them?"

"Miss Caine," said Mr. Raisin, coming round from behind the desk and ushering me into an armchair as he sat opposite me. His tone softened a little now. "I speak regularly to Mr. Westerley's doctor. That man will never leave that room. Ever. Even to attempt to move him would be to kill him. Don't you understand that? He must remain where he is and, while he is alive, the children must remain there too. There is no possibility, none, of that fact changing. You, of course, are free to leave whenever you want, we cannot keep you captive here, but as you have made it clear to me on more than one occasion, you will not leave the children. Does that remain your position?"

I nodded. "It does, sir," I agreed.

"Well then. There is no more to say on the matter."

I looked down at the pattern on the carpet, as if I might find an answer to my troubles there. "Then there is no one who can help me," I said quietly. And in my mind, I thought this. I will never leave until she kills me.

"Help you with what?" he asked, and I was touched by the concern in his voice. I shook my head and smiled at him and for a moment our eyes met and I noticed his flicker just once towards my lips. I held his gaze.

"Miss Caine," he said quietly, and as the words came out he swallowed self-consciously and a burst of colour came to his cheeks. "I would help you if I could. But I know not what I can do for you. If you could simply tell me—"

"There is nothing," I said in a resigned tone, standing up now and smoothing down my dress. I extended a hand in the air and he looked at it for a moment before shaking it. Our connection lasted a little longer than necessary and was that his index finger moving a little along my own, only a fraction, the sensation of skin caressing skin? I could feel a deep sigh at the very core of my being unlike any I had ever known and willed myself to look away from him, but his eyes held mine firmly and I might have stayed that way for a long time or given in to temptation had I not noticed the silver frame on his desk, the image contained within causing me to pull my hand back sharply and look away from him.

"I hope Mrs. Raisin did not protest at your coming home late after our last rendezvous," I said, saying one thing, meaning another.

"Mrs. Raisin had remarks on the matter," he said, turning away, his eyes on the portrait now too. She was a hard-looking woman, somewhat older than her husband. "But then Mrs. Raisin has never been shy to state her opinions."

"And why should she be?" I asked, aware of a faint note of belligerence in my tone. "Of course I've never had the good fortune to meet her."

"Perhaps," he replied, observing the formalities, "perhaps you should dine with us some evening."

I smiled at him and shook my head and he nodded, of course, for he was not a stupid man and he understood perfectly.

I withdrew.

Chapter Twenty-one

I WAS CONDEMNED THEN. If I was unwilling to leave the children, to leave Eustace in particular, that troubled and vulnerable child, then I would have to stay at Gaudlin Hall as long as Mr. Westerley lived. And I was certain that there was more chance of me predeceasing him than the other way around.

Later that afternoon, I sat in the front parlour of the Hall, attempting to read a copy of *Silas Marner* which I had found in Mr Westerley's library. I felt a sense of calm, a quiet feeling of resignation that I was doomed to stay here until I died, however soon that might be. Footsteps on the driveway alerted me to the approach of a visitor and I leaned forward on the couch, peering out the window to see Madge Toxley in conversation with Eustace and Isabella. I watched the three of them, an unusual grouping; Eustace was the chattiest and whatever he was saying was making Madge laugh. A moment later, Isabella started to speak and her laugh faded slightly. She appeared a little disturbed by whatever the girl was saying, a dark shadow crossing her face as she looked towards the house. At one moment, I saw her throw a glance to a top window, turn away, and then in an instant look back, as if she had seen something unexpected there. Only Eustace tugging at her sleeve made her return her gaze to him but she looked thoroughly unsettled by whatever had just taken place. I thought of going out to them but realized that I did not want to take part in their conversation. Eventually, I assumed, Madge would come to me.

And she did, of course, a few moments later, knocking on the front door and looking behind me with an apprehensive glance when I opened it.

"My dear," she declared, stepping inside. "You look quite tired. Have you not been sleeping?"

"Not very well," I admitted. "I am glad to see you though."

"Well, I thought I should stop by," she said. "I rushed off a little the other night when you came back from London. I think I might have been rather rude. And Mrs. Richards—do you know Mrs. Richards? Her husband runs the funeral parlour in the village—she told me that she had seen you emerging from the church this morning looking like you were ready to kill someone before storming across to Mr. Raisin's office."

"There's nothing to worry about," I said, shaking my head. "I assure you that I haven't harmed anyone. Both Mr. Raisin and Mr. Cratchett are quite well."

"I'm glad to hear it. Shall we have some tea?"

I nodded and led her into the kitchen, filling the kettle and placing it on the range for the water to heat. I still felt a certain anxiety whenever I turned the taps on; although nothing but cold water had run from them since the afternoon of my scalding, I was never sure when the presence might interfere with them again and cause me more suffering.

"Your visit to London," said Madge after an uncomfortable pause. "Was it successful?"

"It depends how you define success, I suppose," I replied.

"I expect you were tying up the loose ends of your father's estate?"

"Do you?" I asked, raising an eyebrow, and she shook her head and had the good grace to look embarrassed.

"No, I imagine it was something else entirely. I suspect you went in search of Harriet Bennet."

H. Bennet. It occurred to me that I had never, in all this time, wondered what the "H" stood for. And now I knew.

The kettle burst into a piercing whistle and I filled the pot and brought it, with the cups, to the table. I said nothing for a few moments. "You were talking to the children outside," I said finally.

"Yes," she said. "That Eustace is a funny little chap, isn't he? He's quite sweet really. In a strange way."

"He's a dear boy."

"He didn't want Isabella to tell me anything about your trip to London. He said that it wasn't true, that you hated London and would never go back there. I think he's rather nervous that you're preparing to leave him."

A stab of guilt punctured me and I felt a tear spring to my eyes. "Oh no," I said. "I must disabuse him of that notion if it is what he believes. He has nothing to be concerned about on that matter. Does Isabella think the same thing?"

Madge shook her head. "I don't think so," she replied. "Don't take this the wrong way, but I'm not sure she cares whether you stay or go."

I laughed. How was I expected to take such a remark?

"Actually," continued Madge, "she said the most extraordinary thing. She said that you could leave if you wanted to, that it would probably be best for you if you did, but that they weren't allowed to go, that 'She' wouldn't allow it. I asked her who 'She' referred to but she wouldn't say. Simply smiled at me, an unsettling smile, as if she was the owner of a great secret whose revelation could destroy us all. Shall I be Mother?"

I stared at her and then, realizing what she meant, nodded as she reached for the teapot, pouring two cups of tea and passing the milk between us.

"Eliza," she said. "Why did you visit Harriet Bennet?"

"To ask her about her experiences here at Gaudlin Hall."

"And were you satisfied by her responses?"

I considered this but had no answer. I did not know what responses I had expected from Miss Bennet, nor how I felt about what she had told me. "Madge," I said, changing the subject slightly, "when we last talked you told me about that awful night that Mrs. Westerley, Santina, killed Miss Tomlin and caused such unimaginable injury to her husband."

Mrs. Toxley shuddered. "Don't," she said, dismissing it slightly with a wave of her hand. "It is my stated intention to try to forget that night entirely. Not that I ever will, of course. It will remain with me always."

"But you also said that you saw Santina again."

"That's right. But I told you that in the strictest of confidence, Eliza. You haven't mentioned it to anyone, have you? Alex would be terribly angry if he found out. He expressly forbade me from going there."

"No, I promise that I haven't and that I will not," I said. "You have my word on that."

"Thank you. Don't misunderstand me, my husband is the epitome of kindness and consideration, but on that subject, the subject of Santina Westerley, he would brook no disobedience on my part."

"Madge, your secret is secure," I said with a sigh, wondering why on earth an intelligent woman like this would feel obliged towards obedience or disobedience in the first place. Was she a child, after all, or a grown adult? An image of Mr. Raisin came into my head, an absurd image of the two of us living in marital harmony, neither of us caring for such words at all, and as quickly as it entered my thoughts I dismissed it. This was no time for fantasy. "But it is very important that you tell me about your last encounter with that unfortunate woman," I continued. "You said that you visited her in prison?"

She clenched her mouth tightly for a moment. "I'd prefer not to talk about it, Eliza," she said. "It was a deeply unpleasant experience. For a genteel woman to enter such an environment was quite horrible. To be honest, I've always rather considered myself to be the sturdy type. You know, the sort who can put up with any unpleasant situation if I have to. But prison? You've never been inside one, I presume?"

"No," I said. "Never."

"I wonder that Mr. Smith-Stanley doesn't do something about the condition of the prisons. I've never seen such squalor. Naturally the unfortunate creatures who find themselves in such places are incarcerated for the most heinous of crimes, but is there reason to condemn them to exist in such disgusting conditions? Isn't the loss of one's liberty punishment enough for vice and criminality? And think on, Eliza, this was a women's prison, where one might think that conditions would be a little better. I shudder to imagine what the male equivalent might be like."

She took a sip of her tea and thought for a long time before looking up and catching my eye and smiling a little. "I can see that I haven't put you off. Determined to know about it, aren't you?"

"If you would, Madge," I said quietly. "I don't ask for prurient reasons. I am not fascinated by depravity, if that is what you are worried about, nor am I obsessed with the case of Mrs. Westerley. I just need to know what she said to you that day, when death was upon her."

"It was a miserably cold day," replied Madge, looking away from me and into the flames of the fire burning in the hearth. "I remember that distinctly. When I arrived at the prison I was still uncertain whether or not I could go through with it. I had lied to Alex, something I never do, and I felt a combination of guilt and fear. Standing outside the prison walls, I told myself that I could still change my mind, that I could turn round and hail a hansom cab and spend the day shopping in London or visit my aunt, who lives in Piccadilly. But I did none of those things. There were reporters outside, of course, for this was the day that Santina Westerley was condemned to die and the case had acquired notoriety in the newspapers. They rushed towards me and asked my name but I refused to answer and knocked on the wooden door instead, hammered on it, until a prison officer opened it, asked my name, and let me into a waiting room, where I sat, trembling, feeling like a convict myself.

"It was probably only a few minutes but it felt like an eternity until a warden came out to ask my business and I explained that I had been Mrs. Westerley's neighbour, perhaps her closest female friend, and I was informed that Santina was due to hang in less than two hours.

"'That's why I'm here,' I told him. 'I thought that she could do with a friendly face on her last morning. Her crimes were shocking, of course, but we are Christian people, are we not, and can't you see that a conversation with someone who had once been a friend might soothe her spirits and lead her to the hangman's noose with a clearer mind?'

"He didn't seem too concerned with any of that but said that Mrs. Westerley was entitled to a visitor and as no one else was here he would ask her whether she would see me. 'It'll be up to her,' he insisted. 'We can't make her see anyone if she doesn't want to. And I wouldn't try. Not on a day like today. We try to make her last hours comfortable,' he added, apparently feeling that this was a salve to his conscience. 'She'll pay soon enough for her crimes.'

"After this, he led me through the prison courtyard, which was filthy, Eliza, simply filthy, and in through another door where I was forced to pass the cells of the unfortunate women, walking between them as they threw themselves at the bars. What were they? Pickpockets, thieves, burglars, streetwalkers, most of them. Who knows what suffering they had endured in their childhood that had led them to such an ignominious fate. Almost all of them were screaming at me, thrusting their hands through their cages. I suppose it was a novelty of sorts to see a lady among them, well dressed and whatnot. Some begged me to help them, claiming that they were innocent. Others shouted vulgarities that would have made a gypsy blush. Some simply stared at me with the most unsettling expressions on their faces. I tried to avoid looking at them but it was truly frightening, Eliza. Truly."

"I don't doubt it," I said.

"And the smell! My dear, it was atrocious. I thought I might pass out. Eventually we reached a cell that had no window but was built of four solid walls and the warden told me to wait outside while he spoke to Santina. This, apparently, was where the soon-to-die were housed during their last twenty-four hours.

Of course I was uncomfortable being left there on my own, but as the women were all safely locked away, it seemed certain that I could come to no harm.

"Still, it was a relief when the warden returned to tell me that Santina had agreed to see me. It was quiet inside, Eliza. That was the first thing I noticed. The walls were thick enough to block out most of the noise from the rest of the prison. Santina was seated behind a table, looking remarkably composed for a woman whose gallows were being tested even then. I sat opposite her and the warden left us alone.

"'It was kind of you to come,' she said and I tried to smile. She looked as beautiful as I had ever seen her, despite her imprisonment. I don't mind telling you, Eliza, that I used to grow frustrated with the way that every man paid attention to her, my husband included. But she did not court it, I knew that. She did not tease and flirt as some women would; she simply existed. And she was very beautiful.

"'I thought about it for a long time,' I told her. 'But I felt that I should see you, on this day of all days.'

"'You always showed such kindness towards me,' she said, her voice still tinged as it always was with that Spanish accent of hers. She had learned English perfectly, of course; she was bright, after all, and a quick study. But her accent never left her. I remember staring at her for the longest time, uncertain what to say, and finally breaking down and just asking her why she had done it, what had possessed her to commit such terrible acts, had she been possessed by the devil that night?

"'They were going to steal my children,' she told me, her expression growing grave as she spoke, her lip curling in anger. 'And I will not let anyone touch my children. I swore that from the moment I discovered I was carrying Isabella.'

"'Miss Tomlin was nothing more than a governess,' I protested. 'A young girl. She was there to help you. To take some of the weight off your shoulders. To instruct them in their historical studies and their sums and their reading. She presented no threat to you.'

"When I said this, when I used the word 'threat,' her hands sprang out and they clenched into fists. 'You don't know what can happen,' she said, not even looking at me, 'if a mother loses sight of her children. What others will do to them.'

"'But no one wanted to hurt them,' I said. 'Oh, Santina, no one would have hurt them for the world James told you that.'

"'He wanted another woman to take care of them.'

"'He didn't,' I said, and she stood up, raising her voice now so much that I expected the warden to interrupt us at any moment.

"'No woman will ever take care of my children but me,' she said. 'No woman. I will not allow it, do you understand? And after I am gone, Madge Toxley, if you try to make them yours, then you will live to regret it.'

"I remember feeling a great wave of fear as she said this. Of course there would be nothing she could do from the grave, and somebody would need to take care of Isabella and Eustace. After all, they're still so young. And yet when she said this, I believed that she meant it. Does that make sense, Eliza? And I told myself at that moment that I would not offer to take the children into our house, as Alex and I had already discussed doing. In fact, the knowledge that they were staying with the Raisins was a comfort to me on this count, despite . . . well, I don't know if you've met Mrs. Raisin but I think it would be fair to say that her husband is a saint. But that aside, I knew they would be well looked after. Of course I wasn't to know that James would be released from hospital and sent back to

Gaudlin Hall. I was certain, everyone was, that his death was imminent. And then, of course, when he came back here the children followed within hours."

"Was it a psychosis, do you think?" I asked. "This desperate need to be the only person with control of her children?"

Madge thought about it for a moment and shook her head. "It's difficult to say," she replied. "None of us knew very much about her childhood. She may have confided more in James—if she did, then he never shared the confidence with Alex—and after the attacks, he was never able to speak again to tell us more. We never met her family, her parents were dead, she had no brothers or sisters. She brought no friend or confidante with her from Spain when James brought her back here as his wife. It was as if she had no past at all and yet, of course she did, that painful past of which we spoke. I think it affected her mind in a way that only became apparent after the children were born. What I believe, what I *know*, is that she suffered greatly when she was a girl. And became convinced that if she did not take care of the children herself, obsessively, completely, then they would suffer in some similar, indescribable way. There is cruelty in the world, Eliza, you can see that, can't you? It surrounds us. It breathes on us. We spend our life trying to escape it."

"You believe that?" I asked, surprised by her bleak outlook on the world.

"I do," she said. "Quite firmly. I know something of which I speak. When I met Alex . . . my dear, I was very *fortunate* to meet Alex. It doesn't matter why. But I know something of cruelty, Eliza Caine. By God, I know something of that."

Her face turned cold and I said nothing for a long time; I knew better than to question her on her own experiences. I had always thought myself the most unfortunate of creatures for losing a parent, and an unknown sister, so young, but my childhood had been a happy one, my father had loved me with every fibre of his being and sworn to protect me always. With such love to fall back on, what could I understand of Santina Westerley's past? Or, for that matter, of Madge Toxley's?

"The last I saw of her," continued Madge finally, "was the sight of her marching around her cell, repeating over and over that if any other woman attempted to take care of her children, they would regret it. That she would destroy such a person. The warden was in the cell by then with one of the prison officers and between them they restrained her. No easy task. I left, I didn't even say goodbye, and ran from the prison in tears. It was terribly upsetting. And an hour later, of course, Santina Westerley was dead. They hanged her."

"Only she never died," I said quietly and Madge stared at me, her eyes wide open.

"I beg your pardon," she said.

"Oh, she died of course," I replied, correcting myself. "The hangman did his job. Her neck was broken, her spine was cracked. The blood stopped flowing and she ceased to breathe. But what happened to her after that is something else entirely. She is still here, Madge. Here at Gaudlin Hall. This house is haunted by her."

Madge Toxley stared at me as if I had lost my mind, in much the same way that Reverend Deacons had looked at me earlier in the day.

"My dear, you can't mean it!"

"Can't I?"

"But the idea is ludicrous. There's no such thing as ghosts."

"When Santina Westerley was alive, she killed Miss Tomlin and attempted to kill her own husband. When she was dead, she hanged Miss Golding from a tree, she drowned Ann Williams in her bath, she pushed Miss Harkness out in front of a horse and carriage, trampling her underfoot. She did what she could to end the life of Harriet Bennet but that woman got away. And now she means to murder me. She will not allow me to bring up her children, I am quite certain of it. She has tried to kill or injure me in so many ways already. And I don't believe that she will stop until she has succeeded. Her spirit is locked within these walls, where her children are confined, and while this house stands and woman after woman enters it as governess she will continue to wreak her havoc. But I can never leave, you see," I continued, a tone of resignation entering my voice. "I cannot do what my predecessor did. And so I stand condemned to death. It will come for me as surely as night follows day."

Madge looked at me and shook her head. She pulled a handkerchief from her bag and dabbed at her eyes with it. "My dear, I am worried for you," she said eventually in a quiet voice. "I think you have lost your reason. Do you not realize how preposterous what you say is? Can you not hear yourself?"

"You should go, Madge," I said, standing up and smoothing down my dress. "And please don't talk to the children any more if you see them. It can do you no good and might bring great harm upon your head."

She stood now too and reached for her coat. "I shall speak to Alex," she said. "We will bring a doctor to you. Perhaps a sedative of some sort. You are still grieving, Eliza, are you not? For your dear father? In your grief, your mind has grown bewildered, that's the only explanation, and you are engaged in flights of fantasy. I shall speak to Alex," she repeated. "He will know what to do."

I smiled at her and nodded; there was no point arguing with her, she would believe what she chose to believe and disbelieve what she could not accept. Unless she took over as governess to the Westerley children there was simply no possibility that she could comprehend the things that were taking place at Gaudlin Hall. And I would not wish them on another. Let her think that I was mad if she needed to. Let her think that everything could be cured by a restorative or a bottle of medicine or a long recuperation. Let her blame my ideas on the death of my father. None of it mattered. I was governess here. I had assumed responsibility for these children and, in the same way that Father had refused to cede permanent custody of me to my aunts Hermione and Rachel after the death of my mother, in the same way that he had asserted his rights over me and his commitment to my safety and my care, I had done the same for Isabella and Eustace. I would not let them down, no matter the consequences. Santina Westerley had made her intentions clear before her death and it seemed to me that she was a woman of her word. Soon enough, she would come for me again. And this time it was most likely that she would succeed.

I said my goodbyes to Madge at the front door and watched her for a few moments as she made her way down the driveway before closing it again. At first I rested my forehead against the woodwork, wondering what I might do next, but as I turned round, a hand grabbed me by the neck and threw me across the floor. I hit the wall of the hallway with a scream and felt a body, invisible, rushing towards me. Before it could reach me, however, another presence swept in from my left side and there was a sound like thunder as they collided, one roaring at the other, before both presences disappeared entirely, leaving only one thing, one familiar thing, in their wake.

The scent of cinnamon.

Chapter Twenty-two

A S DARKNESS FELL, I believed that there would be no possibility that Santina Westerley's spirit would ever leave me in
peace as long as it was allowed to wander in its half-world between life and death. I could survive any number of attacks, and
had, but it was surely only a matter of time before she caught
me off my guard and achieved her purpose. Would I see her,
I wondered, as I departed this world for the next? Would our
paths cross for even a moment, as Harriet Bennet's and mine
had at Thorpe Railway Station six weeks earlier? Or would I
simply disappear into nothingness while she lay in wait for her
next victim?

I wondered whether my predecessors had fought so hard,
whether they had succumbed to fear quickly or risen up against
their tormentor. Had they fought back? Had they even realized
who they were fighting? I thought it unlikely. But still, there was
hope for me, for I was certain that I had something that they
did not have: a spirit watching over me.

After the attack in the hallway I lay trembling on the ground
for I know not how long. Of course I was frightened, but being
able to identify who the presence was and why it resented me

so badly had taken some of the terror out of these encounters. I understood it at least. Now it was merely a question of survival. But that scent of cinnamon that lingered in the hallway had left me startled, emotional and terribly afraid. I thought of Eustace and his encounters with the old man and it became clear to me at last who my benefactor was.

I wept as I lay there, and felt a distress unlike any that I had suffered since first entering Gaudlin Hall. Was it possible that Father, like Santina Westerley, had not yet departed this earth? Could he really be looking out for me in this terrible place? There seemed to be no other explanation and yet it left me heartsore, imagining his pain and loneliness, his inability to communicate with me. What was it he had said to me when I returned from Cornwall as a child, when he had at last come to terms with Mother's death? *I will always look after you, Eliza. I will keep you safe.* Somehow he had managed to connect with Eustace but not with me. I knew not why. Were the souls of the dead in closer communication with the young? I could endure these riddles no longer. I was left with no choice if I was to prevail; I must provoke the ghost into action. I must end this.

When I recovered my senses, I repaired to the writing table in what had once been Mr. Westerley's study and, opening some drawers, I located a sheaf of notepaper and envelopes headed with the Gaudlin Hall insignia. Drawing one out, I took a quill from the desk and began to write. When I finished I stood in the centre of the room, speaking to the air with all the oratorical might that I could muster, attempting to equal the confidence of Charles Dickens when he addressed his audience in that hallway off Knightsbridge not so long before. I read the letter I had written aloud in a clear voice, enunciating every word so there would be no confusion as to my intentions.

Dear Mr. Raisin [I began]
   It is with profound regret that I tender my resignation as governess at Gaudlin Hall.
   I am reluctant to go into details as to why I must leave this place. Suffice to say that circumstances here have become untenable. I do not believe that this is a suitable place for children to be brought up and with this in mind I have decided to take Isabella and Eustace with me to my next destination. Where that is, I cannot say. For reasons I will explain at another time I do not wish to commit the name of that place to a letter. Suffice to say that when we are settled, I will write again.
   I assure you that the children will be well taken care of. No one other than I will be responsible for their welfare.
   I apologize for my short notice but, upon despatch of this note, I shall be packing the children's cases for we leave in the morning. I wish to thank you for every consideration that you have shown me during my time here and I hope you will think of me always as your friend,
   Eliza Caine

I reached the end of my narration and waited for a moment. I expected fury; there was a slight movement in the curtains but nothing to make me think that the presence had entered the room and was preparing to attack. The movement might just have been the draught. Nevertheless I believed that wherever it was, wherever *she* was, it would have heard my words and be considering what action to take next.

I slipped the letter inside an envelope and stepped outside into the courtyard, a shawl wrapped around me for the wind had started to rise now. It had grown dark but there was a full moon as I made my way towards the cottage where Heckling lived. His horse was standing inside one of the stables, her great head watching me as I passed, her eyes meeting mine, and I hesitated, remembering how this same horse had been possessed by a devil as it pursued Miss Bennet. I feared that she might break free of her ropes now and chase me down; if she did I did not believe that my chances of survival would be high. But she appeared calm that evening and as I walked past she simply whinnied a little and returned to her hay.

Knocking on the door of the cottage, I regretted not bringing my coat with me for it had grown very cold, and as I stood there, waiting for the door to open, my body trembled. When finally it did, Heckling was standing in his shirtsleeves, lit from behind by a pair of tall candles, an effect which made him seem otherworldly. He did not look best pleased to see me.

"Governess," he grunted, picking a fleck of tobacco from between his teeth.

"Good evening, Heckling," I said. "I'm sorry for the lateness of the hour but I have a letter that needs delivering."

I held it out to him and he took it, peering at it now beneath the light of the moon to read the name. "Mr. Raisin," he muttered. "Aye, good enough. I'll see it gets to him first thing in t'morning."

He moved to go back inside but I stopped him, reaching a hand out to touch his elbow. He turned round, startled by the intimacy of the gesture. For a moment, I thought he was going to strike me and stepped back in fear.

"I'm sorry, Mr. Heckling," I said. "But this is a most important communication. He will need to see it tonight."

He stared at me as if he could not quite believe what I had said. "It's late, Governess," he said. "I'm only fit for sleep."

"As I said, I apologize for that. But I'm afraid it can't be helped. This cannot be delayed. I must ask you to bring it to him immediately."

He exhaled deeply from the very depths of his chest. I could see that he wanted nothing more than to be left in peace in front of his fireplace, his pipe in his mouth, perhaps a tankard of ale next to him, alone with his thoughts, allowing the world to stand judgement before him.

"Aye," he said finally. "If it matters that much, then I'll take it. Am I to wait on a response?"

"Just ensure that he reads it there and then," I said. "I think his response will be quite immediate. Thank you, Heckling."

"Aye," he said, his voice still a grumble as he went back indoors to fetch his boots.

I made my way back to the house and tried the front door but, in attempting to push it open, a force greater than my own pushed against me from the other side. I was being denied access. Above my head, I heard a sound as a gargoyle from the roof of the Hall dislodged itself and spiralled downwards and I was forced to leap out of its way as it tumbled to the ground, its enormous weight of stone smashing into a hundred pieces. As the stones flew up, one caught me in the cheek and made me cry out and I pressed a hand against my skin. No blood had been drawn. Had the gargoyle fallen on me I would doubtless have been killed instantly. But I was not dead. Not yet. I waited, leaning back against the wall as more remnants from the roof fell down to the ground below; Harriet Bennet had been correct, it was in an advanced state of disrepair. When the rain of stones stopped, I turned back to the front door, expecting the force inside to keep me out still, but this time it opened quite easily and I rushed inside, gasping aloud, shutting it behind me, and stood there for a moment, fighting to catch my breath. Was I insane? Was this entire effort a madness? I doubted that I would see daylight again but persevered. Either she or I who could live at Gaudlin Hall but not both of us.

Making my way up the staircase, I entered the children's dressing room, where a wardrobe and dresser on the left-hand wall contained all of Isabella's clothes and shoes, while another on the right-hand side contained all of Eustace's. In the corner stood a couple of suitcases and I chose two at random, filling each with clothes belonging to one of the children.

"What are you doing?" asked a voice from behind me and I spun round in fright to find Isabella and Eustace standing there in their nightclothes, roused from their beds, holding a candle between them.

"She's leaving us," said Eustace in a tearful voice, leaning into his sister for consolation. "I said she would."

"What a shame," replied Isabella. "But she's done well to last this long, don't you think?"

"I'm not leaving you, my darling boy," I said, coming over towards him and taking his face in my hands and kissing it lightly. "I'll never leave you, either of you, do you understand that?"

"Then why are you packing?"

"She's not packing *her* clothes, Eustace," said Isabella, stepping into the room and looking at what was in the suitcases. "Can't you see? She's packing ours." She frowned for a moment and looked back at me. "But this doesn't make sense," she said finally. "Are we being sent away? You know that we can't leave

Gaudlin Hall, don't you? We're not allowed to leave. She won't let us."

"She being who?" I asked, challenging her directly now.

"Why, Mama of course," said Isabella with a shrug, as if it was the most obvious thing in the world. "She can only take care of us here."

"Your mama is dead," I cried, taking her by the shoulders and shaking her in my frustration. A shadow of a smile crossed her lips. "You understand that, don't you, Isabella? She can't take care of you now. But I can. I'm alive."

"She won't like it," said Isabella, pulling away from me and retreating to the doorway, followed quickly by her brother. "I'll not go with you, Eliza Caine, no matter what you say. And neither will Eustace. Isn't that right, Eustace?"

He looked from one of us to the other, uncertain where his loyalties lay. But I had no time for this; after all, I had no intention of taking the children away from Gaudlin Hall. I simply needed it to look as if I was. I needed her to believe that that was my plan.

"Go to bed, both of you," I said, waving my hand to dismiss them. "I'll come in to talk to you soon."

"All right then," said Isabella, smiling at me. "But it won't do you any good. We won't leave."

They went back to their bedrooms and shut their doors and I stood in the dark hallway, breathing carefully, allowing my body to relax for a moment.

As soon as I did so a pair of cold hands surrounded my throat and I opened my eyes wide in fright as I was pushed to the ground. I could feel a body on top of me, an extraordinary weight, but no physical presence could be seen in the hallway. It was dark, of course, there was just one candle lit on the wall halfway down the corridor, but I knew that it could have been as bright as noon-time on a summer's day and I would see no one, there would just be me lying on the floor, my face contorting, my hands scrambling in the air as I tried to release myself from the monster's grip.

I tried to call for help but words would not come and the legs of the body atop my own straddled me, a knee forcing itself into my abdomen and sending a horrible shooting pain through my chest. I thought that it might cut directly through me, split my body in half, and wondered whether this was the moment of my death as the hands closed tighter and tighter round my throat, cutting off my breathing, making the world grow darker and darker.

A great sound above me, a roar of disapproval, and the presence was wrenched from me and I heard a scream, a woman's scream, as the second spirit pushed her to the wall and then a great tumble as she was thrown over the banisters; the sound of a body falling down the stairs was clearly audible to me, and then silence, total silence.

And with it, that scent of cinnamon in the air. I could resist asking no longer.

"Father?" I cried out. "Father, are you there? Father, can it be you?"

But now all was silence again. It was as if neither spirit was present. I coughed repeatedly, trying to clear my throat, but it was terribly sore, as was my chest. I wondered whether she had ruptured something inside me, whether even now the blood was pouring from some sacred vessel within and preparing to haemorrhage and take my life. But there was nothing I could do about that now. I left the children's suitcases on the landing and made my way upstairs to my own room.

The walls on my corridor were lined with paintings and as I began to walk they lifted from their hooks, one by one, and crashed to the floor, making me scream and run faster. One flew directly at me, missing me by inches, and I ran ahead, flinging open the door and pulling it closed behind me, trying not to think about how little difference this would make; the presence did not worry about doors, after all. She might be in here already. She might be waiting for me.

But inside the room, all was quiet. I suffered another fit of coughing and, when it passed, sat on the bed, considering what I should do next. I was relying on one thing. That the presence would attack me so violently that the second spirit, my own father, would bring her actions to an end. I did not even know if it was possible. She had been killed once and lingered on; perhaps she could not be killed again. Perhaps she was an immortal now. How did I even know that Father was stronger than her?

A great roar lifted the window from its moorings, throwing it out of the house entirely and sending it crashing from the second floor to the ground below, the sound of the glass breaking into a thousand pieces competing with the noise of the wind and the scream that emerged from my mouth. My room was now exposed to the elements. I ran to the door, attempting to leave, but was pushed backwards, sandwiched now between two presences, Santina's ghost before me, my father's behind. I cried out, trying to wrestle my way free, but they were too strong for me, their strength was not a human strength at all, but being the weakest of the three I somehow managed to slip down between their bodies and make my way to the door, rushing through it and slamming it behind me. Outside, the corridor was a wreck. The paintings were all smashed upon the ground, the carpet had been lifted from the floor and twisted and torn into shreds. The wallpaper was peeling, the rotting damp swell of the stone leaking some type of primordial ooze down the walls behind. She had grown furious, I realized, because of my refusal to die and was preparing to destroy everything. If my plan had been to provoke her to a fury, I had certainly succeeded. I ran to the end of the corridor, opening the door, uncertain where I might go next.

I was faced with the two staircases.

The first led to the roof, an unsafe place for me to venture, the second to Mr. Westerley's room. I cried out in pity. I should never have gone this way. I should have made my way back downstairs and out to the courtyard. The presence was at her most effective, her most virulent in the house. The further away I was, the safer I would be. I looked back at my bedroom door, from where I could hear a great roar, a scream of fighting, but I sensed that if I passed it again, she would know and I would find myself within the centre of a great complaint from which I might never be released alive. And so I turned round, made a sudden decision, and climbed the staircase, pulling open the door at the top and quickly slamming it shut behind me.

Chapter Twenty-three

THE ROOM HERE was quiet, save for the sound of Mr. Westerley's gasping breath. I pressed my ear to the door and held
it there for a few moments, willing myself not to cry, waiting
for my own breath to be restored to me and then, taking all my
courage together, I turned round and looked at the body that
lay in the bed.

He was a pitiful sight. A horrendous shell of a human being.
His arms lay atop the sheets but his hands were pulpy things,
several of his fingers missing entirely, others little more than
stumps attached to his hands. His face was a confusion. Mostly
bald, the skull was misshapen, a mound of bruising that would
never heal, pulling the left side of his head in a curious direction that my eyes could not fully focus on. The eye on one side
was missing; a dark red and black hole gaped out in its place.
On the other side of his face, his right eye was curiously intact,
the sharp blue pupil staring directly at me, fully alert, the sur-
rounding eyelashes and lids the only part of his remaining face
that looked human. His nose had been broken in many places.
His teeth were no more. His lips and chin melded together; it
was impossible to tell where the natural redness of the former

connected to the unnatural scarlet of the latter. A part of his jaw was missing entirely and I could see enamel and bone. And yet despite the horror I could feel nothing but sympathy for him. His wife's cruellest act, it seemed to me, had been allowing him to survive in this way.

A horrendous cry emerged from his mouth and I put a hand to my own, hating to hear such pain expressed. He groaned again, it was like the dying roar of a wounded animal, and I thought he was trying to say something. The words came but his vocal cords had been damaged so badly that they were almost impossible to decipher.

"I'm sorry," I said, stepping towards him, taking his hand in my own. I didn't care what it looked or felt like; this man needed the touch of another human. "I'm so sorry, James." I used his Christian name despite the difference in our rank; in that room at least, I felt that we were equals.

His groan sounded more defined now and I could tell that he was struggling with every fibre of his being to make himself understood. His head lifted slightly from the pillow and the sound emerged once again. I sank my head lower to his face, trying to hear.

"*Kill me,*" he said with a great effort, the exertion leading him to bubble and foam at the lips as he gasped and struggled for air. I pulled back, shaking my head.

"I can't," I said, horrified by the prospect. "I can't do it."

A trickle of blood emerged from his mouth and made passage along his cheek and I stared, horrified, uncertain what to do as one hand lifted and, with great difficulty, he beckoned me forward.

"*The only way,*" he gasped. "*Break the connection.*" And I understood at last. He had brought her to Gaudlin Hall. He had married her, given her children here. And she had meant to kill him but somehow he had survived. He was as close to a corpse as it was possible to be but he continued to breathe. And she continued to exist in time with it. They could both live or they could both die.

I cried aloud, lifting my hands to heaven in desperation. Why had I been entrusted with this act? What had I done to deserve it? And yet, despite all my misgivings, I began to look around the room for something that might end the man's suffering. If I was to be a murderess, then let it be quick and over. I told myself not to think about it. It was a monstrous act, a crime against God and nature itself, but I could not think or I would be persuaded differently. I had to act.

On a chair in the corner of the room, the chair that I imagined Mrs. Livermore sat in while she was nursing him, there lay a pillow. A pillow that was soft against her back and allowed her to rest quietly for a few minutes. It brought her comfort; so let it bring comfort to James Westerley too. I reached for it, picked it up and turned back to him, holding it tightly in both my hands.

His single good eye closed and I could see at that moment the sense of relief that was coursing through his body. It was finally about to end. He would be set free from this living death. I would be his killer and his salvation all at once. Standing beside him, I lifted the pillow, preparing to bring it down upon his face, but the moment my arms began to descend, the door to the room was flung open, ripped completely off its hinges, and a force unlike any I had ever felt before entered the room.

It was as if I was at the centre of a hurricane. Every dust mote, every item in the room that was not pinned to the floor rose and circled me. Even Mr. Westerley's bed lifted from the floor and rocked as a screaming like the banshee wail of a thousand lost souls filled the room. I stumbled backwards as the wall behind me gave way, the stones ripping from it and flying out into the night beyond, and within a few moments the room at the top of Gaudlin Hall was entirely exposed to the elements. I was staring down at the courtyard below, my feet teetering on the edge even as a hand reached out—oh that hand I knew so well, that same hand that had held my own throughout my childhood, the one that had walked me to and from school a thousand times—and pulled me back in, dragging me to the other side of the room where the second door, the one that Mrs. Livermore used to enter and leave Gaudlin Hall, stood and I pulled it open and threw myself down the stairs.

The steps seemed to go on for ever. I could scarcely believe there were so many of them but somehow I made my way round and round before emerging into the dark night outside the Hall. I was on the ground once again and scarcely able to believe that I yet lived. I ran towards Heckling's stable but he was gone, of course; by now he would have already arrived at Mr. Raisin's house, he would have delivered my letter and be on his way back here, his horse trotting along the road, grumbling to himself in irritation at my night-time messages. I flung the door open but then changed my mind. What was the point of entering, after all? Did I mean to hide? That would achieve nothing. I would not be safe there.

I turned back and ran towards the courtyard and was lifted off my feet, finding myself suspended in mid-air before being thrown bodily to the ground from a height of perhaps ten feet. I cried out, my body aching, but before I could pick myself up, the presence collected me in her grasp, lifted me again and flung me down. This time my head crashed against the stone. I felt a wetness on my forehead and put a hand to it; it came away red in the moonlight. I could not survive much more of this. I looked up and was astonished to see the walls beginning to crumble on the third floor of the house. Part of the roof had collapsed, and to the left and right of the room in which I had stood stones were pouring down. I could see my own bedroom, the window ripped from its socket. I could make out Mr. Westerley's bed near the edge of the precipice above as more and more of the stonework began to pull away from the building, each piece setting another one out of place, a domino effect that would in time, I realized, bring the whole edifice down.

The children, I thought.

I was lifted again and prepared my body for its inevitable thrashing against the stones but this time, before I rose too high, I was released from her grasp and dropped without as much pain. I heard Santina scream and my father roar. Their argument took them away from me, back towards the house, and as I stumbled to my feet I heard the sound of horse's hooves and a carriage approaching and turned to see Heckling and his horse making their way up the drive, the carriage occupied not by just one person as I had expected, but by four. For seated behind Heckling were Mr. Raisin himself and Madge and Alex Toxley.

"Help!" I cried, running towards them, ignoring the pain that seared through my body. "Help me, please!"

"My dear," cried Madge, emerging first and rushing towards me, the expression on her face making clear how bloody and beaten my face was. If I had been an unattractive woman before, it was, I imagined, as nothing compared to how I looked now. "Eliza!" she shouted. "Oh my God, what has happened to you?"

I stumbled towards her but fell into the embrace of Mr. Raisin, who had descended from his seat and ran towards me, his arms outstretched.

"Eliza," he cried, pressing my head to his chest, and even in my pain and torment I felt a giddy delight to be held so. "My poor girl. Not again, not again," he screamed suddenly and I realized that the terrible sight he was viewing reminded him of that awful night when he arrived at Gaudlin Hall to find the dead body of Miss Tomlin and the mutilated body of his friend, James Westerley.

"Look!" cried Madge, pointing towards the house, and we turned to see more stones slipping from the building, a side of the entire structure beginning to fall away even as the ground-floor windows were smashed by the weight of two spirits crashing against them, seeking supremacy. "The house," she shouted. "It's going to collapse."

An unearthly sound emerged from my mouth as I realized that Isabella and Eustace were still inside. I wrenched myself free from Mr. Raisin's grip and threw myself towards the front door even as he called after me, beseeching me to come back. My body ached, I dreaded to think of the damage that had been done to it, but I summoned every part of my own spirit to ascend those stairs to the first floor and ran down towards the children's bedroom.

Isabella's room was first but she was nowhere to be found so I ran to Eustace's door, hoping to discover them both together. But no, he was alone, sitting up in bed, a terrified expression on his face, tears rolling down his cheeks.

"What's happening?" he asked me. "Why won't she leave?"

I had no answer for him. Instead I simply scooped him up in my arms, held him tightly to my body and made my way back down the staircase and out into the courtyard. Alex Toxley took him from my arms and laid him out on the grass to examine him as his wife, Heckling and Mr. Raisin stood staring up at the battle taking place above, two non-existent bodies struggling against each other, crashing into the walls of Gaudlin Hall, pulling the windows down, ripping the stones from the foundations as they sought supremacy.

"What is it?" cried Mr. Raisin. "What can it be?"

"I must go back," I said to Madge. "Isabella is still in there somewhere."

"She's up there," said Heckling, pointing northwards, and all our heads turned to the top of the house, just below the roof, where the entirety of Mr. Westerley's bedroom was visible to us. I gasped. The stones were falling more quickly now; the room was starting to slide away. It would not be long before it fell. And there was Isabella, standing by her father's bed, turning to look down at us for a moment before climbing on top of it and pressing her body close to his. It took only a moment more before the walls and floors gave way entirely and the left-hand side of the house collapsed in upon itself. Everything we could see there, Mr. Westerley's room, my own exposed bedroom underneath, Mr. Westerley himself and Isabella, came down in a surge of stone, furniture and smoke, crashing to the ground beneath with such violence, with such a horrendous speed and implosion, that I knew immediately that he had been allowed to die at last, but that Isabella, who had been in my charge, whose care had been entrusted to me, was gone as well.

I had no more than an instant to consider this though for directly as the collapse occurred, a startling bright light, whiter than anything I had seen before, emerged from the walls in front of us and for a split second, a fraction less than it would take for an eye to blink, I saw my father and Santina Westerley locked together in mortal combat and then, just as quickly, her body blew apart, exploded into a million fragments of light that blinded us all and we turned away, gasping. When we looked back, all was silent. The house was half destroyed and the furies of the ground floor had disappeared entirely.

Santina Westerley was gone. I knew it. All fear had vanished. Her husband had been released from his suffering and she had been taken away too; where she had gone was a question that no man could answer.

I looked towards Heckling and Mr. Raisin, the Toxleys and my own dear Eustace, and they stared at me, each one speechless, uncertain what they could possibly say or how they could explain what had just occurred. And I felt the great pain of my body finally being realized, all the wounds and blood becoming real now, and I stepped a little away from there, back towards the lawn, where I sank to the ground and lay down, offering no words or tears, content to give my life to the next world.

But as I lay there, the voices of my friends muffled to my hearing and my eyes began to close, I felt a body wrap itself around me, those great strong arms that I had known my whole life and that I had spent this last month grieving. I felt them embrace me from behind and I was enveloped in the scent of cinnamon as my father's head pressed itself against my own, his lips found my cheek, and he pressed them to it, keeping them there for a long time, his arms squeezing my body to tell me that he loved me, that I was strong, that I would survive all this and more, and I relaxed into this most tender of embraces, knowing that I should never feel it again. Slowly, it began to grow less powerful, his arms began to loosen, his lips pulled away from my face, and the warmth of his body gave way to the chill of the night as he left me for ever and went at last to the comfort of that place from which no man may return.

Chapter Twenty-four

T HE FUNERALS TOOK PLACE three days later.

Eustace reverted to silence in the intervening time, staying as close to me as he could but never uttering a word. If I left a room he went to the door and waited there for my return, like a faithful puppy, and insisted on sleeping in my bed with me. At first, Mr. and Mrs. Raisin had offered to take him in, while the Toxleys offered me their spare room; I was grateful to accept the latter but Eustace made it clear that where I went, he would go too, and so we both took up residence in Madge Toxley's house and she did all she could to keep the atmosphere light.

Unlike my eight-year-old charge, I did not feel any great sense of trauma regarding the events that had taken place. All of that had dissipated over those last few hours at Gaudlin Hall. Perhaps the adrenalin rush of fully defeating the ghost of Santina Westerley had given me courage that I never believed I possessed. I knew—I had known that night when her husband fell to his death and she disappeared alongside him—that she was gone for ever, that her spirit had been somehow intertwined with his. She had kept him alive for a reason, knowing that the law would see to it that she was put to death for what she had done to Miss Tomlin. And so I did not fear her return and slept soundly, awoken only by the tossing of Eustace next to me, whose dreams, I feared, were not quite as peaceful as my own.

I tried to talk to him about Isabella but he simply shook his head and I felt it would be best not to press him on the subject. For my part, I wept for her the night after she died and I wept for her at her funeral, when she was laid in the earth in a white coffin in the same grave as both her parents, and I took some comfort in the notion that they were together again and would remain together for eternity. She had always appeared to be so in control of her feelings, such an introspective child, but it was my belief that she had suffered a great psychological trauma after her mother's violent actions and death, which could never have been resolved. It was a tragedy, truly it was, but she was gone and Eustace was here and I had to focus my thoughts on him.

"There's a rather good school," Mr. Raisin said when he came to visit me in Madge Toxley's front room the day after the funeral. He had brought a new puppy with him, a playful King Charles of about two months old, and Eustace had been persuaded to go outside with him and throw some sticks for the puppy to retrieve. I was keeping a careful eye on him through the window but he seemed to be in good spirits and enjoying the dog's company; I even thought that I saw him smile and laugh for the first time since I had known him. "It's near Ipswich. A boarding school called St. Christopher's. You have heard of it, Miss Caine?"

"I have not," I said, uncertain why he was telling me this. Had he heard of a position going there perhaps and thought that it might be right for me?

"I think it might be just the ticket."

"Just the ticket for whom?" I asked.

"Why, for Eustace, of course," he said, as if it was the most obvious thing in the world. "I have taken the liberty of making some initial communication with the headmaster and he has agreed to meet the boy for an interview, and should he impress, and I daresay he will, then he will be accepted for the beginning of the new school year."

"I had a rather different idea," I said, thinking carefully how to phrase this, particularly since I knew full well that I had no rights over the boy at all.

"Oh?" he asked, raising an eyebrow. "What sort of idea?"

"I intend to return to London," I told him.

"To London?"

And was it me or did I see a shadow of disappointment cross his face?

"Yes, in a few days' time. I'm hoping that there might be a position for me at my old school. I always had a good relationship with the principal so with luck she might agree to take me back. I'd like to take Eustace with me."

He looked at me in surprise. "But wasn't your school a school for girls?"

"Yes," I admitted. "But there is a school for boys on the other side of the road. Eustace could receive his education there. And he could live with me. I could take care of him. As I have been doing these last six weeks," I added.

Mr. Raisin thought about it for a moment and scratched his chin. "It's a lot to take on," he said finally. "Are you sure that you really want the responsibility?"

"Perfectly sure," I said. "In truth, Mr. Raisin, I cannot imagine leaving him behind. I feel that we have been through an experience together, the two of us. I understand him as well as he can be understood. I believe that he has painful times ahead of him and I would like to help see him through those dark days. I can be a mother to him if the estate, if *you*, will allow me to."

He nodded and I was pleased to see that he did not seem entirely opposed to the idea. "There would be the question of money," he said after a moment, narrowing his eyes. "The house might be gone, but the land is worth a lot. Mr. Westerley's own investments were spread quite wide. That money is locked up in the estate and will one day be Eustace's."

"I don't need any money," I said quickly, in order to reassure him. "And neither does Eustace. Take care of his inheritance until he is eighteen, or twenty-one, or twenty-five, whichever his father's will stipulates, and manage it with your usual thoroughness and propriety. In the meantime we will be able to live quite comfortably on my salary. I am a frugal woman, Mr. Raisin. I do not require luxuries in life."

"Well, there is still your salary to consider," he added. "We could continue to—"

"No," I said, shaking my head. "It's generous of you but if I was to take a salary then I would once again be in the position of being Eustace's governess, a paid employee. I would like instead to be his guardian. Perhaps, if it would set your mind at ease, you and I could be his guardians together. I would happily consult with you on important matters related to his upbringing. Indeed, I would consider it helpful to have your counsel on these matters. But I don't want any payment. Should the estate see fit to help out with Eustace's schoolbooks or things along those lines, I'm sure we could come to an agreement. But other than that, I don't believe the issue of money is one that need concern us."

He nodded and seemed satisfied, reaching out his hand to shake mine. We stood up and smiled at each other. "Very well then," he said. "I believe we understand each other perfectly. And if I may say so, Miss Caine, I think that he will be a very lucky boy. A very lucky boy indeed. You are a fine woman."

I blushed, unaccustomed to such compliments. "Thank you," I said, leading him towards the door. Outside, he summoned the puppy, who looked back at Eustace regretfully as his master called him.

"He's taken rather a shine to you, Eustace," he said. "I expect this is goodbye," he added, turning to me. "I will miss your impromptu visits to my office, Miss Caine."

I laughed. "I'm sure Mr. Cratchett will be pleased to see the back of me," I replied and he smiled a little. Our eyes met and we remained locked like that for a few moments. There was more to say, I was certain of it, but none of it could be said. Whatever it was must remain here, in Gaudlin.

"We shall talk again soon, no doubt," he said finally, sighing as he turned round and raising his cane to bid me adieu. "Send me your address in London when you have it. We shall have to stay in close communication in the years to come. Goodbye, Eustace! Good luck to you, boy!"

I watched as he made his way down the driveway and the puppy followed for a little bit before stopping and turning back, staring at Eustace. He sat down on his haunches, looked back at his master and then at the boy again, and Mr. Raisin turned round and saw what was happening.

"So that's how it is," he said with a smile.

The following Monday, I returned to St. Elizabeth's School and knocked on Mrs. Farnsworth's door.

"Eliza Caine," she said, rather unsettling me with her use of my full name; it put me in mind of Isabella's tendency to do the same thing. "This is quite a surprise."

"I'm sorry to disturb you," I said. "I wondered whether I could have a few moments of your time."

She nodded and indicated that I should sit down and I explained to her how the position in Norfolk had not turned out as I had hoped and I had decided to return to London.

"I seem to recall saying to you that you were rushing into that decision," she said smugly, delighted to have been proved right. "Young women these days are rash in their judgements, I find. They should rely more on the advice of their elders."

"I was also grieving," I pointed out, wishing I could be anywhere but there at that moment. "I'm sure you remember that too. My father had just died."

"Yes, of course," she said, looking a little embarrassed. "Naturally you were not in a position to make the best judgement. I did say at the time that I was sorry to lose you and I meant it. You were an excellent teacher. But of course your position was filled. I could not leave the small girls without instruction."

"Of course not," I said. "But I wondered whether there might be another job opening up soon? I remember Miss Parkin saying that she would be retiring at the end of this term. Perhaps you haven't found her replacement yet?"

She nodded. "That's true," she said. "And no, I haven't yet advertised the post. But you see the position you put me in," she added, smiling at me. "You have proved unreliable. Should I employ you once again, who is to say that you will not walk out on me with scant notice as you did once in the past? It is a school I'm running here, Miss Caine, not a . . ." She struggled to find a way to finish that sentence. "Not a hotel," she added finally.

"My circumstances have changed somewhat," I explained. "I assure you that when I set down roots in London again I will not be leaving. Not for anything."

"So you say now."

"I have added responsibility," I told her. "A responsibility that I did not have before."

She raised an eyebrow and looked intrigued. "Is that so?" she asked. "And pray tell, what might that be?"

I sighed. I had hoped not to have to engage in this conversation, but if it was to be the crux of whether or not I would be allowed back, I had no choice. "I have a little boy to look after," I told her. "Eustace Westerley."

"A little boy?" she asked. She took her glasses off and set them on the table, scandalized. "Miss Caine, are you trying to tell me that you have given birth? That you are an unwed mother?"

Six weeks before, my natural inclination would have been to blush scarlet, but after all I had been through I could only laugh now. "Really, Mrs. Farnsworth," I said. "I realize that we do not teach the sciences at St. Elizabeth's but I could hardly have gone away, become pregnant, given birth and come back again in such a short space of time."

"Of course not, of course not," she stammered, and now it was her turn to blush. "But then I don't understand."

"It's a long story," I explained. "The son of the family I was employed by. Unfortunately his parents have died quite tragically. He has no one in the world. He is alone. Except for me. I have undertaken to bring him up as his guardian."

"I see," she replied, considering this. "How very thoughtful of you. And you don't think that this will interfere with your work here?"

"If you are kind enough to take me back, then I hope to enrol Eustace in St. Matthew's across the road. I don't envision any problems pursuant to that."

"All right then, Miss Caine," she said, standing up and shaking my hand. "You may have Miss Parkin's position when she leaves us in a few weeks. But I take you at your word that you will be reliable and not let me down."

I agreed and left, relieved; it seemed as if my old life was returning to me, albeit without Father's presence, but with Eustace's.

Chapter Twenty-five

SEVERAL MONTHS PASSED and Eustace and I set up home in a small house in Camberwell Gardens, with a garden at the back for the puppy to run around in. Our days passed in quite a regular fashion. We ate breakfast together in the morning and then walked the ten-minute distance to our respective schools, me standing at the gate until Eustace had entered his, then crossing the road to begin my own day. Afterwards, we met again and walked home together, ate our evening meal and sat reading or playing games until bedtime. We were content with our lot.

Eustace thrived in his new school. He appeared to put the events of the previous few months behind him, and I learned in time that he did not wish to discuss them at all. I tried on occasion to bring up the subject of his father, mother and sister, but it was pointless. He would shake his head, change the subject, close his eyes, walk away. Anything to avoid discussing it. And I learned to respect that. In time, I thought, perhaps when he is older he will want to talk to me about it. And when he is ready, I will be ready too.

He made friends, two boys in particular, Stephen and Thomas, who lived on our street and went to the same school as him. I liked it when they came to the house, for although they were mischievous, they meant no harm, had good hearts and, besides, I rather enjoyed their nonsense. Of course, I was only twenty-two years old by now; I was still a young woman. I enjoyed the company of these children, and the fact that they brought Eustace so much pleasure was a delight to me. He had never had friends before; there had only been Isabella.

In short, we were happy. And I trusted that nothing would come into our lives to disturb that happiness. We would be left in peace.

Chapter Twenty-six

A S I WRITE THESE last few paragraphs, it is late at night in December. Outside, the night is dark and the streets are filled yet again by this awful London fog. The house is chillier than usual, it has been for some nights now, despite the fact that I load extra coal in the fire and keep it stoked throughout the evening.

Eustace has been quieter these last few days and I do not know why. I asked him whether everything was all right and he simply shrugged and claimed not to know what I meant. I chose not to insist upon an answer. If there was something wrong, then he would tell me in his own time.

Tonight, however, as I tried to fall asleep I was distracted by something. A noise of some sort from outside the window. I rose and looked outside but could see nothing out there through the haze. I stood still and listened and realized that, no, it was not coming from outside at all; the sounds were coming from inside the house.

I stepped out into the dark corridor, holding a single candle in my hands, and made my way to Eustace's door, which had been closed in the night despite the fact that I always insisted he leave it ajar. I moved my hand to the latch, preparing to open it, but before I did so I was surprised to hear noise emerging from within. I pressed my ear to the door and realized that it was voices, two voices, locked together in a serious and quiet conversation. My heart skipped a beat. Was Eustace playing a game of some sort? Putting on a false voice and holding a conversation with himself for some perverse reason? I pressed closer and tried to hear what the two were saying, and it became clear to me that while one of the voices was definitely Eustace's, the other belonged to a girl. How could that be? There was no girl in this house; no female except myself had set foot in it since we had moved here.

I listened more closely, not wanting to open the door until I could understand what was being said, but the words were too muffled through the oak. And then one word came through to me, as clear as day. Just one, a clutch of syllables, stated in Eustace's clear tone and passing from his lips through the air, beneath the door and to my ear. I stood there, my blood freezing, my expression growing cold, a sense of incomprehension and terror filling my body when I realized what it was he had said.

A single name.

"Isabella."

John Boyne was born in Ireland in 1971 and is the author of eight novels, including the international best sellers *The House of Special Purpose* and *The Absolutist*, as well as three novels for younger readers, including *The Boy in the Striped Pyjamas*, which won two Irish Book Awards, topped the *New York Times* bestseller list, and was made into a Miramax feature film. His novels are published in more than forty-five languages. He lives in Dublin.

www.johnboyne.com